Witch

Witch

A Cranky Little Tale

Ann Robinson

Peter E. Randall Publisher
Portsmouth, New Hampshire
2020

ISBN: 978-1-942155-09-6
Library of Congress Control Number: 2020916847

Published by:
Peter E. Randall Publisher
PO Box 4726
Portsmouth NH 03802
www.perpublisher.com

Book Design: Grace Peirce

Back cover photo: Albert Karevy Photography; Witch sculpture by
Artist Bethany Lowe

Dedication

I am indebted to my wonderful husband of sixty-one years, Jim, for his love and support. It's not easy to be married to a writer, nor is it easy to listen to him practicing his violin. But when I see the pleasure it gives him, I can relate.

Life is a journey, not a destination.

—Author unknown

Contents

Introduction

Two women, mother and daughter, tell this story, which begins on Halloween and ends one year later. The setting is an imaginary town in New York's Hudson River Valley in the mid-1990s. In the portion of the novel that deals with the Catskill Mountain region, some actual locations are named. The circumstances and principal characters in the novel are products of the writer's imagination.

Acknowledgments

I would like to acknowledge the faculty of Vermont College of Fine Arts for giving me two wonderful years from 1995 to 1997, when I pursued my Master of Arts in Writing. I was so happy to be a graduate student (except for the times in workshop when I felt like crawling under the rug). At graduation, when I was surrounded by my family and was asked to give a speech, I was so proud of me! I would particularly like to thank Abby Frucht, my mentor and friend, for encouraging me to put joy in my writing. Did I say I pursued my degree? No. It pursued me!

Part 1

Halloween

Tricks Are Treats

Irene

I used to hate Halloween—teenagers coming to the door; big, bruising football players wearing macho-message T-shirts, their faces hidden by werewolf masks, scaring the shit out of me; toilet-paper-draped branches and dog poop on the patio; tipped-over bird baths and soaped-up windows. But this year I can't wait for those pustule-faced creeps to come around, because I've got surprises of my own. Now even the big bruisers, the ones too cool to wear costumes, will get a thrill from touching a withered hand so pockmarked with age spots it looks boiled. They'll want to feel the heat of my rancid breath upon their skin. They'll want to tell their friends they've looked the Devil's daughter in the face and lived to tell the tale. They won't linger, but if they do, I'll threaten to boil their bones for soup and make wreaths of their hair. I'll threaten to suck out their entrails and paint pictures with their blood, and their fingernails will end up pressed flat beneath the glass on my bedside table to be used later in potions. I'll tell them their little brothers and sisters are in the greatest danger because their flesh is so sweet and tender.

I wasn't always a witch. For the first half of my life I fulfilled the promise of my name, Irene, which means peace. I was born here, in the Hudson River Valley of New York, to a mother who raised chickens and a father who sold vacuum cleaners. When I was twenty-six, a young doctor who'd just come to town cured a rash on my inner thigh, but infected me with desire. We stoked the flames for a while, then settled for the steady, dependable heat of married love. I continued to trace the simple, familiar patterns of rural life and soon found joy in motherhood. It seemed Teddy had found bliss, too; but then our lives twisted in directions we'd never anticipated. We moved to Miami, where my husband had a better career opportunity. Oh yes, better: He had an affair with his nurse and lost his license in a malpractice suit. Where was peaceful Irene then? Bitter and resentful, I wanted revenge, but didn't know how to get it until now. Now, in my sixty-fourth year, as new possibilities present themselves, I settle myself in a comfortable chair beside the door and prepare to practice my art.

Here come the first ones, dressed as ghosts and devils, costumes straight out of Walmart, boring. I have my wooden bowl heaped high with miniature Hershey bars, Reese's Pieces, Starbursts and Mallo-mars. Only one to a customer, you greedy little slimepots. Of course, all they care about is digging their grimy paws into the bowl and scooping out teeth-rotters. This little devil's here with his father who plows our driveway and gets rich from throwing gravel up on the lawn. That snot-nosed brat, the one who throws popsicle wrappers under my bushes where she thinks I can't see them, is here with her grandma, my next-door neighbor Mabel. The old lady's done up like Bela Lugosi in drag, her normal getup.

Oh, I love the parents who drive their kids around! Those kids always have the biggest sacks, as if you're going to throw in a kitchen appliance or two. Hey, one to a customer, you little pisser. Two more fistfuls and I'm gonna have to break out the Wheat Thins. Whatsa matter, you don't like bat's breath? Here, take home a tarantula.

I've gotten so I can sit right here in my chair and do everything by remote control. I watch the bowl float towards the twerps in Frankenstein masks and hover just long enough for them to stick in their trembling paws. Oops. Sorry, we're all out of Wee Musketeers! Don't like Wheat Thins? Stick around for my specialty—cockroach croutons.

Time for the ones too big to bother with costumes, the testosterone tanks out for a kick playing Scare the Old Lady Done Up Like a Crone. RAID cocktail, anyone? Just the thing to wash down those spiders. Oh, come now! Don't puke on my front step. Remember me? I'm the old lady you hit with a snowball last winter.

★ ★ ★

Any minute now my daughter, Shirleen, worried about me being alone, will arrive to protect me from the mean old trick-or-treaters. Six months ago, I wheeled her smiling, heavily sedated father through the doors of the Rip Van Winkle Extended Care Facility because, among other confusions, he thought our front hall closet was the elevator in the office building where he and Nurse Rosalie used to get it on. Shirleen and I figured he'd be safe at the Rip, but one night, he climbed into his wardrobe, pushed an imaginary button marked sixteenth floor, and suffered the stroke that now keeps him prisoner of his bed. It gives me satisfaction to see him lying there, knowing I didn't have to cast a single spell.

In past years, Teddy, Shirleen, and I would have a cozy little threesome once a month. She'd pick up a pizza, loaded, no anchovies, and a video, and it'd be just us, like in the old days. Then Teddy entered his soporific stage, falling asleep and wetting the couch, and it just wasn't fun anymore. Jesus. At least I have my bladder under control.

Good thing Shirleen's bringing supper because my cupboards are bare, thanks to my sweet son-in-law Deke who took away my car. I'm now down to two cans of chicken noodle soup, three pieces of stale bread, and one-third of a jar of peanut butter. My freezer is full of little packages I forgot to label: eye of newt, tongue of frog, toe of bear—who knows? The other night I goofed: I heated something in the microwave in a metal pie plate. I've been known to put microwave dishes in the big oven and have them melt all over the shelves. My eyes are punk due to cataracts, but my hearing's okay—worse luck.

Half the time I don't want to answer the phone because it's either Shirleen, the nursing home, or a woman looking for somebody named Frank.

If it wasn't for Shirleen insisting that I leave my house, I'd be fine staying here, thanks to sorcery. Who needs a car when you've got powers? The other day I practiced getting a shopping cart full of groceries, and sure enough, one came to my door. Unfortunately, it was loaded with diapers, baby food, and infant formula. Next time I'll get it right. I'll concentrate on pulling in beer, bagels, and bologna. Keep it simple, that's the idea. I'm not into frills.

★ ★ ★

The phone rings. It's Teddy's nurse wanting to give him oxygen to make him more comfortable. I'm wondering if it'll prolong his life. "How long is this going to take?" I ask.

"To get the oxygen? About five minutes. We have the tanks here. All we have to do is hook him up. Five minutes, tops."

Talk about dense! But then I guess the really smart nurses get to work in private hospitals. "I mean, how long will it take for him to die?"

The nurse pauses. "That, my dear, is something none of us has the power to predict," she says in a voice that drips with honey. I recognize her now. She's the older woman on the night shift, really kind of sweet in a Bible Belt sort of way.

I know I have to cover up, make her think I really care. "Of course. Uh, I'm only anxious for him not to have to suffer any more." I remember my last visit, when Teddy "came to" for a minute. He opened his eyes, looked up at me and said, "Rosalie? Is that you my darling?" Something to make him more comfortable? I don't think so. But I tell the nurse, "Certainly, dear. Give him anything he needs."

★ ★ ★

When Shirleen gets here, I'll show my gratitude by planting a cunning little rat in her overnight case. Shirleen hates rodents. Concentrate, concentrate. You don't need a fancy spell, my textbook says, only one that works for you. *Sallagadoola, menchacaboola, bibbity-bobbity-boo.* Shirleen is really turned off by witchcraft. I can picture her reaction if she opened my oven and saw half a head roasting in a pan. She'd think twice about having me live with her! But that won't be an issue, if I have my way. In my first-ever Halloween grand finale as a witch, I plan to whisk her away to some subterranean shopping mall where all she has to think about is whether they take plastic. I'm only two lessons away from lycanthropy. Shirleen hates snakes as much as she hates rats. I'd really like to be a boa constrictor tonight. I'd give her a hug she'd never forget. Just for kicks I'll give it a try: *Ipsi pipsi domenic*, try your best to make me sick. No, no, that's not it. Wait a minute: *Inka slinka minka doo*. I know it starts like that. Oh, shit. It'd be hard to open the door, anyway, and how would I present the candy bowl? Balanced on my tail? Nah. Better to be me. Scarier, really.

★ ★ ★

The phone rings. "Frank does not fucking live fucking here!"

★ ★ ★

No sooner did we get Teddy settled in the nursing home than Shirleen started in on me. Wasn't the house too big? Didn't I mind being alone?

"Oh no," I told her. "I like solitude."

"You never used to. You used to be with people all the time, Ma." These days when she says "Ma" she bleats the word like a disgruntled sheep. She used to call me Mother or Mom; her husband, Deke, damn his cretinous soul, is the one who always calls his mother Ma. When we were first having this conversation about me moving out, Shirleen was taking me grocery shopping. The day we took Teddy to the home, Deke borrowed our car and he's never given it back, so you can bet I have it in for him! "Anyway," Shirleen continued, "we've been talking,

Deke and me, and we think you ought to move in with us. Deke says he'll finish the back room for you and you can share a bathroom with Junior."

The back room at their house is where Deke keeps all his hunting stuff. It's really just an oversized storage area with a window. And my grandson, Junior, is your average messy sixteen-year-old with some disgusting personal habits. I panicked. "Pardon me?" I managed to blurt, just when we arrived at the supermarket parking lot. Shirleen swung into a handicapped space and whipped out the placard we'd used for Teddy. "What the fuck are you doing?" I said, trying to grab the card before she hung it from the rear-view mirror and declared to the world that her mother was a helpless old fart.

She pushed my hand away. "Jesus, Ma. Don't do that! And don't say fuck. Mothers aren't supposed to say fuck."

Well, she was right. Mothers aren't. And I haven't always. It just seems the right word for me now, when my life is like one big cesspool.

"Now, where's your cane? You know you're not supposed to go without it."

There's a perfect example of what I mean. Suddenly she's the mother, giving orders like a drill sergeant, and I'm the child. If that isn't living in a cesspool, I don't know what is.

"Oh, never mind! I'll get you one of those scooters with a basket."

Scratch child, insert baby. That's what I am, a blubbering, slobbering, idiot baby. Wheel me here, wheel me there. Good, I thought. I'll follow her into the store limping obediently, then I'll get me one of those motherfucking scooters. I'll bump it into the produce counter and spill fruit all over the floor, just to get even.

And I did run the cart up against the fruit display hard enough so that apples, oranges, pears, and grapefruit went bouncing all over the place. It caused a real commotion, and Shirleen was pissed. So there.

★ ★ ★

When I got home from shopping with Shirleen, I made myself a double Scotch on the rocks even though it was only two in the afternoon, and I picked up a copy of Ladies' Own Journal, that useless piece of pap Shirleen reads. As usual, I headed straight for the Classifieds where, amidst the X-rated videos masquerading as sex improvement tools and the ads for chemical peels, I usually find something to order: useful gadgets, nothing exciting—an elastic gizmo to keep my bra straps from falling down, a rubber grip for opening jars, everyday items. This time, however, the phrase "Sorcery for Apprentices" caught my eye. A correspondence course in witchcraft! Delight coursed through me like brandy on a winter's night. At last I'd found a way to make Teddy and Rosalie pay for their sins!

A month later I was performing such simple telekinetic feats as opening my garage door with the blink of an eye. I thought I was being clever, choosing a trick that wouldn't arouse suspicions (how would anyone know I wasn't flipping the switch located inside my house?), but even such subtle forays provoked reactions. At the super-market one day I overheard my neighbor hiss, "Something's going on over at Irene's," so I started thinking of little ways I could discourage her from snooping. Without inflicting major harm, I figured a blister could fester, a bunion erupt, but it was my first such attempt, and it fizzled. The next day, my neighbor's podiatrist speedily removed a puny plantar wart without so much as an extra Medicare form.

Meanwhile, Shirleen continued to get on my case about leaving the house. In my textbook I looked up Meddlesome Daughters, but all I could find listed were some pranky little frogs-in-beds type of things. I wanted something that would teach her a lesson big time. To do that, I assumed I'd have to summon You-Know-Who (you're never supposed to actually utter His name.) I'd have to brush up on my Latin; *veni, vidi, vici*, wouldn't cut it. And there'd be a lot of mumbo jumbo involving gizzards and altars and daggers and smoke. Most sorcerers are careful not to reveal the exact wording for fear just anybody will use the Summons, so it looked like I'd have to make up part of it myself. What was that rhyme from childhood? In pine tar is, in oak none is; in mud eel is, in clay none is. Fake Latin might come in handy, assuming He wasn't the scholarly type.

As for dealing with Shirleen, it was clear I'd have to set a target date. Halloween came to mind immediately. I'd have a whole month to get ready. In studying, my biggest challenge became what to ask for when He arrived. I had to ask myself, what do I want most in all the world? The answer came easily: to stay in my own home. That would involve getting rid of Shirleen forever. I knew the inconvenience it would cause Deke and Junior, who didn't like to cook or clean for themselves, but there seemed no other way out. Shirleen would just have to disappear. But first I'd have to learn the Summons.

Easier said than done! I found all sorts of spells to summon other people. For instance, I could get three gentlemen to appear in my bedroom and have dinner with me by issuing the conjuration that begins *"Hunkulum testicum masculim beastie..."* They'd come right on cue and be very polite, the book promised, and one of them would even stay and make love to me, which I certainly wouldn't mind, especially if he looked like Brad Pitt. But why would Brad Pitt want to get it on with an old crone? And then there was the business about getting rid of the famous Mister Pitt. There had to be a spell for that, too, but I couldn't find one. Poor Brad. He'd be condemned to live forever in my underwear drawer!

In the weeks that followed, the progression of events just confirmed my resolution. As predicted, Deke made good his promise to transform the hunting storage unit into a stuffy little sleeping cubicle. Shirleen talked to Junior, and he swore he'd put the toilet seat down after each use and clean the snot from the sink. But the most crushing blow occurred when I awoke one morning to find a "For Sale by Biddell Realty" sign plunked in the middle of my front lawn. I couldn't believe Shirleen had acted without even consulting me! What I needed, I decided, was definitely a Summons.

* * *

It's Halloween, and finally, the last of the tricksters have spun their toilet-paper webs on the tree branches, and my picture window is a soapy swirl. I can hear Shirleen's car rolling into the garage. She's only two hours later than she said she'd be. (What else is new?) "Baby, that you?" I call in my best little quavery voice.

"You've left the door open again, Ma. Haven't I told you to lock it? Just anybody could creep in, especially on Halloween. Jesus. Well, soon we won't have to worry about keeping you safe. You'll be with us, snug as a bug in a rug."

Ignoring that last remark I coo, "Aren't you nice to be giving up your bowling league to visit me!"

She puts the pizza down on the kitchen counter and brushes her hair back with both hands, using her fingers as combs. Her hair is stringy and shoulder-length, a brittle bottle-blond shade. She wants to be like the ads on TV. "Honey, your hair is so pretty," I lie. "Who's doing it these days? Linda at Kindest Kut?" Linda is Deke's old girl friend from high school. I know Shirleen'd rather die than go to her. "Let's go inside and I'll help you make up the bed in the spare room."

Shirleen looks hurt. "I want to sleep in the big bed with you, Ma. Just like old times. When I was little and used to have bad dreams, and you used to make them go away."

I look at the wiggling overnight case and can see, with pride, something moving inside. "Sure, honey. But don't you want to unpack your things?" I've never been the patient type. I want her to get her surprise NOW.

"After we eat. I'm starved. You got any beer?"

I'm thinking all I have is a case of the liquid pap she bought for me. "There might be some in the frig. I'll get it."

"Thanks, Ma. Hooey! I'm sooo tired. What a day! I had to take Junior to the dentist after school, and then he had to have a new pair of sneakers for basketball practice, and then, since it was bowling night, I had to have Deke's supper ready real early. Actually, it's a relief to be here." While she's talking, she's walking around, snooping. "Where are all the boxes I packed up, Ma? They were all stacked in the living room."

"I did like you suggested. I had the stuff I wanted to keep put in storage and the rest I sent to the Salvation Army." Of course, everything is actually stewing in stagnant puddles in the cellar where I heaved it yesterday in a rage. And to think that Teddy almost fixed that leaky bulkhead years ago!

"Well, good for you." She comes over and sits down beside me, taking my hands in hers. "You know, I gotta say, Ma, you've been such a good sport about this all. Deke and I thought you'd put up a fuss about coming to live with us, but much to our delight, *au contraire*."

"I just know it's best for everyone," I say meekly, peeling off a wedge of pizza and stuffing my mouth. For the next few minutes, we just concentrate on eating. Every once in a while, I sneak a peek at her overnight case, which has moved to the other side of the room. I can hardly wait. Meanwhile I play at being lovable. "Sorry about the beer," I add. "I never drink it."

"Hey, no problem. This stuff is pretty good. What did you say it was?"

"It's a kind of, ah, milk shake." If I tell her it's nutritional supplement, she'll think I've really lost it.

"Mmm. Do they make it in chocolate? Never mind. Chocolate gives me headaches. Uh, Ma. Do you have enough stuff for breakfast? Cause I could run out and get us bagels."

I grasp her wrist. "Don't bother. I've got what we need."

"Ow, Ma. You're hurting me! Christ, when did you cut your nails last? They're like claws. Look. You made me bleed!"

Instantly, I switch into my helpless mode, complete with doe-eyes. "Sorry. I know I haven't been taking care of myself like I should."

"You can say that again! Look at your skin, it's green. And you smell funny. Don't you ever bathe? Eeyeu." She backs away. With any luck she'll stumble over the case, the catch will fly open and a giant rat will crawl out. In fact, the rat does crawl out, but by that time Shirleen is in the bathroom disinfecting herself from my touch and the effect is lost. "Begone," I whisper, and the rat disappears in a puff of smoke. Too bad it's not that easy to get rid of humans. Still, it's good to know I can conjure up a rat when I need one and not have it end up in my underwear drawer.

Shirleen comes out of the bathroom with gauze wrapped around her wrist. "There's slime in the shower," she says, "and the toilet bowl is filthy. When was the last time Mrs. Baker was here to clean?"

Mrs. Baker was the cleaning lady Shirleen hired to keep me tidy. "Oh, didn't I tell you? She took another job across town. To be near her daughter. I guess I should have gotten somebody else, but you know how hard it is to find good help." Actually, I fired her. Oh, I tried changing her into a rabbit. I planned to send her scurrying into my garden where she'd OD on foxglove, but I wasn't up to a prank of that magnitude. Too bad. It would have been a great way to graduate, magna cum laude.

"What's this in my case?" Shirleen asks, shaking rat turds from her nightgown.

I have to struggle to keep from snickering. "Looks like Deke needs to do a little exterminating. It's that time of year, hon. You know. Critters come in looking for food."

"Not in my house! I keep everything in containers. This is from your place, Ma. I don't know how it got in my overnight case, but it did. You've let everything go to pot, including yourself!"

Why thank you, babycakes. Fuck you. "I know," I say, all cow-eyes. "I need to be someplace where I can be cared for. I just bless you and Deke for making all the arrangements."

"Well, at least you and I will be together." Shirleen bends down and hugs me cautiously, taking care not to get clawed.

I can see tears in her eyes. How touching. For a split second I feel my ice melt as I remember the loving duo we used to be, a century ago. As if I even liked being around my son-in-law and his clone for an evening, much less the rest of my life. What do children really know about their parents? You have to wonder.

"At least you'll be well cared for in the years to come. Oh my God, Ma. Will you look at the time? It's almost midnight. That clock can't be right!"

I'd moved the hands ahead when she wasn't looking, the better to issue my Summons. Time flies when you're having fun.

"I'm gonna get ready for bed," I say. "You do the same. You look beat."

In this business you're encouraged to improvise, so here goes. "*Besticum beasticum* quick as you can, *flimulum flamulum* send me a man.*" Shit, that's not right. Wait. I've got it. "*Denizen venizen Hepzibah Quinn, flatular, spatular* let Him come in." Is that a doorbell I hear? "Shirleen. Somebody's at the door. Can you get it?" I can hear her humming and flossing and gargling and spitting. That's the doorbell, all right. "SHIRLEEN. WILL YOU ANSWER THE DOOR?"

"Christ, Ma. I'm not deaf. But who could it be at this hour? I'm gonna keep the chain on, just in case." Shirleen is wearing her bunny slippers with the ears that stick up and wobble around her ankles. I think of Mrs. Baker, who could have been belly-up in the herb garden. "Who's there?" Shirleen calls, cracking the door. I hear a muffled response. My blood heats up and I can feel a tingling in my bowels, a good sign. Whooee. I'm nervous as a schoolgirl on her first date. I get up from my chair and wobble over to the door so I can get a glimpse before the two of them disappear forever. Wait a fucking minute. That's no Prince of Darkness. That's... "Ma," she says, turning away from the door. "You got a nutcase out here says he's Elvis. Want me to call the cops?"

I count to ten, stinging with defeat. Sure enough, he's wearing his rhinestone-studded jumpsuit. "Buzz off, Buster," I say, fixing him with my darkest glare. "Hasta la vista, baby. So long, partner. Hit the road, Jack. In other words, begone." The King looks hurt, but only for a second, then *pouf!* he's gone, just like the rat.

"You know, he looked really real," Shirleen says. "I didn't know they had costumes that were so authentic. And he sounded just like him! It gives me the creeps."

Not bad for my first celebrity, I think, patting myself on the back, but there's got to be another way to get rid of Shirleen. Suddenly it dawns on me. "Have you checked the cellar, hon? We never did get to bring up all those Christmas decorations. I was hoping you and Deke could use them." A quick peek at the old textbook reveals the spell for floods. All I have to do is get her down there, and *Shazaam!* Death by drowning.

"I took them weeks ago, remember?" she says impatiently, convinced I have Alzheimer's, counting me out already. "Here. Have a…whatever this is." She hands me a well-done piece of toast, or is it a burnt offering of another kind? I've lost track. "You know me, always hungry. By the way, I threw out that jelly in the back of the fridge. It had mold on it."

It's clear I'm going to have to buy some more time because tomorrow Biddell Realty is supposed to be bringing over a hot prospect. "What time are they coming to see the house?"

"Oh God, Ma. I knew there was something I forgot to tell you! Biddell had a heart attack! Out of the blue. It was really strange. They said he'd never had any health problems before. The thing is, they don't know if he'll make it, so I guess we're gonna have to find another agent."

My heart bleeds for Biddell. And I didn't even have to lift a finger! The power of negative thinking. The wheels are turning, turning. Aha! Another plan to get rid of my pain-in-the-neck progeny. "Shouldn't we take the trash out to the garage?" I say, pointing to several swollen trash bags sitting in the corner of my kitchen.

"I'll do it, Ma. You have a bad back, remember?" She drags the plastic sacks which leave a watery pink wake. "Phew. Did you have fish in your freezer? Something yucky is defrosting."

In one of my darker fantasies, I caught the Fed Ex man snooping around the house and uttered the spell to get rid of everyday nuisance types ("*Tintinaboobulous, tintinabomb,* we're gonna crud every Harry and Tom.") "Oh, that. That's the horned pout Teddy caught five years ago fishing in Maine," I say. "Definitely toss it."

Shirleen deposits the sacks in the one remaining empty trash can in our garage. If I'm right, she'll take a cigarette break, giving me a little window of opportunity. While she's lighting up a cigarette, I'll utter my super-duper made-to-order incantation. I'll bring the garage doors crashing down with such a force the whole house shakes. I'll squash her like a grape. "*Incumous nincumous wobbledy woo…*" Before I can finish, the whole house shakes with the force of the impact. Then everything's quiet.

I wait a few minutes before punching 911. "Something awful (gasp), accident (sob), send help (choke.)" Within minutes there's a big vehicle outside my house and floodlights are turning night into day. I hobble to the door to take a peek. What I see is Shirleen talking to the neighbor as if nothing in the world has happened. They're looking in the direction of another neighbor's lawn where, of all things, a well is being drilled at half past midnight. Bang! goes the rig and my house shakes again. Shirleen glances over her shoulder, sees me looking at her and gives me a big fat wave. I remember a little girl getting on a school bus, riding a two-wheeler, going to the prom, and suddenly my eyes fog up so I can hardly see the big keys on my phone. "Never mind, operator. Everything's okay here," I say, thinking, shit, where did I go wrong?

Mommy Dearest

Shirleen

The morning after the worst night of my life, the night my mother, who thinks she's a witch, went completely berserk, I realized she could have the upper hand no longer. I came to this decision knowing Ma would continue to do everything she could to thwart me. But she and I are made of the same strong stuff and I know how to dish it out as well as she does, so I came right out and told her she was coming to live with us. Period.

She stuck her stubborn Polish chin up in the air, stamped her size-nine clodhoppers, crossed her beefy arms over her sagging chest and said, "I'm not leaving this house until it's sold, and that's that!"

"You're packing your clothes and coming with me, and that's that!" I insisted. I ran into her bedroom and started throwing things from her bureau drawers into a big suitcase. Ma has more stuff than anyone I've ever known, including her mother, who was completely senile by the time we moved her into a nursing home. We needed a derrick to clear out that woman's house. But Ma goes her one better: She has hats from the 30s, shoes from the 40s, and purses from the time they were called pocketbooks. She has long black gloves and angora sweaters and a poodle skirt. This woman never throws anything out! She's a stranger to the collection bins at the Salvation Army, and she would never, ever give anything to Catholic charities because she was raised to believe that Catholics were evil. Quite simply, my mother is the queen of pack rats.

When she saw what I was doing, she was on me like some wild animal. "Give me that!" she screeched. "That's mine! You have no right, you stinking little pisser!" (Her language has gotten more vulgar as her interest in witchcraft has grown.) "Put those things back where you found them!" And she proceeded to unpack the suitcase.

"Fine! Leave everything here. We'll come back at a later time, or, better still," and here I paused for effect, because I knew how this would anger her, "The nuns from Our Lady of Mercy can come in and take the whole damned mess."

"Over my dead body!" she shouted, hurling Cuban heels against the wall. "I won't have strangers pawing through my things!" Then, almost as if someone had flipped a switch inside her head, her mood changed abruptly. She began putting things back in the suitcase. "I won't need any of this, will I? Not where I'm going! You people never go places where I'd need to dress up in fancy clothes! I'll only need a few things, some old outfits…who cares what I look like, anyway?"

Well, I didn't have the time or inclination to deal with her self-pity so I said, "Why don't you take some basic things, like slacks, a couple sweaters, underwear, a robe, slippers? We can deal with the other stuff tomorrow. But hurry, Ma. I told Deke I'd be home for lunch today."

She mumbled something about always having to fit in with my husband's schedule. I wasn't going to let her get away with bad-mouthing Deke, which she does all the time. "I beg your pardon?"

"Oh, never mind. Look, Shirleen. Here's the deal. You go about your business, and I'll go about mine. Come back in, say, a couple hours, and I'll be ready to go."

Seeing her sitting there on the edge of the bed she'd shared with Pop for so many years, I began to sense how hard this was on her, so I agreed, even though my better judgment told me not to leave. "Okay, Ma," I said reluctantly, thinking I had a lot to do and this was probably a better idea in the long run, even if it was hers.

I went on my errands, then dashed home to fix lunch for Deke. The next thing I knew, I was getting a call from the police department saying Ma had stolen the next-door neighbor's car!

Mabel Gallagher's car—what was Ma thinking? For Christ's sake, Mabel's son is a big-shot California lawyer. But then, as if he had read my mind, the policeman said, "No charges are being pressed. Your mother is one lucky lady. You want to talk to her? Never mind: She doesn't want to talk to you!"

I never did find out what Ma had in mind when she stole the car, but I've got a feeling Mabel won't be leaving her keys in the ignition anymore. Ma was contrite, or acted as if she was, and Mabel, bless-her-heart, was forgiving.

I brought Ma and her suitcase here to our home, promising her we'd start weeding though her things slowly, that she could decide where everything would go, and that if there were possessions she couldn't bear to part with, we'd find some place to store them. I didn't have the heart to tell her I'd heard from the real estate agency at noon. They had a buyer who wanted to know how long it would take us to empty the house.

★ ★ ★

Having Ma under my roof is stifling. It's only been a few days, and already I feel she's using up my space, even though she stays in her room most of the time, sulking. It's sad. But it could be much worse: She could be with Pop in the nursing home. If she didn't have us to take her in, that's definitely where she'd be. And in less than a year, all the money would be gone. This way, Pop can be private-pay for a while longer. Although they tell you it doesn't make any difference in the quality of care, I think it probably does.

Having her here also makes me think of my childhood. The other day, for instance, I remembered that when I was in the third grade, I sat next to a girl named Bonnie, a stuck-up little prig who told me her name meant pretty in Scotland. The thing I remember most about

Bonnie was that she picked her nose. She may have had the highest IQ in the elementary school, but she had a disgusting habit that drove me crazy.

Well, just as I was remembering Bonnie, the most amazing coincidence occurred—my mother brought up her name in conversation! It was after lunch, the first meal Ma had eaten in a couple of days of hunger-striking. We'd been working hard to clear out her house, and the more time we spent packing up, the more she got depressed. Then, out of the blue she said, "I wonder what ever happened to Bonnie McCullough? You know, that cunning little girl who won the spelling bee and went on to the county final and then to Washington, D.C., where she lasted until the final round? That Bonnie McCullough. Mm, this soup is delicious. I think I'll have some more."

At first, I was so relieved Ma wasn't suicidal, I ignored the fact she'd uttered the name of my nemesis. Ma knew only too well I'd never forgotten that spelling bee when I, the best speller in the third grade, had goofed on a simple word: depth. "D-E-B-T-H!" I crowed loudly, and everybody laughed. "Well," I explained lamely, "It sounds like it's got a B in it…" My embarrassment turned to agony as I watched Bonnie stagger off the stage under the weight of the bronze trophy that was supposed to sit on our living room mantle.

"You know, the girl who won a full scholarship to State but whose family sent her to Radcliffe," Ma continued between slurps of soup. "The girl who got a Fulbright?"

By then I was seething with jealousy. "Can't say that I do remember her," I lied.

But Ma has the tenacity of a pit bull terrier. "Oh, you must remember Bonnie," she continued, watching my face for a response.

I stormed out to the kitchen, my mother's empty bowl in my hand. It was clear to me she thrived on confrontation. Too bad I couldn't say the same about myself.

★ ★ ★

The other day when I went to visit Pop, he was smaller than ever. The nurses tell me he hardly eats at all. They say it's common in cases like his. It's clear to me he wants to die. I don't blame him. What's he got to live for?

Sometimes he seems to know I'm there. The other day he formed the words "hello darling" with his mouth, but no sound came out. I hope he knew it was me, but I suspect he thought it was his darling Rosalie.

These days he only wears sweatsuits. His waist is so swollen from edema he can't fit into normal clothes. As a consequence, my poor Pop, who was always so careful about his appearance, looks like a slob in an oversized jacket that says "Champion" and pants that are stained with urine. They're pretty good about keeping him clean, but there just aren't enough aides to handle every accident.

My visits usually begin like this: "Hello, Pop. Feeling any better today? You're looking better. They keeping you comfy? You're looking comfy." I always pray for some response because it's difficult to carry on a one-way conversation. Yesterday, I was surprised to hear him grunt. "Is that a yes? Well, good. The nurses think you're pretty special, you know." Actually, they do. When he first came to the home, he still had enough gumption to flirt and tease, and right up until his last stroke he retained some of his old spirit.

They tell me that touch is important, so when I visit I always hold his hand. I caress his paper-thin skin, so easily bruised. A minor brush against the guard rail is enough to produce bleeding. In his professional days, Pop would have known just what to call it—a subcutaneous something-or-other. I'm glad he's disoriented. It would be awful for him to know the truth about his condition, to be able to see into the future and realize what horrors lie ahead. Of course, he seems to be aware of what's happening. The other day as I was leaving, his sad eyes sent me this message: Excuse me for being a smelly old man.

* * *

When I was eight, Pop had his license revoked for prescribing diet pills and tranquilizers for his obese patients. He was such a softy. If some poor fat lady came to him wanting to be thin, he'd try his damnedest to oblige. Unfortunately, one of them died from an overdose, and her family came after Pop. Afterwards, he couldn't even get a job doing physicals because no company would insure him. That was a bad time. I was in the third grade, sitting next to Bonnie McCullough, who beat me at spelling and picked her nose. "My mom and dad called your dad a drug dealer and a murderer," Bonnie said one day.

"Shut up, you liar!" I yelled, bursting into tears.

Bonnie narrowed her eyes. "Your dad should have gone to jail for what he did. Instead they just gave him an iddy-biddy slap on the wrist." She tapped her left wrist with her right hand to demonstrate the insignificance of the punishment. "Just a little old slap for killing that poor obeast woman by feeding her ill-issit drugs."

"Snot-eater," I hissed. "You make me sick." Then the bell rang for recess and we went our separate ways on the playground, which was a good thing because I probably would have beaten her to a pulp.

★ ★ ★

When I get back from visiting Pop, I tell Ma what I always tell her: "He's just the same, only smaller." This time I add, "Actually, I think he's getting sicker. He won't eat."

"Well, that's one way to go," she says bluntly. These days when we talk about Pop's death, we always say "go." It seems more cheerful, somehow; as if he's on a trip and looking forward to reaching his destination. Neither Ma nor I really believe in an afterlife, though what witches would say about that, I'm not sure. Since Ma's gotten hooked on the occult, I suppose anything is possible. "Well, I hope he goes soon," she says quietly, and sighs.

We sit in silence for a while, and then it comes, the question she always poses. "Did he ask for me?"

"Of course," I lie, thinking she knows he's in a twilight state and not in a position to make conversation, polite or otherwise.

"You're a fucking liar," she says.

"Fine. Next time you want to know if he's talking, you go there yourself!"

She hasn't been to see him in over a week. Of course, the way she talks and dresses is disgraceful. If Pop were with it, it'd send him clear over the edge to see her like this. So, once more, I'm glad he's pretty much gonzo. "You want to know the truth? I'll tell you: he just sort of grunts. At first I was excited, thinking that it was the beginning of something, but then he didn't make another sound the whole time I was there."

I decided not to tell her about his mouthing hello, because we might get started on Darling Rosalie, who was Pop's nurse at the time of the trial. It came out during questioning that they were lovers and that they used to have sex after hours on the examining table. Somewhere Ma has a stack of newspaper clippings, though why she'd want to save them is beyond me. There's one story that features a big two-column picture of Rosalie posing on the table, a real tabloid shot. She was a babe, Deke says. Naturally, both Ma and I hate her for ruining our lives. As if Pop had nothing to do with it!

Before Mrs. Peabody (the fat lady who OD'd) and Rosalie, we were pretty happy. I can remember we took a lot of trips. Ma and Pop were always laughing and fooling around, touching each other every chance they got. Ma was a full-figured sexy blond with a page-boy hairdo and big, eager eyes. Pop was handsome in a clean-cut athletic way and he looked younger than his age. Although he wasn't very tall, he carried himself well, with his shoulders squared and his head held proudly, and he had a wonderful smile. His sandy hair was cut in the flat crew style of the day. When he wasn't working, he liked to wear chinos and colored shirts with the sleeves rolled up to reveal his muscular arms. He lifted weights, which wasn't all that common back then.

Once I caught them making love in the kitchen. It was late at night when they thought I was asleep. I'd come downstairs to get a glass of milk and some cookies and there they were, heavily into it. I was about six at the time and I didn't know what was going on. As soon as they saw me, they got flustered. In her hurry to pull down her dress Ma bumped her elbow on the counter. "Oh, Irene honey, did you hurt yourself?" Pop asked, as he kissed her arm.

Of course, after the trial, everything changed. We sold our house in Florida and moved to New York, to a small town in the Hudson River Valley, where we've stayed. It was a year or two before Pop got back on his feet and took a job with a medical supply firm. I think they were very brave to hire him, considering that the story of his professional misdeeds had appeared in papers all over the country. Fortunately, Pop's new job kept him out of the limelight. Working behind the scenes, he helped them decide what to order and how much, and became involved in some of the key decisions regarding the running of the business.

By the time he retired, he was a vice president, and the firm had grown large enough to have branches across the nation. He and Ma moved into a smaller house where they continued to live quietly. They had long since signed a truce, but Rosalie continued to make her presence felt in our lives. Even after she married a stockbroker named Bixby and moved to Short Hills, New Jersey, she actually had the nerve to send Ma and Pop a Christmas card every year.

Right after we moved up here to Riverton, we heard she'd taken a job with our former dentist. As I grew wiser about such matters I used to wonder if she and the tooth doctor had sex in the office, and if so, where? In the reception area, on the small couch next to the potted palm; or in the little dark room where he used to develop x-rays?

"Hey," Ma says, jabbing me with her fist. "Wake up. I'm talking to you. I was just saying I think I'll wait a couple days to visit your father." She always refers to him as my father, never her husband or Teddy, which is his given name. "Might as well spread things out, you know? I mean, since you were just there."

★ ★ ★

By the time I was in high school, I had pretty much forgotten about the family scandal. I worked hard at getting good grades, and tried to make everyone like me. I was elected vice president of my class; in those years boys still got to be president of everything. I played basketball. And then, in my junior year, I started going out with Deke McClure, a jock. In a couple of months, we were in love and sleeping together every chance we got, in the back of his father's big Chevrolet and, when we were lucky, on the small bed in my mother's sewing room very late at night when my parents were asleep.

I didn't care what people thought. It was after the hippies and the yippies and even in our small town, things were changing. I was crazy in love, so much so that we never used a condom. I guess I was too stupid to go on the pill. Consequently, I got pregnant. I had to leave school the first semester of my senior year. Deke stuck by me, and we were married in his parents' living room, with Ma and Pop both in tears, convinced I had ruined my life. Deke went on to graduate, but he never went to college. Although he never says anything about it, I think he has regrets; after all, he could have had a full football scholarship.

Getting my high school diploma gave me a boost, but I'd like to get a college degree someday. Meanwhile, I keep busy taking Adult Ed courses: French, Quilting, t'ai chi. I've always wanted to study law or be a teacher. There are a million things I'd like to do.

When Donald Kenneth Jr. was born it seemed as though we'd be happy. We hadn't planned to have a baby and I certainly hadn't counted on having to drop out of school, but Deke and I loved each other, and Junior was adorable. I was suddenly the envy of all my friends. They thought Deke and I were so romantic, and they couldn't wait to take turns caring for the baby. I could have told them it wasn't all that great living with your in-laws in a little apartment over their garage. That place was so crowded that Deke and I fell over each other every time we got up and moved around.

After graduation, Deke went right to work for his dad who owned a commercial cleaning franchise. At school, he got paid a little to help coach the football team. My folks helped us out, too. It took a while for them to get over the feeling I'd gotten pregnant on purpose, but when they finally understood, they stopped blaming me and started trying to be helpful.

It was hardest for Ma, who'd never been what you'd call a natural mother. I think at one time she had career dreams. She had a good singing voice and studied dancing from the time she was little. If she hadn't been needed to help at home, to run the chicken farm, and, eventually, to take care of her mother, she might have done something interesting with her life.

I can remember her trying out for amateur productions, taking the smaller but still significant roles, but after Rosalie, she lost interest in acting—and practically everything else. Gradually, she let herself go until her beautiful shiny blond hair turned brittle and her eyes became dull from watching daytime television. Ma rarely left the house. She wore print dresses that were too tight and needed shortening. And she drank too much.

When Pop had his first stroke, a miracle occurred: Ma came to. It was as if she'd been comatose. After Pop had made a full recovery, people said that the stroke was actually a blessing, because it brought my mother back to life. Within a couple of months, she was her old self. She even went to Pop's office and handled the accounts so he wouldn't fall behind. She lost weight and stopped drinking. She cleaned the house and bought herself a new wardrobe. As the Bible says, Pop and I rejoiced, and were exceeding glad.

* * *

Over the years I've had regrets, but hasn't everyone? There's always something we wish we'd done differently. In my case, I've often felt

I was cheated out of a regular grown-up life. I was really little more than a child when I married Deke. These days it's different because kids mature much earlier. I see this in Junior, who's sixteen going on thirty. For instance, I know he started having sex when he was fourteen. I knew he was hanging out with Tuffy Carter and Tuffy's older sister, Cissie, who had her eye on practically anything that wore pants. Junior has always looked more mature than the other boys his age. He has his daddy's big athletic build and he seems to have inherited his grandpa's way with women. Worse luck for the woman he marries! Anyway, Junior stayed a lot after school that spring, and I knew he wasn't getting that many detentions. He didn't run track or play baseball, so I knew it wasn't sports-related. Where he and Cissie went to have sex I don't know, but I can recall from my younger days that when those hormones start to rage, there's no denying the urge.

My suspicions were confirmed when Junior came to me complaining of certain telltale symptoms. I took him to the doctor, who diagnosed a whomping case of genital warts. I made Junior call Cissie, considering it my civic duty to halt the spread of STD in my community. Junior's never forgiven me. Whoever said that being a mother was easy?

About my regrets: I really do wish I'd been able to stay in school. Nowadays, if a girl gets pregnant, she stays until the baby is born and then goes back as soon as possible after the birth. They even have daycare. In one coed home-economics class, the kids carry around eggs so they can get used to caring for something fragile. Fortunately, you can't scramble a baby!

After Junior was born, I think I had a postpartum depression. I remember I didn't want to do anything but lie in bed all day. That's when Ma came over and yelled at me. "What in heaven's name do you think you're doing, Shirleen?" (In those days she didn't use the F-word.) "You have a husband and a baby to care for. This place looks like a pigsty!" The apartment was so small I couldn't really do a whole lot to mess it up, only leave dirty dishes in the sink and diapers in the trash. It was more a case of me being messed-up. After a couple days of Ma picking on me, I decided it was time to pull myself together, so I began to make an effort. But no matter how hard I tried to be cheerful, there was a lingering sadness that prevented me from feeling happy.

It wasn't that I disliked being a mother; it was just that I'd see my friends walking home from school or getting together on weekends to do the kinds of fun things that young girls do, and I'd be jealous. It didn't take long for Deke and me to get into a major rut. Basically, all he wanted to do when he wasn't working was eat steak sandwiches, drink beer, and watch TV; looking back, I can see my biggest mistake was that I let him.

* * *

When Junior entered grade school, I had a chance to go to work as a lunchroom aide. Without a high school diploma, my options were limited, so it didn't surprise me that what I'd be doing in the high school cafeteria would be serving food to all the football slobs and cleaning up after the rich kids who thought it was beneath them to take their trays to the window. Thank goodness I had sense enough to say no to that employment opportunity! I realized then that if I'd ever have a chance at a decent job, I'd have to finish school.

So, I did. I only had a year to go, so it didn't take much effort on my part, and I got to like studying. Deke was a little impatient at first, maybe even jealous, but I think Junior liked to see his ma doing homework, and when I got my diploma, everyone was proud—mostly me. In the years since then, I've considered working towards a college degree, but somehow I always get sidetracked. Fortunately, there are courses offered through adult ed that really appeal to me—like ornithology, which I've signed up to take in the spring, taught by a zoologist from the community college.

Deke now thinks my passion for learning is a good thing. "Instead of sittin' around on her butt watching QVC she's out there learnin' stuff," I heard him tell his buddy Carl. When they're together, Deke talks like a country boy.

"But what about them teachers? Doncha worry about them puttin' the make on her?" Carl still thinks like a caveman. He's married to Martha, who has agoraphobia, which is fine by Carl. "At least I know where my missus is all the time."

"You ever see any of 'em? They're mostly fags. I don't think I got anything to worry about from fags." The minute I heard Deke say this I lost the warm fuzzy feeling I usually got when he boasted to others about my schooling. Oh, it's true that Stanley Frobush, who teaches painting, is very effeminate, and that Harvey Millhouse, the poet, has been seen at the diner holding hands with his housemate. But at the other end of the spectrum there's Judd Madison. When Judd isn't teaching t'ai chi to housewives, he's coaching soccer at Miss Emily Paulson's School for Girls. Rumor has it that he's slept with half the team. They don't come any more stud than Judd; if Deke saw him, he'd really be worried.

To tell the truth, I don't think it would occur to Deke that I might cheat on him. I certainly haven't thus far. Not that I haven't been attracted to other men, but I think Pop's affair with Rosalie taught me a lot about what infidelity can do to a family.

Not that I haven't been tempted. Recently I hired a guy to paint and paper Ma's room. He was maybe in his late twenties—bearded, tall, and muscular, stomach like a washboard (he took off his shirt once so I observed), musical (played the guitar on his lunch break), blue-eyed, and from Montréal. His name was Rolfe, and when he smiled, I got all weak in the knees. If that guy had made a pass at me, I'd have responded in a minute.

Towards the end of his assignment, Rolfe apologized for not getting the job done on time. "Ah cood come an work on zee wick end eef you like," he said.

"Oh, no," I said quickly, thinking that Deke and Junior would be around and it wouldn't be any fun. "There's no big rush. You can finish next week. Actually, there might be another couple of small jobs you could do when you're finished in here..." But Rolfe had paused for coffee (which I brewed fresh for him whenever he wanted it) and was singing something sexy, and how could I concentrate on redecorating? I just slid to the floor and sat, transfixed, until the petcock on my pressure cooker started to hiss. How long had it been since I'd had an orgasm? I couldn't remember. I got up slowly, feeling all heavy in the legs, and forced myself to walk into the kitchen, where I rescued my corned beef and cabbage.

The next week Rolfe finished papering Ma's room. He said he didn't have any more time to give me because he needed to go visit a friend. "Une amie?" I asked. He smiled. Would he be back in our area soon? He shrugged his shoulders. Did that mean maybe? I hoped so. Maybe was good enough for me.

That night I seduced my husband for the first time ever. He was surprised at first, maybe even a little shocked. But when he got used to the idea of me taking the initiative, he lost his shyness and we had a good old time. Afterwards he looked at me in amazement and said, "Whooee, woman. What got into you?"

* * *

Now that Ma is living with us and Pop is dying and I've still got my normal responsibilities to tend to, a weekend with Rolfe sounds pretty good to me. I often think about him. In a way, it's better than if something had really happened. This way I can continue to fantasize about how and where and what it would have been like. In my daydreams, Rolfe's transformed into a Fabio-like hunk, and I am a Southern belle, all scented and slim and virginal.

"What are you thinking about? You nearly let that stew boil over, Shirleen. If I hadn't been here beside you, you'd have some mess to clean up."

"Mm, yeah, Ma, thanks, what would I do without you?" the words come tumbling out of my mouth automatically. At this moment Rolfe and I are in a cave, riding out a storm, and he is about to ravish me. At a time like this I can hardly be concerned with stew.

"Watch it! You turned the heat higher instead of lower! Here. Let me finish. You go lie down. You feeling okay? Your face is all flushed."

So, I leave her alone in my kitchen, something I simply never do, while I run into the bathroom and splash cold water on my face. She's only been with us a couple of weeks, but it feels like forever, and there's no end in sight. She's my shadow. Everything I do, she's right there doing it with me. It isn't that I don't understand. I know she's lonely. I've tried to get her involved with the church women. But she doesn't like being with other people.

"What am I going to say to them?" she responds.

"Well, you start off with hello and the rest just follows. Since when did you become a recluse, Ma? You used to love being with the girls." No sooner are the words out of my mouth when I realize she'd never been what you'd call gregarious. She was always a loner. Still, I press on. "Those church ladies are nice. They'll make you feel right at home. You'll see." But I sense I'm wasting my breath.

The next day she surprises me by saying she's changed her mind; She's heard there's a sewing circle at the parsonage, and she wants to go. "All right, Ma! Good for you. Uh, how about taking a shower, washing your hair, changing your clothes? You know, best foot forward…"

"I took a shower Monday," she snapped. "This is Thursday. And my hair looks fine!"

"Here. Let me just comb it a bit. It's such a rat's nest."

"Hey! Hands off! I don't tell you how to dress and how to wear your hair. If they don't like me the way I am, the hell with them."

So, I put my slightly smelly, borderline-soiled mother in the car and drive her to the parsonage, where the minister's wife is hosting the sewing circle. "Well," hoots Mrs. Donderhook, head of the Ladies' Aid Society and an influential member of the Dutch Reformed Church in Riverton, "we were wondering, Shirleen, when you were going to introduce us to your mother. And here she is! Does that mean we'll see her on Sundays from now on?"

"Don't bet on it," Ma mutters. I notice she smells like soured milk.

"I beg your pardon?" chirps Mrs. D. "Didn't quite catch what you said. Hard of hearing, you know. I do have one good ear, though. Sit on my other side. There. Now what was it you said?"

"She was wondering when I should come back to pick her up," I say hastily. "An hour or two?" The prospect of two hours without Ma was wonderful.

"I'll bring her home," Mrs. D. says. "I know just where your house is, Shirleen. My cleaning lady lives across the street. Betty Green. You must know her."

"Is she the one who has a fifteen-year-old who..." Ma interjects.

I glare. "That one, yes. Well, Mrs. D., that's really very nice of you, but I can just swing by here after I pick Junior up at football practice. I wouldn't want to have you go out of your way."

"It's not out of her way," Ma says. "She wants to do it. So, let her."

"Well. Thanks. I guess I'll see you all...soon, then."

Ma hardly notices when I leave. She and Mrs. D. are busy picking nuts out of the brownies. Ma has a thing about walnuts. "The Mormon Tabernacle Choir Sings Songs of Inspiration" is blasting on the stereo. "Don't bother to get up," I say, but they are deep in concentration.

★　★　★

At 6:30, when Ma still hasn't come home, we sit down at the table and have our dinner. "I can't imagine where she is. I called the parsonage, and that meeting broke up hours ago," I say for the third time.

"Doesn't Mrs. Donderhook know where we live?" Junior asks.

"She said she did."

"Maybe they went to a movie," Deke suggests. "Although, they don't usually have matinees on weekdays."

I keep getting up and going to the window, hoping by some miracle to see Mrs. D.'s Olds come barreling down our street. Knowing Ma and her propensity these days for getting into trouble, I'm beginning to have a bad feeling.

"I'll do the dishes," Deke offers, sensing my anxiety. "Maybe you and Junior ought to go out looking for her. God knows what she's gotten herself into now. Jesus, Shirleen. Your mother. She's certainly unpredictable."

At that minute we hear a car pull up to the curb and we run to the window. Sure enough, it's the Olds. We watch as Ma, somewhat unsteadily, gets out of the back seat and staggers up the front walk. "Holy shit!" Junior says. "Grandma's toasted!" Deke opens the front door and catches her as she falls in.

Ma sits on the floor and looks up at us with the air of an innocent, slightly dopey child. "Well, what have we here? A welcoming committee? Don't say it. I know what you're thinking, but Mrs. D. and I just stopped in at Bugsy's Tavern for a teensy little pick-me-up, and before we knew it, we were plastered! You know, she's all right! I mean, for someone whose ancestors once owned Manhattan. Oh, don't worry, the bartender wouldn't let her drive. He called her son, and Barclay the Bank President came to get us. See?" She rolled over and opened her jacket, exposing her well-stained outfit, "All in one piece! What a gas! Well, don't just stand there with your mouths hanging open. Help me to my room. And forget about dinner, Shirleen. I've had enough beer nuts to last me till tomorrow." She hiccoughs. "Also, I think I may have wet my pants."

Then she throws up.

This woman doesn't need witchcraft, I think. She's perfectly capable of wrecking my life without it.

Settling In

Irene

"**T**his is the deal," I say to Junior. "You stay on your side of the world, and I'll stay on mine." We're sitting on the edge of my bed in the little room at the back of his parents' house, just across the hall from his room. He looks at me with love in his eyes, the kind of non-judgmental, adoring love you expect to receive from your progeny but which I don't get from Shirleen. This kid is different. From the day he was born, he was mine. I captured his spirit, and that was long before the thought of practicing witchcraft ever seized my imagination.

"Deal," he says, and grins broadly. He's not what you'd call handsome, but he's got definite appeal. He can't help it if he's gotten most of his features from his dad, like the broad, flat nose of a prize fighter and the wide-set eyes. He has his mother's golden hair—her natural shade, that is, not the brassed-up tone she favors now—and her generous mouth. He's got good teeth, too, if he doesn't knock them out playing football. The kid has a heart; look how many times he's been to see Teddy. It can't be easy for a sixteen-year-old to visit his stroked-out grandfather in a nursing home—the smells alone'll get you—but he goes, and he's cheerful about it. Now he stands up, towers over me like a big bear, and bends over to give me the softest kiss. "You'll get used to it here, Grandma. I did." What's not to love?

I know one thing. I know I won his respect when I got arrested last week. Now Mabel Gallagher, that stupid bitch, was just asking to have her car stolen. I mean, how dumb can you get? She leaves the keys in the ignition. Well, duh. She's lucky the person who finally stole it was me and not some lowlife who'd strip it for parts. If it hadn't been for Howie Bender, that snoop who lives across from her, she wouldn't have noticed it was gone until Thursday, when she goes to get her hair done. By that time, I would have accomplished my task, which was to burn my house to the ground. Hey, I figured if I can't stay there, nobody can. I was on my way to buy kerosene when Howie reported me to the police and, as they say, the rest is history.

Now Mabel won't talk to me. Who the fuck cares? I don't live next to her any more. Shirleen has seen to that. Besides, Mabel and I have zero, zip, zilch in common. She's a good Catholic, down on her knees every chance she gets, but, if you ask me, it's so she can keep her ear to the ground. That woman knows more about the neighborhood than anyone else. She kept track of who was doing what to whom, and she wasn't a bit shy about sharing the info with anyone who wanted to listen. Get me! I'm talking about her in the past tense, as if I could make her disappear, when I know that stuff is all in the past. After all, I promised Shirleen.

The other day, when Mrs. Donderhook and I got tipsy, I was tempted to break my promise. Now, as a result of misbehaving, I've had my telephone privileges revoked for a week. I'm not even allowed to answer the phone, I have to let the machine get it. (Of course, this way I can listen to all the messages, and some of them have been very interesting.) I wonder what Lavinia's family did to her? I bet that's the only time she's ever been in Bugsy's Tavern. The minister's wife came to call yesterday, but Shirleen told her I was ill. I'm a prisoner. The only place I'm allowed to go is down to the nursing home to visit Teddy, which is punishment enough, I say. My cell is a converted closet with a single bed, a night table, and my mother's boudoir chair, a small upholstered relic from bygone days, the only possession she ever really liked. I was touched when she said she wanted me to have it. Oh, I have Teddy's bureau, too. Would you believe I found a picture of Rosalie in the top drawer? "To my Teddy, Always yours, Ros," is written on the back. I ripped it in five pieces and threw it in the wastebasket, then retrieved it. You can never tell when it might come in handy, spellwise. Of course, I made a promise to Shirleen.

This place sucks. My clothing just barely fits in the closet. There's no window. The door doesn't shut completely, so that when Junior's pals are over, I feel I have no privacy. I should be living by myself. If they won't let me stay in my own house, I could get an apartment somewhere. If Teddy would only be a good sport and die, I could use the house money to set myself up quite nicely; instead, it'll all go to pay for his stay in the nursing home.

I hate to say it, but the last time I went to visit him he looked better than the time before, when I'd put my mouth down next to his good ear and urged him to speed things up. "Croak, you old fart," I'd said. The nurse's aide nearly caught me stage-whispering sweet nothings, but I just smiled and said sweetly, "Doesn't he look peaceful?"

That little Irish colleen who talks as if she's just stepped off the boat trilled, "Oh, yes, ever so peaceful. He's one of our treasures. You two must have had a wonderful life together." I nearly puked. But then, I had to admit, before the slut and the fatty, we really did have a pretty good life. The girl continued, "Do you know, we thought himself was coming to yesterday. Did the head nurse tell you? He fluttered his eyelids and raised his right hand. One of the orderlies saw it. I always say, the good Lord works in wondrous ways. Thanks be to God!"

If she'd gone on like that any longer, I made my mind up to leave, but she had the good sense to shut her yap and finish her chores in silence. Then she left the room. It was then I noticed that Teddy's left eye was blinking. Shit, I thought. He's gonna make a recovery and spoil everything. But then I noticed the eye was closed again. Whew.

"Oh, Mrs. Richards," the head nurse called as I passed her desk. "Could I see you for a moment?" I pretended not to hear her. Instead I headed right for the front hallway where I could see Junior was waiting for me. "Yoo hoo." The nurse slid in front of me, blocking my exit. "I wonder if you know the payment for Dr. Richard's room and board is overdue."

"You'll get your money," I snapped. My voice echoed in the hallway, causing folks to look up from their noodle craft projects. Right on cue, one of the poor lost souls (as Miss Killarney calls them) grabbed his crotch, and when the nurse took him to the bathroom, I made a break for it. In my haste, I forgot you have to push a button to open the sliding doors. My nose hit the glass with a significant impact, and I reeled backward. Junior, still dressed in his football uniform, rushed to steady me. Above the dark protective smudges, I could see genuine concern in his eyes. If it weren't for him, I don't know what I'd do, but as we rode home, I couldn't help thinking that if I hadn't promised Shirleen I wouldn't fool around, I'd be outta this mess for sure.

★ ★ ★

This is Shirleen's day to help Deke out at the office. "Ma, I worry about leaving you alone. You're not going to do anything stupid, are you?" she says as she pulls on her jacket and gets ready to leave.

"Without wheels? Don't be ridiculous."

"I don't want you calling a cab. If you have errands to do, Junior can take you after school."

"Okay, okay." I would have said anything to get her out of the house. Today is the day I'm going to mix potions. I know I promised I wouldn't, but I was awake for most of last night, tossing and turning, and I finally reached a decision. Witchcraft is like sex; you use it or lose it. And I don't intend to lose it. "Don't worry about me. I'll be fine."

"Oh, Ma. Look at you. You need some new clothes. Well. Next week we'll take a day, go into the city, do some shopping. Just like old times. What do you think?"

Ick. "Terrific." I watch her skip out to the garage and get into my old car. Then, when I'm sure she's out of sight I run out to the back yard, looking for Frisky the cat, who's going to donate a key ingredient. "Frisky!" I call, at first sweetly. No answer. "Frisky!" Then I remember: Frisky is an unaltered male, and the neighbor's kitten is in heat. Guess it's back to the books to do a little improvising.

In the kitchen, alone, I'm in my element. I swear I never had so much fun cooking. You have to use a lot of pots, which you later have to scrub, and the odor is horrific, but you get such a sense of power! And improvisation is called for at every turn. You have to be resourceful. For instance, who has hen's teeth lying around the house? And furthermore, do hens have teeth? I'm not sure. For a cauldron, I substitute a lobster pot. Phew. This one is really bad. I'm going to dump some of Shirleen's Devastating Love bath oil in it to improve the aroma. There. That's better. Now, just simmer until done.

While I'm waiting, I'll check the messages:

Beep!

Hello. This message is for Irene Richards. Really, I hate talking into a machine. Uh, the thing is, Mrs. Richards, we find ourselves unable to add your name to our current Ladies' Aid membership roster. Perhaps if you try again in the spring. That's when we get busy planning our program for the coming year. There'll be vacancies, I'm sure. Well. I tried to see you to deliver this message in person the other day, but your daughter said you weren't feeling well. Hope you're better. On behalf of Ladies' Aid, Pastor Elsie Froembech. I hope this all gets recorded. I do hate to talk to a machine. Well. Goodbye. And God bless.

Beep!

Mrs. McClure? This is Mabel Gallagher's son Fred. The family is pretty upset about the, ah, incident the other day. Since I'm out here on the coast, I've asked a friend of mine to handle the matter. George Rafferty. I think you went to school with him. Anyway, if you call his office, he'll tell you what we have in mind.

Beep!

Mrs. McClure? Biddell Realty calling. We need your mother's signature on some papers. Just a formality having to do with the transfer of properties. And there's just one little wrinkle. About the boundaries. We can't seem to find the pins. So please give us a ring. Oh, and by the way, Mrs. Biddell wants to thank you for the nice flowers you sent to the funeral home. Such a tragedy! Have a nice day.

Beep!

Mrs. McClure? I hope I have the right number. I've been trying to reach your mother, but her phone has been disconnected. I do hope she's okay. I heard that your dad is in a nursing home. I'd like the address, so I can send him a card. I hope you remember me. I understand you have a son. Maxwell and I have a fifteen-year-old daughter who goes to Miss Emily Paulson's School. Isn't that near you? My goodness, we might even have a chance to visit you some day. After all these years! Anyway, I hope your life is going well. I'll try to reach you again soon.

The last caller forgot to leave her name, but I'd know that voice anywhere. Rosalie Light. Only now her name is Bixby. If I hurry, I can finish mixing this potion and then start on something more ambitious before Junior gets home.

Life Goes On

Shirleen

Friends ask me how we're getting along now that Ma is with us, and I don't know what to tell them. On one hand, it's nice to be able to repay her, in part, for all the years she cared for me. On the other, caring for Ma is something of a nightmare. For instance, after the episode with Lavinia Donderhook, I had to punish her by taking away her privileges. No outings for two weeks, I said. And no telephone, either. That way, if I'm out of the house, I know she's not pulling any tricks.

So today, I get home from work and find her sitting in the living room reading, with her legs crossed primly and a shawl around her shoulders like anybody's mother, and immediately I'm suspicious. "Any messages for me?" I ask. I know she listens to the answering machine while I'm gone.

Ma looks up from the newspaper and smiles. "Not a one."

"Not even from the realtor? We were supposed to find out the date of the closing."

Another smile. "Nope."

"So, Ma," I say, playing it cool, rifling through the stack of junk mail and catalogs that normally fill our box this time of year, "what did you do all morning?"

"A little this, a little that."

"Meaning what?"

The smile fades. "What is this, the third degree? I cooked. I made some soup."

"That's what I smell. Soup. Good. We'll have some for supper."

"No, we won't. It didn't turn out right, so I dumped it. Actually, I put some in Frisky's bowl. Where is that cat, anyway? Never mind. Let me guess. Next door screwing. Just what this neighborhood needs—more kittens."

I'm picturing the empty vegetable drawer in my refrigerator. Damn! I had spent a bundle on produce just yesterday. "You wasted perfectly good ingredients? Ma! You know I have a food budget. How could you?" Then a little voice tells me to lay off. At least she was trying to be helpful. "Oh, well. Forget it. It must have been frustrating, huh? All that time and nothing to show for it. Making soup is a pain."

"You have no idea," she sighs. "I tried to clean the pot, but there's still some gunk stuck to the bottom. Maybe if we soak it."

"Sure." I'm hoping she didn't use my new stock pot, the one I've never even used. The little voice says, so what? You can get another pot. "Well. Let's go see what we can rustle up for supper."

"You go. I'm really tired. Must have been from all my earlier efforts. Think I'll take a nap. You don't mind, do you? Sometimes I think two's too many in that little kitchen." She sighs again. "It was different in mine. Plenty of room."

Whenever she starts in with the old refrain—how much better her house was than mine—I tune out. At first, I tried to be sympathetic, but then I found myself dreading the broken record of regrets which she plays constantly, reminding me of a chorus from one of those dreary Country love songs: I'm so lonely, lonely, lonely. I watch her get up slowly and move out of the room. She seems so frail these days. I feel guilty. Have we broken her spirit, I wonder? All that bravado and bluster associated with spellmaking and curses? My Other Car is a Broom, indeed. I'll have to get Junior's help in removing that bumper sticker from Ma's car. Oh yes, I tell my friends, having Ma here is a blast.

Something, I don't know what, has died in my kitchen. Burnt vegetables simply do not smell like this. When Deke comes home, I'll get him to look under the sink. There's a crawlspace, and sometimes mice go in there to die, crazy with thirst from eating D-Con. I've got the windows open and the fan going; somewhere I've got a scented candle that I'll burn to get rid of the stench. I'm tossing out the stuff in Frisky's bowl. Not even a cat should have to eat this. Where is he, anyway? He always shows up for his dinner.

When I go to wake Ma from her nap, I hear her voice coming from Junior's room. His door's closed. I know he's at a friend's house, so, at first, I think she's talking to herself, probably not so unusual for someone in her situation. Then I realize she's on the phone. She's not supposed to be on the phone. "Yes, hello," I hear her say. She speaks loudly because her hearing is going. "Is this Miss Emily Paulson's School for Girls? I wonder if I could speak with Miss Bixby. No, I don't know her first name. Antoinette? Oh, thank you. Who am I? A very close friend of her mother's family. No, it's not an emergency, but I would appreciate it if you could get her to come to the phone. Yes, I'll wait. Yes, I understand you don't like to interrupt classes. Thank you for making an exception." Bixby? Why does that name ring a bell? And why would Ma be calling a student at Miss Paulson's? Jesus. This is worse than having another teenager.

She continues. "Antoinette? Is that you, sweetheart? I'm your Auntie Irene. Well, I'm not really your auntie. You see, your grandmother and I were close enough to be sisters. Your mother never told you about me? It must have slipped her mind. She's such a busy bee! Anyway, I was thrilled to hear you're practically in my backyard, and I was wondering if you'd like to come and visit me, and get a taste of my famous home cooking. It'll be a nice change from dormitory life. You would? Oh, I'm in heaven! Now, I've looked into bus service, and you can catch an Express right across from your school at nine o'clock Saturday morning. You'll be here before noon. I'll have my grandson meet you. Oh, I should tell you that I'm staying temporarily with my daughter, Shirleen, while my house gets fixed up for the winter. What does my grandson look like? Oh, he's tall and blond, about your age. His name is Junior. How will he know you, dear? I see. Long black hair, about 5'4", carrying a red duffel. Wonderful! Can't wait to see you. Until then!"

As soon as she hangs up, I burst into the room. "Ma! What are you doing inviting some kid we don't know to spend the weekend?"

I've startled her, but she looks more annoyed than surprised. "Don't you knock? Can't a person have any privacy around here?" she sputters. "And P.S. did you ask permission to eavesdrop?"

"Excuse me, but this isn't your space, it's Junior's. Did you ask permission? And don't try to evade the issue, which is who is she, anyway, and why is she coming to our house?"

"She's the daughter of someone your father and I used to know very well."

"Someone I know, then. Who?"

She stalls. She smooths out the wrinkles in Junior's spread. She puts the phone back on his desk and straightens the cord. I wait for her in the doorway, impatient and curious. As she reaches up to turn off the light she says, "Antoinette is Rosalie's daughter. Rosalie asked me to look out for her. I decided it was time to make peace. What else can I say? Of course, it's your house, Shirleen. If you don't want her here, I'll understand."

"I don't believe you! This woman ruins your life—our lives— and you want to do her a favor? After all these years of bitterness? I don't understand!" All my personal grievances against Rosalie come rushing to the fore. I'd thought of revenge so often that it was almost a comfort to imagine all the hells we could put her through. But it was really my mother's vendetta, not mine; I realized that a long time ago. "Look, Ma. If you say you want to forgive her, then I guess it's okay," I hear myself saying. I should be proud of her, but my problem is, I don't really believe she's doing this. The little voice says give your mother some credit. So, I do. I say, "Ma, I'm really proud of you."

"Then it's all right for her to come?"

"Of course. Oh, wait a minute. Where will she sleep?"

"She can share my little room. I'll sleep on that old cot of Deke's."

Suddenly I can only worry about specifics. "Is Junior supposed to meet her at the bus station? Does he know? Christ, I hope he doesn't have football practice. There's a big game that afternoon." We walk to the kitchen, where I'd decided to read her the riot act about using my cookware without asking permission. In the light of her generosity towards Rosalie, that seems a little petty. Still, she did ruin the pot. Oh, what the hell. Deke can get me another one for Christmas.

★ ★ ★

After dinner Ma and I corner Junior and present him with our request. His response is immediate and, as I've guessed it would be, negative. "Ma, I can't meet this girl on Saturday. I promised Jerry and the guys I'd help them set up the bleachers. It's Homecoming, and you know what a big deal that is. Besides, I've gotta be in uniform by noon."

Ma beams. "Homecoming? Good! You can take Antoinette to the dance. She'll love it. And you have plenty of time to meet her bus at ten and still get ready for the game, so don't hand me that crap for an excuse."

Junior patiently explains, "I've already got a date for the dance, Grandma."

"Not that sleaze who gave you the clap!"

"Grandma! Mom, did you tell her about my warts? You weren't supposed to tell anybody! Shit. What happened to confidential? It's probably all over town by now." Suddenly Junior's rugged, usually pleasant features are contorted with anger. He's feeling betrayed, though I'm innocent. Ma must have overheard something. The woman has ESP, so it's impossible to keep secrets. "Okay, sure, I'll pick up your little friend, Grandma. Why not? My life is finished, anyway. But get this. Both of you. I'm picking her up and bringing her back here. Period. That's right. No dance. And Grandma, no funny business at the game. Don't pretend you don't know what I'm talking about. I saw what you did last Saturday when we were trailing by one point in the last quarter."

And now I'm thinking, what does he know that I don't know? "What's he talking about, Ma?"

"I haven't the foggiest."

"Ask her about the books in her closet, Mom."

Now it's Ma's turn to be outraged. "The scrapbooks I brought from home? The last vestiges of my inheritance? The only record I have of my early years? Those books, Junior?"

Junior rolls his eyes and flops down on his bed. "Yeah, sure."

I'm beginning to feel edgy. "Is there something going on here I should know about?"

Ma looks down at the floor. Junior stares up at the ceiling.

"*Monday Night Football!*" Deke yells. "Anybody interested?"

Whoosh. In seconds I'm left alone in the room to sort out Junior's dirty laundry and to contemplate the future, which is looking pretty dicey. Since when did my mother become a football fan? Since she started going to Junior's games.

★ ★ ★

The rest of the week goes by in a blur, as it seems to when I'm excited about an upcoming event, and before I know it, it's Friday and I'm cleaning and shopping in anticipation of Antoinette's arrival. "Ma! Did you unpack the groceries? Where's my chopped meat? All I can find is fish. I didn't order fish. Did you? And so much of it!" Damn. I knew I shouldn't have left her alone to finish the shopping while I went to the drug store. She screws up every time.

"I thought fish would be a nice change. Healthier, you know."

"Well, I have to say I've never seen any fish quite like this one. It's whole, for one thing. With the eyes still in. Ugh."

"So fresh. You can tell by the firmness of the eyes. Look. They don't jiggle when I pick up the head."

"Where on earth did you learn that? Dad hated fish. We never used to eat it, except in restaurants, when you and I would order seafood. Eeuw. What kind of fish is it, anyway?"

"Oh, I don't know. What difference does it make? Fish is fish."

"Schrod is supposed to be nice. Why didn't you get that?"

"It wasn't fresh."

"No fish is fresh here, Ma. This is upstate New York, remember? The fish sold here is all frozen. We don't live near the ocean."

"Well, this fish is fresh. So, don't worry."

"I still think everybody would prefer Swedish meatballs."

"Fish is healthier. And fewer calories. Young women are into eating right these days. I bet Antoinette watches her diet. It wouldn't hurt some of us, either."

Ma gives my waistline the once-over and I think, please dear God let's not get into another confrontation. Meanwhile I continue to make my case for eating beef. "I think meatballs are nutritious. Fish is brain food. People eat it because they have to. And P.S. it's loaded with bones, which people tend to choke on." I'm getting annoyed. She could lift a finger to help me, like dust or vacuum or straighten the couch cushions. "Oh Christ. Look what I found—a condom! You'd think we lived in a pig pen. What's Antoinette going to think? She goes to that fancy school. Where did you say her home was? Short Hills? Oh, yeah. It figures. Rosalie would marry for money. This place is like Tobacco Road compared to Short Hills. Here. Do something with Deke's cigars. And hand me that rug cleaner. What time did you say she was getting here? Ten? Well, that gives us some time tomorrow morning, if we get up early. Ma, what's that on your face—a wart? And your skin is still that funny shade of green."

"It's the water here. At my house, we had our own well, and the water was so nice and pure."

"Bullshit. Remember when we found out that the chemicals were seeping in? That was right after Pop had his first stroke. I'd rather have city water any day. At least they purify it, and test it all the time. I think your skin color comes from eating weird things."

"Maybe you're right. In that case, we're doing the right thing by having fish instead of beef tomorrow."

I flop down on the couch and swing my feet up onto the coffee table, pushing the pile of magazines to one side. "Yeah. You win. But then, Ma, you always do."

★ ★ ★

Late that afternoon, while Junior is taking Ma to the hairdressers (I finally convinced her to get a perm) I set up the cot in her room. There's just barely enough space. Maybe we should have had Junior sleep on the living room couch. Anyway, while I'm in here I'll just take a peek in the closet and see what Junior was talking about when he mentioned books. Ah, here they are. Big deal. Scrapbooks! I've seen these many times before. Some date back to her childhood on the farm which had belonged to my grandfather's family. As I understand it, he wasn't interested in running it, so my grandmother Sylvia took charge. Grandpa got a job selling hardware to little stores across the state, and was gone much of the time. There must have been Rosalies in his life, but if my grandmother knew of them, she never let on—at least not to hear Ma tell it.

Then there's another group of pictures taken when Ma was in high school and just getting interested in boys. To look at her now, you'd never guess she was sought after, but to hear her tell it, and judging from these pictures, she was. She married when she was twenty-six. I once heard her say she knew the minute she saw Pop that he was the one for her. He'd come to town to replace the old general practitioner who was retiring. Ma was one of Pop's first patients. She said she looked right away to see if he was wearing a wedding ring. Remembering how good-looking he was then, and what a catch he must have been, being a doctor, I can't understand how he'd stayed single. Ma had this rash on the inside of her thighs. She said she was embarrassed to take her clothes off in front of this handsome stranger. Not long after that, they started dating. It must have been her skin that got to him—milkmaid's skin, Ma used to call it. She said, "You'd think with all the hard work handling chickens I'd have a rough hide, but I didn't. My skin was smooth and white. What was it your father called it? Luminous."

The next album is full of our early years as a family. I was born during their second year of marriage when Ma was, by her own accounts, still starry-eyed with the glamour of being a small-town doc's wife. By then they'd moved to south Florida where Pop had gotten a chance to further his career. Ma became involved in community theater, playing ingenue roles.

Pop became very interested in nutrition and the problems of obesity, and soon he had a large practice of mainly overweight women. Poor Mrs. Peabody. Undressed, she must have looked like a beached whale. She was desperate to be thin, and Pop was determined to help her. Unfortunately, amphetamines weren't the answer, and soon Pop was at the center of a major scandal involving Mrs. Peabody's untimely demise, and his after-hours romance with Rosalie. We were forced to leave Miami and our good, soft life in the South.

There's a scrapbook from this period, filled with newspaper clippings. When I asked Ma why she bothered to save these painful reminders, she said, "When you're out to document your life you have to include the bad as well as the good. It's all part of the same mix."

The next group of pictures are painful to look at. They show how Ma was affected by the double whammy of having her husband accused of murder and discovering his infidelity. I remember those years. Young as I was, I took on the role of caregiver, bathing her, setting out her clothes, pleading with her to eat. Now I realize she was severely depressed. Pop tried to help, but she wouldn't let him. That was his punishment. There were no miracle drugs back then, except for tranquilizers, which made her fat and sleepy. Something happened. It was as if her heart, which had always been loving and generous, turned into a clenched fist. I remember reading "The Snow Queen" and identifying with the little girl.

Junior's birth mellowed her. She might have slid gracefully into the next stage of her life if it hadn't been for Pop going to the nursing home. At the time, we thought he'd bounce right back, but as the months went by we could see he wouldn't. In her desperation she turned to sorcery. Thank God that's over! I sent those books to the dump, which is where they belong—squished to smithereens in the trash compactor and buried in the bowels of the earth where nobody else's mother can ever find them.

* * *

I'm so nervous. I keep on looking out the front window to see Junior drive up with Antoinette, even though they're not due for another half hour. Ma is in the kitchen making sandwiches for lunch, a safe enough assignment. Deke is picking up something special from the bakery—cookies or tarts. "Who is it we're entertaining? Royalty?" he asked. We never have dessert with lunch.

Junior and I cleaned up the bathroom and hung fresh towels. I got him to promise he'd shower in the locker rooms after the game so as not to make a mess.

Ma comes in. "Did I hear a car?"

"They're here." We rush to the door, eager to catch the first glimpse of the young woman who walks behind Junior.

"Oh, my God, Shirleen. She looks exactly like her mother. Only not so coarse."

I've been told that Rosalie was actually very beautiful, petite, with exquisite features, black hair and those big, deceiving pools of eyes that registered so dramatically in the newspaper photos. Can Ma stand the shock, I wonder? But I don't have to worry, because she is pushing past me, eager to greet Antoinette, whose smile dazzles all of us. Junior, red-faced, stumbles into the house. He's clearly enthralled. "Welcome to our house," I say. "I hope you had a pleasant ride."

"Actually, it was bogus. There was this absolute barfball sitting next to me. He smelled! I guess I could have switched my seat, but I was kind of shy. I've never ridden public transportation before, you see."

"Oh, my. Shirleen, did you hear that? Her very first bus ride! How ghastly for you, dear!" Ma can't help herself; the urge to mock is overwhelming. "Tsch, tsch. Junior, dear, take Antoinette's bag to my room."

"I hope I'm not putting you out of your room, Auntie Irene."

"Oh, no," Junior says. "Gram'll be sleeping there, too. I'll be right across the hall." He blushes.

"Nothing's far away from anything in this little house," Ma snaps. She gives Junior a look, as if to discourage any shenanigans.

Antoinette pauses. "Do you think I could use your Little Girl's Room?"

"Oh, I don't have a little girl," I say. "Junior's our one and only."

"She means the bathroom, Mom," Junior whispers, blushing again. "It's, uh, right over there." He puts her duffel on the bed in Ma's room. "Wow. She's a babe."

"Just like her mother," Ma and I chorus, *sotto voce*.

"What a darling little room!" Antoinette says. Her lipstick's darker and her hair's pulled back. She is a very cute girl. Junior is drooling.

"It used to be a closet," Ma blurts. "My son-in-law fixed it over for me. I'm staying here. Temporarily. Just until I can find a place of my own."

Junior and I exchange glances.

"Well, I think that's sweet, all of you in this teeny house together. Where should I hang my things, Auntie Irene? Oh, look! I probably brought all the wrong clothes!" She holds up a party frock, a little slip of a dress, red, that has Junior's tongue hanging out. "Silly me!"

I bet all her clothes come from expensive catalogues. It occurs to me that she's her mother's daughter, and that Rosalie was only three years older than Antoinette when Pop first hired her. Instinctively, I pull Junior over and give him a protective hug.

★ ★ ★

So, we all end up going to the football game—Deke, Antoinette, Ma, and me—and much to my surprise, instead of being totally bored and disgusted with the locals, the girl screams her head off rooting for Junior and his teammates. "Ooh, they've just got to get that point," she squeals. "I'll just die if they don't!"

Ma gets this weird look on her face, as if she's concentrating really hard.

They get the point. "Say what?" Deke says, an expression of utter surprise on his face. "It was a first down for the other team. Did I miss something?"

Ma smiles.

"Oh, Auntie, I'm having an absolutely fab time," Antoinette gushes. "Thanks so, so much for having me." She looks so happy and so lovely that I feel pangs of remorse for disliking her, but then I remember Rosalie, who single-handedly wrecked my young life. I'd long ago stopped blaming my father. After all, Rosalie was the temptress who got him to stray, the siren who caused our ship to crash against the rocks.

"I still don't get it," Deke mutters. "The other team had the advantage."

Wait a minute, I think. Something's not right. "Ma." I turn to her and squeeze her arm, pinching it tight enough to get her attention. "You didn't."

She looks at me with clear, innocent eyes. "Didn't what?"

"You promised you wouldn't!"

She sends me a message: Would this old grey head lie to you? "I don't know what you're talking about," she says, then dismisses me. "Oh, look," she says to Antoinette, "Junior's just lying there. He's not getting up. I hope he's not hurt!"

If she were using her powers, I think, she'd never let him be hurt. For a minute I'm relieved. Then my maternal side kicks in and I'm frantic. Why can't she use her powers? I don't give a damn. I just don't want him to be injured.

In a matter of minutes Junior goes from unconscious to frisky, raising his arms in triumph and blowing Antoinette a kiss; the ref declares a first down, and the Ramblers are leading 14–7. There are only two minutes left in the game.

Antoinette is crying. "I thought he was really hurt," she sobs. "But he's okay, isn't he?" Before we know it, the game is over and the team is carrying Junior on their shoulders, right over to the section where we're sitting. They practically dump him in Antoinette's lap. "Ooh baby, you're a hero," she croons.

Junior spits out his mouthpiece. He has this big dumb grin on his face, a look of complete adoration. He hugs Ma. "Thanks, Gram, for everything. For bringing her here. And for, well, you know what."

"What?" Deke and I chorus. But the three of them are already on their way out to join the crowd in the center of the field. "Yeah, Ramblers!" Ma yells. I can hear her voice above all the others. It works its way around the bleachers and bounces off the scoreboard, larger than life, just like the woman who owns it.

★ ★ ★

Well, of course they go to the dance together, and of course they don't come home until 3 a.m., and of course they spend the rest of the night on the living room couch, though what Junior does when he reaches for his condom and can't find it, I don't know. I only hope she doesn't give him warts.

★ ★ ★

The next morning we all sleep late. When the kids drift in for breakfast, I notice Antoinette's neck is pockmarked with hickeys and her lips are swollen from kissing so much.

"Coffee?" Deke asks, oblivious to the evidence. Men never seem to notice things like that. He offers me a cup. "Should I scramble up some eggs? You got any bacon?"

He's such a good-natured soul. Pop always liked him; Ma was the one who found fault. I know she thought he wasn't good enough for me. Now she sees that he's a good husband and father, and she's got to appreciate the fact that he welcomed her into our home.

Breakfast sounds great, but we're going to be eating dinner in a couple of hours. "Gee, honey, we're having an early dinner," I tell him. "Antoinette has to leave by three, you know." But he's already got the frying pan out and is cracking eggs into a bowl, and Junior and Antoinette are looking starved.

"Hey. Catch the love birds," Deke says. "And they barely know each other!"

Ma creeps into the kitchen bringing with her a chilly aura. Ever since yesterday when I discovered she's been using her powers I can't bring myself to face her. I wonder what she's got up her sleeve next? "Of course, at this age they blow hot and cold, if you know what I mean," she says. "Next week he'll probably be screwing someone else."

"Irene!" Deke never calls her Mother, because he's already got one of his own. It's okay. I understand, and so does Ma.

"Sorry." She sits down at the table. Her new permanent is tight, and the top of her head looks like a steel-wool pad. I have a feeling that if I touched it, I'd get splinters.

★   ★   ★

"I wish you'd let me help you, Ma." She insisted on preparing dinner herself and now I watch her wrestle a very large fish. "Aren't you supposed to gut it first?" I ask, feeling squeamish.

"This is a recipe I got from one of my books."

Oh, I have a bad feeling about this dinner. "Which book?"

Ma gives me a look that says will you never trust me? "Fanny Farmer. Boston Cooking School. Joy of Cooking. James Beard. I don't know. Some cookbook. Don't be so nervous! I've been cooking since I was eight. Remember? My mother was always busy with the chickens. My job was to see that all the humans got fed. So, leave it to a pro."

This is a story I've heard many times before, and its familiar content has a calming effect. I retreat into the living room where Deke is reading the paper and Junior and Antoinette are necking. At the sound of Ma's voice calling us to the table they separate reluctantly and move slowly toward the dining room. I can feel the heat emanating from their bodies. Deke and I were like that once, I think. So were Irene and Teddy.

"Would you say grace, Donald?" Ma asks demurely.

Junior's in shock. "Grace?"

"Junior, please! We have company," Ma says.

We bow our heads obediently while Deke intones, "Dear Lord bless this food to its use and us to thy keeping in Jesus' name amen." Where did that come from? I have to hand it to him. He must have remembered the words from his childhood, because we rarely say grace. Junior looks stunned. For once, he isn't reaching across the table with both hands to grab the rolls and butter.

Ma says, "Now, dear, I've prepared something very special, and I want you to have the choice piece." To everyone's horror she serves Antoinette the head. It's true she's replaced the repulsive eyes with olives, but the pimentos have a ghastly effect and we gag collectively. Ma ignores us. "Help yourself to mashed potatoes and peas."

"I, uh, never eat fish," Antoinette says in a small, weak, voice. There's a look of disgust on her pretty face.

"Nonsense. It's good for you." Ma says, glaring fiercely.

"That's okay. We never eat it either," Junior says. Then he looks at me. "Mom. What's going on here? I thought we were having Swedish meatballs."

"Maybe some other part of the fish would be more to your liking," Deke suggests politely. "Pass the platter, Irene."

Ma gives him this look that says butt out. "No!"

Antoinette looks very pale. "That's okay. I'll eat it." And she starts picking away at the cheeks. Suddenly she's gobbling it down, picking up the bones and licking them clean. "This is really delicious, Auntie. Can I have some more?"

"Of course you can, dear." Ma gives me a triumphant smile. O ye of little faith.

Soon we are all scarfing down the fish, smacking our lips and asking for seconds. "Ma, this is really terrific," I say. I am, truly, in awe.

"You should spend more time in our kitchen," Deke says.

Antoinette burps. "Excuse me." She belches again and again, a rumble that comes from the very depth of her stomach. "Oh, my. I don't feel very well," she says, and keels over, landing in a pile of mashed potatoes.

"Dial 911," Junior says, looking panicked. "She's out cold."

Ma remains calm. "It's just a touch of indigestion. I'll get her some of my remedy."

"Sit right there, Ma!" I command. "We'll take care of this." Junior's right. Deke runs to the phone, and I feel for a pulse. It's there, but just barely.

Junior carries Antoinette over to the couch and lays her gently on the cushions. "She looks awful, Mom. What're we going to do?" He wipes her forehead with a damp cloth. "She's the most beautiful, wonderful girl I've ever met," he says, and starts to cry. "If she dies, I don't want to go on living."

I watch Ma. She sits at the table, looking down at her plate. Her hands are clenched. She's mumbling something—praying, I hope, that whatever she's done can be undone.

Carpe Diem

Irene

"**T**akke one fragrante fleshye fishe," began the recipe I found in *The Cooke's Byblle*, a creepy text written by Moldred of Breste, apparently the Julia Child of twelfth-century western Europe. "A carpe is beste, but almoste anye fishe will do." There was a lilting ring to that phrase which set me to humming. Soon I was making up lyrics: "Anye fishe will do, I told my own true love. Anye fishe will do." As if I had a true love!

So off I went to cruise the waters of the Grand Union Supermarket. Of course, since it had to be a whole fish, any fishe wouldn't do. Being used to fillets, I figured my choices would be limited. Imagine my surprise when I saw, nestled in ice chips and looking as though they had been caught in a time-warp log jam, a cusk, a monkfish, and a salmon—complete, snout to tail, except for their innards! I chose the monkfish because it was ugly, grey, and pale pink, with a snout the size of Philadelphia and little feelers curling up around an angry-looking jaw. Yuck. I could smell Moldred's fetid breath as she whispered, "If you cannot gette a carpe, a monkfishe is the nexte beste thynge." Well, sure. I mean, what daughter of Satan wouldn't be tempted by a monkfish? I snapped a number off the roller and waited my turn. "Have you got one that isn't eviscerated?" I asked.

"Say what?"

"You know, one that hasn't had its insides stolen."

The fish peddler stared across the counter at me, incredulous. "You say you want a whole fish?"

"That's what I said, honey."

"Nobody ever wants a whole one," she grimaced.

"Well, I do."

"You ever clean a fish? It's disgusting. You want one that's already cleaned."

"Look. I know what I want, and I want a whole fucking fish! Now do I get one or do I have to kiss your ass?" I puckered my lips in readiness.

"Wait a minute. Uh, I think there may just be one fish that came in whole." I watched her disappear into the back and come out seconds later with a very large, ugly monkfish which she hoisted up on the counter. Its morbid stare was enough to frighten off the other customer, who backed away skittishly. "This here's what you wanted, right?" the sales clerk said, wrinkling her nose in disgust. I nodded enthusiastically. Just thinking about all those formerly-steaming entrails still oozing their magical juices made me salivate. Fish guts, according to Moldred, are tastiest when steamed on seaweed and served with a light sauce of eel's blood and mead. I wonder if I should lay them on top of the pool of sauce, California style. She's not specific when it comes to presentation; it takes someone like Martha Stewart to tell you how to serve up a dish. One evening I'll make myself a special treat—cod liver, shark bladder, whatever I can scoop up from the available catch of the day—probably on Deke's bowling night, when Junior's out with his friends, and Shirleen is learning how to tat or prune. I'll set up a tray table in the living room and watch *Tales from the Crypt*. Even witches like to be pampered.

Anyway, that monkfish was a heavy sucker, almost eight pounds, and ditz-brain had trouble encasing it in the special wrappers Grand Union uses for fish. Moldred, skinny little crone that she probably was, wouldn't have been able to heft it. She'd have asked the apprentice to carry it home for her. She'd never have paid as much as I did—seven bucks a pound, more money than I had with me. In those days they bartered—a frog's eye for a newt's tail, a sow's ear for a goat's hoof, that sort of thing.

Once home, I had to sneak the fish into the kitchen, which wasn't too difficult because Shirleen was knocking herself out vacuuming, poking that nozzle into every nook and cranny. Antoinette's impending arrival had sent her into a frenzy of mopping and dusting. Normally a neat housekeeper, Shirleen was determined to present her house as super-spotless, which meant she'd probably be sniffing my armpits and checking for rings on my collar. I shoved the monkfish to the back of the refrigerator, hiding it behind Deke's beer and Junior's Ring Dings. Then I snuck into my lair to chill out.

★ ★ ★

"Makke a brothe from the entrailles and flavore it with frogge's eyes," Moldred instructed. Well, okay, I'd anticipated that frogs' eyes would be needed somewhere along the line since they're a staple in conjurer cuisine. Before Shirleen's cat Frisky fell into the brew, he caught a toad which I rescued (but not in the nick of time, thank badness.) Those little eyes popped out like tiny jewels. I dropped them in a grip-lock sandwich bag and pushed the bag to the back of the freezer for safe-keeping. "When the brothe is the color of bloode, throwe inne a full-growne hare with one blue eye and one browne." Being hareless, I knew I'd have to improvise. If only I'd succeeded in changing Mrs. Baker to a bunny! Frisky, bless his dear departed heart, would have to do.

Down to the cellar I went, deep into the crawlspace where, beneath a goodly layer of soil and lime, lay the decomposing body of that curious cat. Holding my breath, I extricated the carcass and dumped it into a Macy's shopping bag. "Not so frisky any more, are you?" I whispered. Then, employing a little trick I'd learned from detective novels, I dumped coffee grounds into the bag to mask the smell. How virtuous I felt! Eating household pets is the ultimate in recycling. Too many kittens? Make a Mewling Stew. Too many puppies? Wrap their little tails in phyllo. Moldred has a recipe for puppies, I'm sure. But when it came time to dump the carcass in the pot, I just couldn't desecrate the household pet. So back into the crawlspace went Frisky, or what was left of him. *"Pax vobiscum,"* I said. Rest well, my family's little furry friend.

* * *

How content I was, stirring that brothe. The sounds of simmer, the burble of boil made me want to soar with happiness. I grabbed a broom and jockeyed it around the room. My feet were skimming the floor when in comes Junior to get his morning snack. He'd just taken a shower. His hair was wet and prickly, shedding drops of water on Shirleen's newly-waxed floor. "Eeuw. What are you making, Gram? It smells like a dead animal," he said, gulping a toaster pastry. "Put a lid on it or something." But before I could make up a story about Halloween soup that smells like goblins but is good for humans he turned away and headed down the hall to his room. I swept his puddles into claws of water, blotting them with a paper towel. Then I took his suggestion and covered the pot. Ten more minutes and the brothe would be donne. I only hoped I hadn't compromised the outcome by turning faint-hearted.

* * *

So, sue me. I hadn't meant to do Antoinette in, only teach her mother a lesson. I'm actually relieved the girl is going to be okay.

Someday I'll see Rosalie again. By then I'll have devised a better way to get even, but it's clear now that Antoinette won't be the victim. Junior's in love. And I'd never do anything to hurt my Junior.

From now on, Antoinette will be under my fond protection. Yes, there's a flip side to evil that most people can't even guess. I can be loving and sweet, and even, yes, almost genuine. It's scary when I think of it, this side of witches that few people see. I think of it as a vestige of my ordinary self. Beneath the dark is a layer of light that shines through every once in a while. Junior suspects it's there. And although I try hard to keep Shirleen from glimpsing that old, sweet side of me, she does. Occasionally.

In Harm's Way

Irene

Once a week I visit Teddy.

When I see the shrunken, sleepy shadow of a man I used to love it almost makes me cry. But only almost. What keeps me from going all mushy with sentiment is the conviction that beneath this sleeping shell lurks passion. Not for me. Never for me. I imagine—I know—of whom and what he dreams, and it drives me batty. He dreams he's young again, lying on a beach beneath the hot Caribbean sun. Next to him lies guess who? She is bronzed and luminous in her cocoon of baby oil, her breasts, butt, and crotch encased in tiny floral triangles. The stretch fabric of her bikini is lush with miniature pink and orange blossoms that flourish in Teddy's neglected garden of desire. He gets erections. Even now I can see that underneath the sheet stamped "Ace Linen Service" his flaccid penis betrays his age, pushes stiff and taut against the sheet's restraint, then flops back. I'm guessing he has to pee because the Caribbean water has warmed his feet and heated up his blood. You might say that Rosalie gives him a seminal emission.

In other words, he wets the sheets. "Hey there, honey," the black aide says. She's built like a linebacker but her name is Lily, no doubt a reference to the purity of her soul. Today she's wearing a bright pink smock—chocolate wrapped in fuchsia—not Teddy's type, too old and too fat, like some of the women who used to be his patients when he was a diet guru in Miami Beach. "You done wet your bed. No need to fret. I'm gonna change you, wash you, buff you up. I'm gonna comfy your butt." Her fingers are strong, her intentions just so. Teddy, always the gentleman, would thank her, but all he can do is eke out a tear or two. Lily knows that all his orifices weep these days, and she seems to understand.

I can tell by his slow, rhythmic breathing that Teddy's dreaming again. Now he and Rosalie lounge in a room watching the curtains balloon onto a patio. The patio overlooks a pool, their own private mirror of absolute bliss in which floats a single giant hibiscus, a flaming red invitation to fuck. Rosalie climbs on top the way he likes her to, at least to start. This I know from experience. He likes to finish up the old-fashioned way because it makes him feel strong. The whore rides him hard, her voice an aphrodisiac: aah, ooh.

"Why you old sly devil you. Look at you! There's life in the old boy yet." Lily sponges his penis, massages it with her capable fingers, but even a professional hand job can't sustain his erection. "Let Miss Lily roll you over now. Mmm-mm! You even skinnier than last week. Not like Mister Whale over there." She indicates with a nod of her head his roommate, whose giant belly threatens to overflow the narrow bed.

Teddy and Rosalie have finished making love, and now he lies on his stomach in a sweet pool of stuff, the sticky product of their joint effluence. Rosalie massages his back. Let me do something more for you, he says. He wants to hear her say aah, ooh, again and again. Having turned him over gently, Lily deftly kneads his poor, frail spine, aligning her thick thumbs and moving her palms slowly up and down the knobs. When she finishes, she turns him on his back and says, "Tonight we're havin' mashed potatoes and meat loaf. Put some beef in your tummy, get some flesh on those bones. Let me raise your head so you get used to the idea." Lily. Pitch-black, yet named for a fragrant white flower that must remind Teddy of his mother's Easter funeral. He was only six when he stood beside her casket and almost puked from the sickly sweet smell of the lilies. For the resurrection. There it is again, a flutter of hope, but Lily's left the room and there's no one but me to see his boner wiggle the sheet. He doesn't notice she's gone, probably because he's thinking of how his mother abandoned him. He once told me he thought of crawling into the coffin beside her. "They could have closed the lid on me. I thought my world had come to an end anyway, what did I care?" Well, Teddy grew up despite his sorrow.

Of the two of us, I was definitely more miserable. My parents were poor chicken farmers. I can still remember getting up at five to hack the ice off the watering pans. I remember going to school smelling of chicken shit. I remember a house that was colder in winter than the barns where we kept the hens. There were times when, just to keep warm, I sat in the corners of the incubator rooms, cradling in my hands the disfigured runts, the chicks whose beaks were crooked, the ones who couldn't push and shove their way to the mash.

★ ★ ★

I know exactly what happened in that Caribbean hotel room because I hired someone to follow Teddy and Rosalie to St. Thomas. The PI's name was Joe Spitowski, the only business tenant on the fourth floor of a walkup that should have been condemned. I paid him one thousand dollars plus expenses to nail the happy couple who were attending a medical convention devoted to the study of weight loss in obese post-menopausal women, Teddy's specialty. I once told Rosalie, just think: when he's finished with you as a lover, you can come back as his patient.

When he told me he'd been invited to speak, he said, "Ordinarily I'd encourage you to come along, but I'll be really busy with lectures and workshops, and you know what the tropical sun does to your delicate skin. So, I've asked Rosalie." When I didn't balk Teddy felt cheated; he'd been counting on the rush of adrenaline he felt when we collided, but all he got was an alibi. I told him I couldn't possibly go anyway because 1) I was chairman of the upcoming PTA supper, and 2) Shirleen's dance recital fell during the dates we'd be gone. I had reasons to suspect that something was going on: late nights at the office, a sudden spring in his step, the elusive aroma that didn't remind me of his aftershave. I just hadn't decided what to do about it. Rosalie was very popular with Teddy's patients. She was an inspiration to them, a role model. Even her name conjured images of the miniskirted sylphs they all wanted to become. She'd been born a Lichtenstein but her father had the good sense to change the name to Light.

As it turned out, Spitowski was a sound investment. He returned from St. Thomas laden with tapes and glossies documenting the many times they played hooky to drink mai tais and enjoy their cozy little private oasis. As I requested, he continued to monitor their office shenanigans, offering proof they had wild, inventive sex after hours on his examining table where, I would see from the photos, the delightful addition of stirrups led to imaginative variations. I soon gathered that our sex had been too tame for Teddy. Even if he'd asked, my Catholic upbringing (to say nothing of my forty-something body) wouldn't have permitted gymnastics.

"Do you suppose Irene knows about us?" I can imagine Rosalie saying. "Do you suppose she's hired a private detective to catch us in the act?" Thanks to Spitowski's sleuthing, I became an enthusiastic voyeur. Thus, I can picture her small, round face aglow with excitement. They are about to have their semi-weekly romp and she's already stripped down to her panties and bra. It's Valentine's Day and she's wearing red satin hearts. He can hardly keep from drooling. "You sound positively disappointed that she wasn't angry," he responds, unzipping his fly carefully so as not to snag Cupid. "Personally, I was relieved. A little puzzled, maybe, but definitely relieved." She slides into place on the examining table and waits for him to nip the hem of her panties. And no sooner does she utter "Aah, ooh" in that adorable little Betty Boopish voice than Teddy becomes giddy and forgets all about me.

It often occurs to me that Teddy must have enjoyed grazing two separate pastures. We were as different as any two women could be. Rosalie's ancestors were Sephardic Jews. She was petite and dark with small yet tenderly rounded breasts and a perfect little bottom; I was big-boned and blond, ample-bosomed, with an ass that had begun its gradual slide into infinity. As a physician whose practice was largely devoted to older women, Teddy had seen tushes disappear. Where did they go, he must have wondered. Was outer space afloat with wavering half-moons of dimpled flesh?

So, Rosalie was full of girlish giggles, whereas I tended to be moody, the dark side slipping always into view. I know Teddy often prayed that Shirleen wouldn't inherit my bipolar tendencies.

Thanks to Joe's diligent snooping I had enough ammunition to sue Teddy for divorce, but when he was charged with Flora's death, I began to feel sorry for the bastard. I soon realized that the trial would destroy his career and punish him to a degree that I couldn't. At least at the time, that seemed enough revenge. Only after years had passed and we'd rebuilt our lives could I see it would never be enough.

As Rosalie would testify in court, Flora Peabody was Teddy's greatest challenge. She came from a respectable GP who sent Teddy referrals as if women were gift baskets of delectable cheese. At thirty-eight years of age, Flora stood 5'3" and weighed 280 pounds, but beneath the rippled landscape of cellulite Teddy knew there lay beauty, and he was determined to exhume it. As with all his patients, he was careful to maintain proper protocol, insisting that Rosalie remain in the examining room to protect against charges of impropriety.

Word of Teddy's success rate spread. Of the twenty-four cases he'd handled, over half lost a minimum of fifty pounds in a year's time, and most had kept the weight off. Never mind that they were jumpy, had trouble sleeping, and developed signs of thyroid disease. They were on the path to waifdom, and that's what mattered to the world. A couple of unhappy husbands complained, however. They wanted their sweet, lazy, love-handled, satchel-assed beanbags back in their arms.

As Flora dwindled to a size twenty, her family hardly recognized her. According to her husband and children, she no longer sat at the table for meals. She was always skittering about, sliding her portion onto everyone else's plates. Hardly anybody saw her eat, except for late at night when they sometimes came upon her munching celery in the dark like a furtive rodent. She seemed to take extraordinary delight in such secretive behavior, crunching down on the stalks, closing her eyes in ecstasy as she chewed.

Rosalie claimed she warned Teddy of the danger signs. Here again, I fantasize. "Honey, I think Flora has a great big crush on you, and you'd better do something to set her straight before disaster occurs."

"What're you saying, babycakes?" I can see them buttoning and zipping after one of their sessions. He's just ripped off the section of paper where their secretions pearled and is wiping the Naugahyde clear of any telltale moisture. Room deodorant will be spritzed later, a pleasant, long-lasting lemony scent.

Rosalie pulls on her shimmering tights. Teddy notices she isn't wearing underwear, which usually drives him crazy, but given their conversation and the fact that he's just knocked himself out satisfying her, it has the opposite effect. "I'm saying she has the hots for you, lover."

"Mm. You jealous?" He feels his interest piquing and wonders if they have time for a post-coital quickie.

"You're kidding."

He watches her comb her long, black hair, then twist it into a French knot. She is absolutely the sexiest woman he's ever seen, and it's hard to resist the urge to cover her with kisses, beginning with that sweet little spot at the nape of her neck. "Well, yeah, sure. I guess I am. I mean, she doesn't begin to tempt me the way you do."

She turns to face him. "Just remember that. And don't give her any reason to think otherwise. I know danger when I see it, and that woman spells trouble."

A year later I would hear him tell the lawyer, "I should have taken Rosie's advice. I just didn't see it coming. Honestly. If I'd only been more perceptive, I probably wouldn't be in deep shit now, right?"

I listened to him describe Flora's last office visit. "She'd been using a tanning booth and was looking surprisingly healthy for February. I should have recognized the signs of abuse—the gaunt stare, the squirrelly behavior. What can I say? Instead, like a schmuck, I took her picture. 'We have a before shot. How about an after?' I said. Something like that. Then she said, 'I owe everything to you, Doctor. You've given me back my life.' My God. She was probably already planning to kill herself, when she said that."

Teddy wiped his glistening face with the tissue I handed him. The lawyer shook his head. "What a waste. That woman coulda done something with her life. Go figure. All that effort to lose weight, and for what? So her family could purchase a smaller coffin?"

As far as I was concerned, the biggest blow fell on the day Teddy testified that he found nothing wrong in having an affair with his nurse. He actually said: "Our love is pure," then scanned the crowd for a glimpse of his beloved who was next door posing for photographers. The press would portray her as the shameless hussy who ruined a good doctor's reputation. At that moment, I longed for my own death. In my desperation I placed the blame on Rosalie. I made up my mind to take the lovesick idiot back and rehabilitate him. Within a week Shirleen was begging Teddy for bedtime stories, and two months later we moved up to Riverton. There, in the orchard-studded valley of the Hudson River near where both of us had grown up, we began our new lives.

* * *

On visiting days, I usually hang out in Teddy's room or in the lounge where there's a big TV with closed captions. Right now we're watching *Lifestyles of the Rich and Famous*, or rather I am; the others are snoring so loud I can't hear the script. The nurses and aides buzz in and out of the room delivering pills, positioning wheelchairs, exchanging gossip. It seems one of the patients was moved to another nursing home by court order at the behest of a disgruntled guardian. The man across the hall yells "Marsha!" all day long and into the night as well. Sometimes they give him a pill to shut him up. I guess Teddy's gotten used to all the sounds, all the yellers and moaners and farters and crappers. It doesn't matter what sex you are or what condition you're in; everybody contributes to the general din.

It's so hot in this place it makes me sick. I went into the dining room for lunch, which they call dinner. Months ago, the combination of smells—fish fried in rancid oil, octogenarian poop, and some faded beauty queen's sickeningly sweet perfume—killed my appetite, but now that I've stirred a wicked pot or two, I find them almost pleasing. At the moment I'm being tempted by a gelatinous mass masquerading as a molded salad which shudders at the prospect of sliding down my craw. They know how to tempt me here. How they love me! If they elected a Pin-up of the Week, I'd be it. Oops. Somebody farts, a great ripping explosion, followed by a stink strong enough to fell Goliath. Come on, Junior. What's keeping you?

* * *

He finally appears, the answer to a grandmother's prayers. "Hey, Gram. It's me. "Look who I brought."

"Who? I can't see. Come over here in the light, honey." They expect me to be frail, and I don't want to disappoint them. "Why, is it really you?" Sure enough, I see it's Antoinette, who seems all recovered from our recent episode. The bloom is definitely back in those cheeks. Adorable. All the male aides are lined up in the hallway to pay homage. She'll be Pin-up of the Week, but I won't mind; I like her now. "So nice to see you, sweetheart." I pull her down to kiss her cheek and notice another hickey on her neck. Junior's been busy again.

"Eeuw. What's that awful smell?" She wrinkles her pretty little nose. At once Earl the aide appears with a can of Lavender Spice Air Freshener. He also opens a window. How disappointing to have to breathe fresh air again. "How sweet," Antoinette flirts. Earl's a goner. He stumbles, looks backward adoringly and waves goodbye. "Can we go see Mister Richards now?"

"Anytime, dear. He's asleep, you know. I guess Junior's told you. So tragic. He'll never, never be our old Teddy again." I eke out a tear or two, and it has the desired effect; she cries, too. So does the old crone in the corner, but she cries all the time. "Come. Help me up. We'll walk slowly down the hall together." I grasp Antoinette's dainty elbow with my hand and she and Junior pull me up. I manage to work up a palsy. Soon my head is nodding, and my hands are shaking, and I'm one helluva mess. Ya gotta love witchcraft.

★ ★ ★

Just an hour earlier I was in Teddy's room having a little chat. I squeezed his hand with all the force I could muster just to see if he'd wince. He didn't, thank badness. When we're alone I try to send my thoughts where they'll interfere with his dreams. Today I'm totally pissed, so I let him have it.

"Teddy, you son of a bitch. Why don't you die? You're so close. Anyone can see it. Just a little more to the right—or left; maybe up or down is more to the point. Anyway. You wanna know what your darling daughter Shirleen did to me? She kicked me outta our house. Remember our house? No, of course you don't, you mushbrained old fart, you only remember beaches and hotel rooms. Oh, yes, and maybe an examining table or two, eh? Take that." I pinch him on his cheek where, if he had any sensation, it would really sting. "She's selling everything out from under me. I have to live with her and that jerk of a husband and our grandson who's a chip off the old blockhead but also a good kid, if you remember, but you don't. Why am I wasting my breath on you? Speaking of Junior, he's coming to visit this afternoon. Last week he was too busy screwing the neighborhood cuties. Oops, I forgot. He has a steady girlfriend now. She's the daughter of somebody you know very, very well.

"You know that front hall closet that never managed to get you to the sixteenth floor? Well, Shirleen sent everything in it to the Thrift Shop, even the old leather jacket I found the condom in all those years ago. I should have guessed then that something was going on between you and randy Rosalie. I shoulda junked that jacket right there and then but I knew how much it meant to you, coming from your father and all. You know your toolshed? Stripped to the screws. The tractor you used to mow the lawn? Sold for zilch to Bogus Boy, the kid who used to charge a million bucks to do odd jobs. Shirleen's killing me, Teddy. All these years she never lifted a pinky to get back at you, and now she's getting back at me. For what? That's what I need to know.

"Remember how we named her? *Shir* for my mother, Shirley; *leen* for your mother, Arleen. Ah, but she was gorgeous. Coulda crawled right into an Ivory Soap commercial. That pink skin, those golden baby curls. You should see her hair now. What am I talking? You do see her hair. She comes to visit. She wants your money. Well, she's not gonna get it. I have power of attorney now that you're out in left field. When you die, I'll get everything you owe me for being such a shit, and off to Florida I'll go and buy a condo and lie on the beach all day cooking my skin but what do I care? I'll die, too, one of these days, but not until I've spent every penny, you fuck.

"Oh, why waste my breath on you? Look at you lying there, being waited on by Lily as if you knew all your life you had this luxury coming to you. I say you're one of the lucky ones. The rest of us have to fight our way, tooth and nail, every minute of each day. But I've been learning things you wouldn't believe. Dark, evil, fun things! You hear me, Teddy? Of course you don't. Well, on the outside chance that you do, I want to tell you that I have powers, Teddy.

"Hey. What happened to Blubber, your roommate? Never mind. I'll ask at the desk. Look. When I leave this afternoon, it may be a while before I see you again. I have some nifty plans to make. D'ya get my drift, lover? Oh, don't tell Shirleen what I said about getting even! Oops. That's the biggest laugh of all. You're a speechless blob and I'm begging you not to rat on me. I guess my secret's safe with you, eh, Teddy? Oh, look. I've gone and bruised your dear little wrist. Here, let Momma kiss it better. Why, Lily! I do believe he's coming around! He won't let me give him a kiss, the naughty boy. Oh, Teddy. I see your gruel has arrived on its gilded tray. Ta, ta, sweetheart. If you need anything, just whistle."

* * *

Late afternoon, as we enter Teddy's room, supper's being served. Earl does the honors. He bends to stage-whisper in Teddy's ear. "Looks like you got some important visitors. The quarterback is here with his girlfriend, and let me tell you, she's a babe."

Antoinette blushes like a ripe peach. She moves closer to the bed.

Earl wipes mashed potatoes off Teddy's chin with a corner of the sheet, providing a painterly touch to the canvas on which are smeared yesterday's raspberry Jell-O and pea soup. Here in Rip's place they're pretty clean, but not too. The bottom line is that the staff is kind. Teddy probably likes it when the men are on duty. They usually stink from b.o. but they're gentle, like Lily. Once a week, Earl gives him a whirlpool bath.

"Go on, Antoinette," Junior urges. "Hold his hand. He likes it when we hold his hand."

"Would you like to feed him?" Earl asks. Suddenly I have a picture of Antoinette tossing fish to a seal at the zoo.

She hesitates. "I...don't even know him," she says. Then, shyly, she touches his left hand. "Oh, he's got bruises! Look."

"Yeah," says Earl. "I noticed that. On his cheek, too."

From my pinching. *Mea culpa.*

"His skin is so soft, like a baby." Her glossy black hair masks her profile so I can't see her expression. Earl is transfixed. Junior is proud. I am amazed at a Short-Hills-stuck-up, nasty-neat kid like Antoinette showing compassion for a smelly old shell of a man like Teddy. "There," she says, yanking her hand away. "You need to get your rest, Doctor Richards." She straightens the sheet. As she steps back, Teddy sighs.

Sighs!

"Did you hear that?" Earl says, jumping up and spilling peas on the floor. The tray tips off the bed and Junior just manages to catch it before everything slides off.

"I heard something," Antoinette says.

I feel numb all over, and clammy. I think I'm having a panic attack.

"Did you hear anything, Mrs. Richards?" Earl is puzzled. "I could swear I heard him sigh, but I know that can't be so, unless…"

"Unless what?" The words creep out of my mouth, barely loud enough for others to hear. "Unless what?"

"Unless he's beginning to wake up!" Junior says triumphantly. "Isn't that so, Earl?"

Earl shrugs. "I dunno, kid. That's pretty unlikely. Look at him now. He's sleeping."

We look. Teddy sleeps, surrounded by food stains and green peas, some of which have rolled into the collar of his pajamas. One by one Antoinette collects them and puts them in the bowl of half-eaten lime Jell-O where they tremble, like my legs, on a wiggling sea of green.

"Don't worry. If anything does happen tonight, I'll let you know," Earl says, reaching for Antoinette's dainty hand with his big paw. "It's been a pleasure to meet you, Miss…"

"Bixby."

At the sound of her voice, Teddy opens his eyes. We all stare. He turns his head and looks at Antoinette. "Ro-see," he says. Then he closes his eyes.

A Way Out

Shirleen

Good morning. I'm very happy to meet you. *Bonjour. Je suis très heureuse de faire votre connaissance.* Adult Education is going on a spring field trip to Montréal. I've got these cassettes I practice with, in the kitchen at night when nobody can hear me. Deke can't help himself—he makes fun of me. What does he know about French? *"Voulez-vous coucher avec moi?"* is the extent, and you can bet I won't be saying that on this trip. I guess I should consider myself lucky that I'm even going. At first, I thought no way, with Ma here and all, but then she and Lavinia started planning a bus trip to Williamsburg that same weekend, so I figured why not?

These days Ma is seeing a lot of her new best friend. She and Lavinia get together almost every day. Once a week they meet at Bugsy's Tavern for cocktails, but they're careful not to overdo. It wouldn't pay to cause another ruckus and ruffle feathers at the Ladies' Aid, although Ma really made points with Junior—"Wow, Mom! Did Gram really hit Bugsy over the head with a beer bottle?" Personally, I can't imagine what the two women have in common, but I'm simply grateful that Ma has found something other than witchcraft to occupy her time. I got very nervous after the incident with Antoinette. Oh, I know the county health inspector said it was mercury poisoning, but I strongly suspect otherwise. And Ma promised me she was through with that shit! When I confronted her with her misdemeanor last week she insisted, "The girl is fine. She made a complete recovery. I don't understand what you're carrying on about. Anyone can get stuck with a tainted fish."

"Is that what you call it when you put a spell on something? Tainted? Look, I don't care if you are my mother, ever since you took up this peculiar hobby you've gotten totally weird, and scary things have been happening. Just try something else and see how long it takes me to kick you out."

Ma just sat there and took it. What else could she do? She has no one but me, and no place to go but here. She started to cry. "Please don't be angry with me, sweetheart," she sobbed. "I can't bear it when you scold me."

She sure knows which button to push. In an instant I was down on my knees, begging her forgiveness. "Ma. I didn't mean to upset you. Remember when I used to misbehave and you'd take away my privileges? Well, this is like that. Sort of. Except now I'm the parent and you're the teenager. Or you're the teenager and I'm the babysitter. Or we're both, both. Christ, I don't even know any more. But the point is, you can't poison people, no matter who you are. It's simply not allowed." By this time I was crying too, wiping my eyes and then Ma's, dabbing away with the Kleenex. When I was growing up my girlfriends and I used to make each other cry so we could blend our tears. This was our feminine version of Blood Brothers. "Look at that, Ma. We're sisters."

She remembers the rites. "Yes, sisters." But I could read her mind: If this is sisterhood, I'd rather be an only child.

* * *

I'm an American. Where's the subway? Where's the police station? I don't speak your language well. *Je suis une Américaine. Où est le Métro? Où est le commissaire de police? Je ne parle pas bien votre langue.*

Sometimes I wonder if the person who wrote this language course is trying to scare me. I mean, I know Montréal is a big city, but I'm a big girl. I can take care of myself. Never mind the dangers lurking. What if I like it there? Is there a phrase for, "I don't ever want to go back home?" Ha ha, only kidding, Deke.

Please repeat. *Répetez s'il-vous-plaît.* Damn it, the phone always rings when I'm just getting going. "Get the phone, will you, Hon?" He's in the living room watching *Monday Night Football*, eating popcorn, sucking on a beer, missing Junior who's gone to the nursing home to pick up his grandmother. Lately I haven't been able to get through to Junior. "I can't live without her," he said the day after Antoinette returned to school. "Look, Ma. I can't breathe." I had to promise him he could take the truck down to visit her the next weekend just so he'd get his lazy butt in gear.

Deke cruises in, pops open the refrigerator, takes out a frosty Bud, rummages around for some leftover meatloaf, *viande*, scoops up the bread, *pain*, and the mayo, and closes the door by kicking it. "Wrong number," he says. "Damned nuisance. Made me miss the kickoff."

"Did I hear Junior say Antoinette was coming up today?"

"Oh, yeah," Deke says between mouthfuls. "Didn't I tell you? She came up on the afternoon bus. Something about her classes being cancelled. Lover boy was thrilled. This meatloaf is somethin' else!" He stops in mid-chew. "Christ, Shirleen. Your mother didn't make it, did she?"

I give him a look: Get real. "You know Ma isn't cooking these days."

"Thank heaven for small favors. Mm-mm! Dee-licious."

He leans against the counter and stuffs his face and I'm thinking, he's a lovable pain in the rear, this guy who's crazy about meatloaf sandwiches and football and who's gonna let me go to Montréal. He should have told me Antoinette was coming, though. "Junior will be bringing her back here tonight. How'm I gonna get this place cleaned up? It's a mess."

"You think they care? They only have eyes for each other, babe. Like we were in high school." He picks me up and we nuzzle like puppies. I'm not that fat that he can't still lift me. Ma should be here to see this. When he puts me down, he gives me an extra squeeze. I follow him to the living room where Bryant Gumbel's younger brother is doing color commentary, as if we didn't know every little detail about the players already. Deke pats a place for me to sit down next to him. Won't you sit down? *Veuillez vous asseoir.* "My little honey," he says—the name he used to call me when we were first seeing each other. We snuggle together on the couch. He scoops up popcorn to feed me. I'm a million miles away, going through customs. Here is my luggage. I don't have anything to declare. *Voici mes bagages. Je n'ai rien à déclarer.* "Hey. Penny for your thoughts." He gives in and pushes mute on the remote. "You're not fretting over your folks, are you? Forget it. You were always trying to make things right between them. It's not going to happen. If your dad's lucky, he'll just pass away, and then she won't have anybody to nag, except you."

"Quit feeding my face. I don't even like popcorn." I have a feeling that if I tell him what I'm really thinking of—the trip to Montréal— he'll think I don't love him anymore. I guess I feel a little guilty for wanting to go so much. "Do you think this thing with Junior and Antoinette is moving too fast?" I ask, changing the subject.

"Oh, come on. They're teenagers. It'll be over just as fast as it started."

"You know they're having sex."

"Yeah. I had a talk with him."

"And?"

"He said he would...you know, use precautions."

"I'm not just talking about sex. I'm worried he'll lose interest in school, and in the scholarship."

"Yeah. His chance to get outta here."

"The chance you never had, because I got pregnant."

"I didn't say that."

"You didn't have to. I can see it written all over your face every time things don't go well and you remember how much you hated going to work for your father. You coulda been something other than an armchair quarterback, and you know it."

I watch his face for some sign that will tell me he knows I'm right, but he's watching the game, avoiding eye contact.

"I say it won't last. Junior and Antoinette are worlds apart, Shirleen."

"So?"

"So, sooner or later, we'll have to get together with her parents. What a nightmare that'll be. The rubes from Riverton meet the stuffed shirts from Short Hills. Hey. Now you've got me worrying. I thought we were gonna relax, get into the game." He brings back the crowd with a click, and I settle into the curve of his arm. The receiver fumbles a crucial pass. Actually, it's the quarterback's fault, but Deke'll never admit it. He loves the Bronco's star quarterback. I think he has delusions of grandeur for Junior. When the crowd roars, he imagines it's because our son has just won the game for Denver. But first we have to get him through Syracuse. And before that, we have to get him away from Antoinette. "Jesus! What the fuck. Everybody has off days. We got any of that Rocky Road ice cream?"

I guess we're both worried about Junior's future. But who can compete with raging hormones? When they get here, he'll want to have her all to himself. He'll take her to school, show her off, then bring her back here where they'll screw up a storm on this very couch where popcorn falls between the cushions where he keeps a condom hidden, just in case. I know my Junior. If getting on with his life means losing Antoinette, he won't budge. He'll be a grease monkey in his friend's dad's garage before he lets her get away. Deke said it to his parents, and Junior will say it to us: This is my life, and I'm gonna live it the way I want.

Click. "Hey," he says, surprising me by getting rid of the game. "I have an idea. Why don't you go warm up the sheets while I take a shower?"

* * *

He slips into bed beside me and we hug, not a sexy embrace, but a comfortable warm exchange of affection. "Nice," he sighs. His skin is still slightly moist from the shower. He smells good. Must be the cologne we bought him for Father's Day. "I can't use this," Deke said, embarrassed. "I'll smell like a pansy." But Junior convinced him it was just the thing he needed to drive me wild. "Do you wanna make love?" he asks now. Since we did that Couples' Encounter Weekend he's been careful to ask me, and I've been careful to give him an honest response. "If you don't wanna, I understand. You've had a lot to think about tonight." Bless him. I know how hard it's been for him to change. I never hoped for New Age Sensitive, only someone who'd respect my feelings. I know I should say yes, if even just to reward him. Relax. Take a deep breath. "Is that a yes? No shit!" he says, pulling me close. "I'm crazy about you, honey. I hope you know it." How to tell him I'm not in the mood without actually saying it? Oh yes, we're supposed to use body language. I pull away, leaving him with a big erection. Should I feel guilty? Nah. "Yeah," he says sadly. "Okay. I understand." No guy has to like being sensitive. That was one of the things we learned in therapy. He turns on his side and pretends to go to sleep.

It was a charming evening and I thank you very much. *Merci pour tout. J'ai passé une charmante soirée.* I'm not in the least sleepy. French phrases are running through my head, and all I can think about is getting on that bus.

Où est le téléphone? Where is the telephone? The telephone is right here, on the night table beside my bed, and it's ringing. What number are you calling? *Quel numéro appelez-vous?* "Oh, Earl. Sorry. I'm practicing my French, learning how to use the phone in Montréal. What's up? It's late. Is everything all right? Ma and Junior were there, but I guess they've left by now. What? What? Wait a minute, I have to turn down the volume on my Walkman. There. That's better. Pop woke up? Are you sure? I mean, can it happen after all this time? Oh, my God! Thank you for calling." When I hang up, I realize I'm still wearing the earphones pushed back on my head, like a runner crossing the street not wanting to miss the honk of anyone's horn.

"Something wrong?" Deke mumbles.

Even with the volume turned way down on my Walkman I can still hear the instructor's patient voice: Operator, will you please get this number for me? May I use your telephone? Long distance, please. Of course, with this latest development, who knows what the future will bring? I might never get to use those phones in Montréal.

* * *

The next morning, I wait until Deke leaves for work, then enter Ma's room to test the waters. "Antoinette spent the night with Junior, in his bed," she starts, hoping to pick a fight. "I hope to God he's using a rubber." She's sipping coffee from a large pottery mug. I recognize her book, *The Cooke's Byblle*, a dividend from the Sorcery Book Club, which Ma quickly hides under the blankets.

"Something spicy, Ma?" I tease. "It's okay. I know a thing or two. I even like a good hot read myself, from time to time. Lemme see." I reach under the covers but the telltale lump is gone, whisked away. *Poof.* "Ma. You promised. No more hocus pocus, remember?"

"Whatever are you talking about?" She holds up a copy of vintage Victoria Holt. "Since when are romances taboo?"

"Ma. The one you got the fish spell from. Hand it over."

"I don't know what you mean when you say fish spell. Go ahead. Look." She whips back the covers. Sure enough, there's nothing to see.

Un, deux, trois, quatre... I count to ten in French. What can I do with this woman? Why am I even trying? *Cinq, six, sept...* I should be at my aerobics class swaying to Michael Bolton. *Huit, neuf, dix.* "Earl called last night. About Pop."

"Oh, yes." The jacket illustration, a couple dressed in Victorian-era clothes embracing on a cliff with the stormy ocean roiling beneath them, commands more of her attention than I do. "Teddy woke up for a while when we were there."

"For a while?"

"Well, they don't know how long he'll stay awake, exactly. It might be, well, like a last gasp or something."

"They don't know? Who's they?"

"Did I say they? I meant we. We don't know how long he'll be awake. For heaven's sake, Shirleen, you're so irritable. And why? You should be delighted. Your darling daddy is back from the dead. Too bad he looks like shit. He was so vain about his appearance in his cheating years."

"Ma." I sit down beside her and take her hands in mine. "You don't have to pretend. I know how hard this is on you."

She pulls her hands away. "What are you talking about?"

"The fact that he's going to get better."

"Who says?" I watch in awe as her denial turns to rage. Her hands become karate weapons. She hits the mattress so hard her Oil of Olay bottle clatters from night table to floor. "There's some mistake," she says icily. "You said yourself he was…deteriorating."

"Well, like it or not, Earl says he's talking."

"If you can call it talking. Ga ga goo goo. Babytalking," she laughs.

"Come on, Ma. Get dressed. Have some breakfast. We'll go over and see for ourselves."

Her color has gone from ruddy to pale. "You go. I need to stay here and think. What am I gonna do? It's a shock. One day he's deteriorating, the next day I have to listen to him calling out Rosalie's name. Yes! He opened his eyes, looked straight at her clone, and said…oh, never mind. Nobody else understood him but me." She clutches her chest. *Au secours!* Help! For a minute I think she's having a heart attack, but then her breathing slows. She pauses for a moment. "When you're old, you get used to thinking in a certain way. You understand, I'm sure." *Ça va bien.* It's okay. "You want to know the truth? I wish he was dead! There. I said it." She smiles as if she's just unleashed the world's biggest secret.

Conflicted, a word that popped up often in our therapy group, comes to mind. "Ma. I know you're conflicted about Pop but think how this will look. This will look bad! You've gotta put up a front, if only for Junior. How about it? Pretend. Be the actress you always said you wanted to be. You can wear the new outfit we bought at Macy's. Pop always liked you in red." As I'm saying this, I realize that Ma doesn't give a shit about what Pop likes, but I go to the closet anyway and pull out a polyester pantsuit with the tags still attached. When we shopped last month, Macy's was having a big pre-season clearance. There were only a couple of things in Ma's size, and for one horrible minute I was afraid she was going to duke it out with another senior citizen eyeing the same merchandise. In an instant, the other woman disappeared. *Kapoof!* All that was left were her shoes and her rolled-down stockings, right in the place where she stood contemplating the sale rack. I'll never forget those shoes. They were custom-made orthotics with broad toes and wedge heels, built to last into the next geologic era. "Tell me you didn't," I pleaded with Ma, but she only shrugged and marched her outfit to the register.

But Ma's not interested in her hard-won pantsuit. "Tomorrow," she sighs, getting back into bed. "You tell him I wasn't feeling well today, that I'm happy to hear he's back to his old wonderful self again. Lavinia can give me a lift to the nursing home tomorrow. That'll give you a break. You can go have your hair done. And do me a favor. This time, have the girl cut it shorter. It's a rat's nest. You're getting too old to have one of those curly permanents. And honey, have you been putting on weight? Or is it just that sweatsuit? You better watch your-self. Deke's a good-looking man. A bit of a slob, but then, some women find body odor very arousing."

★ ★ ★

All smiles, the nursing home administrator is waiting for me at the Rip's front door. "Mrs. McClure. We're all so happy with your father's progress." With strong hands used to having their way with patients she guides me into her office, then sits me in a chair. "Have you thought about the future? Father will soon be ready to upgrade. Perhaps Mother might like to join him in our Rip Van Winkle Manor. We have twenty-four-hour back-up nursing support in our assisted living quarters. And the cost for all this is really quite..."

I notice the framed certificates of commendation. There's even a letter signed by the governor, attesting to the high quality of care at the Rip. "Well, I don't know. This is all happening kind of fast. I'll have to talk to both my parents. Unfortunately, their house has been sold, or they could go back there, with home-care providers. Do you really think Pop will be ready to leave here so soon? He seems awfully frail. And his speech! His senility! How will Ma be able to manage? I suspect he'll be just as confused as before."

The administrator's face lights up. "Oh, not necessarily. I've seen folks come out of these things clear as a bell. Of course, that's not usually the case, but...with your father, I suspect we'll just have to wait and see. As for speech therapy, he'll have access to the same services he receives as a nursing home patient."

"I see." Assisted living sounds expensive. Where would the money come from? Of course, there's the house sale, but we realized much less than we hoped to on that.

The administrator reads my mind. "Well. I only wanted you to start thinking about some options. If you do, uh, decide, we'd need to know soon, so we can free up the bed. You understand."

"Yes. Now, if you'll excuse me, I'd like to see him."

"Perfect timing! Here he comes now. Lily has him in a wheel-chair. Why, Dr. Richards. It's just grand to see you out taking a stroll," she gushes.

For months Pop has been trapped in bed, a prisoner of his body, and now I can hardly believe he's out of his room. I kneel to meet him at eye level and hug his bony legs which Lily's wrapped in a lap robe. "Well, look at you, Pop. Do you know who I am?" I search his poor, pinched face for an answer. He's lost so much weight that the skin stretches over his skull, creating the illusion of a death's-head. This wheelchair dwarfs him. He looks at me cloudily with eyes that have receded far into their sockets. I repeat the question, yelling over the roar of the rug-scrubbing machine.

Pop smiles on cue. Lily has dressed him in clean pajamas and someone else's too-big robe; I make a note to pick up a robe that'll fit him. What happened to the one he brought in here? Last month there was a pair of slippers that disappeared from Pop's wardrobe. Just the other day I saw them on Harold Barnes. I put Pop's name on everything but it doesn't help. It makes me think of summer camp where one day I'd see Brenda Smith wearing my khaki shorts, and the next day I'd see Sally Ann Blackwell wearing my Shetland sweater.

The rug is finally clean. Good thing, because Pop touches my face and says, "Shirleen. Gootaseeoo," in a weak voice.

"It's good to see you, Pop. Oh, is it ever." I embrace him cautiously, fearing that his brittle bones might snap if I overdo. How can they even think of discharging this ghost of a man? Who will care for him if they do? Ma? "Lily, do you mind if I take over for a while? I'd like to spend a little time with him." The maintenance man begins scrubbing the rugs again. "Somewhere quiet." I want a quiet room. *Je veux une chambre tranquille.* At least the place doesn't smell of pee.

I push Pop down to the end of the hall and into a room that's used for storage and sometimes for crafts. It's a kind of sun porch, a cheerful windowed enclave smelling of dust and Elmer's Glue. "This okay, Pop?" He nods, reaching up to touch my arm. What lovely pale green eyes he has. Ma's voice comes back to me: He was so vain in his cheating years. It's clear a warning is called for. "About Ma," I could begin. But how to continue? You should know that Ma has it in for you, still. She still blames you for Rosalie. She wants revenge. I don't know how, exactly, she plans to get it, but I do know she's determined, and I'm afraid for you, Pop. Here, you're safe. Out there are trap doors and hens' teeth, dungeons and lizards' tails.

I place his chair in a shaft of sunlight, turning it so that he doesn't squint, then I sit on a bench across from him. I bridge the space to hold his hands. His skin is surprisingly cool, and loose as well-worn gloves. I mustn't pull too hard. "See, it's this way, Pop," I begin. My throat suddenly feels dry. I can't do this. "We all want you to be safe," I finally say. *Sauf.* How foolish this sounds. Safe from what? I need to spell it out. If I only knew enough French. It might seem easier to tell him in another language. But does he understand French? I don't even know.

"Ahk oo."

Don't thank me, Pop. I'm only trying my best to warn you. She's not the person we used to know. Years of hating you have made her crazy. She ought to be locked up. In a dungeon. "I'm sorry Ma isn't here. She said to tell you how happy she is that you're feeling better. She'll be here tomorrow." *Elle viendra demain.*

He pulls away. With surprising strength, he turns the chair so that I can't see his face. He puts his head down. He shivers.

It's then I realize I don't need to translate. He knows.

Close Call

Irene

I always thought when a woman got to be my age the bloating would quit, but no, I'm a regular water balloon, a funhouse freak. I can't fit into the pantsuit I bought at Macy's, the one I went to all that trouble for. At first, I thought they switched sizes on me, gave me a twelve instead of a sixteen, but no, the tag says sixteen; of course, they make mistakes, it could be a twelve. It fits like a ten. I can't even pull the pants up over my hips. The matching blouse—if I could find the fucking thing in this closet, which is so small I can't jam even half of my wardrobe in it (Shirleen had to store my off-season clothes up in the attic where the moths will probably get them)—won't button across my ballooning boobs. It's Shirleen's fault. She talked me into getting this godawful shade of red. Shit. I just split the seams. The blouse is here somewhere. I never even removed the sales tag. "Lady Lovely, for the Woman Who Cares." I care, all right. Okay. Here goes: shoes, purses, raincoat, umbrella, slacks, blazers, dresses (which I never wear but which I can't bear to throw away), fur stole (ditto). No blouse. Up on the shelf, what've we got here? Oh, yeah. Scrapbooks, the hatbox containing my witchcraft study aids, another box of controversial texts. Where's my drug stash? I swear I've got some ancient diuretics that some doctor prescribed a million years ago when I was still flowing. I never throw anything away. Do diuretics have a shelf life? They're here, somewhere. Somewhere.

Okay. Bureau drawers: jewelry box, scarves, underwear, night-gowns, bed jacket, sweaters, cardboard file with supposedly important papers (though who gives a damn about them?): marriage license, outdated passport, Shirleen's birth certificate, IRA, key to safe deposit box, clippings from the trial, etc., etc. Here's a paperweight Junior made for me when he was a second-grader. And here's my wedding picture. God, I had a waistline then. What a stunner.

Well, I can see there are no quick-fix pills in here. Moldred will have a potion to get rid of excess fluid. Even damsels in the Middle Ages must have needed to pee away those extra pounds, and dammit, I will find a way, even if it means emptying chamber pots out windows like they used to do. Here's my *Byblle*. There'll be time, before Lavinia comes to pick me up.

Here's the blouse, underneath the raincoat. Yech, paisley. I never wear paisley. Who designed this? Who cares? I'm only going to see Teddy at the Rip.

★ ★ ★

Lavinia picks me up in her new Mercedes, a seventieth birthday present from her family. "What do you think, Irene? Isn't it something? Won't the truckers at Bugsy's be surprised?" She's all puffed up with pride.

"Well, yeah, I guess it's quite a car, Vinnie. I mean, if you like ostentation. Me, I'm more of a background kind of person." As I hand her this drivel, I know how ridiculous it sounds coming from a person decked out in red paisley. She can probably see right through me, knows how jealous I really am. In six years, when I turn seventy, Shirleen will buy me a straw hat and some hankies.

"I've been thinking that when we go on our trip, we should take this instead of the bus."

Fine. But you'll have to let me do the driving. I can't stand the way she drives—all over the road, tailgating, running lights, scaring the hell out of people. The looks on their faces right before she doesn't hit them! Priceless. "Jesus! Look out! You almost plowed into that truck!"

"Oops," she says with a coy smile.

Oops, indeed.

"Well, what do you think? Shall we go south in style? You know, I've never ridden a Greyhound bus in my life. I hear they smell. And the people you have to put up with. Did you see that movie *Midnight Cowboy*? Dustin Hoffman died on a bus."

I listen to her babble, and I understand why Hendrik Donderhook kicked the bucket before his time. He couldn't stand her incessant yakking. Me, I've got other things to think about, other problems to solve. Our trip to Williamsburg may not be possible if I'm stuck playing nursemaid to Teddy. So, at this point, I figure it's a moot discussion. Still, I hate to burst Vinnie's bubble. "Sure," I say finally, averting my eyes as she sideswipes a van. "Let's live it up."

She swings her arm to protect me as she slips back into the lane after passing a semi in a no-passing zone. "We'll have a wonderful time."

If we live that long.

"You seem distracted, Irene. Oh. It must be something to think of Teddy coming back from the dead. Thank God it never happened to Hendrik. He just slept his way into paradise. I'll never forget what Pastor Brinker said at the funeral. He said..."

"Hendrik Donderhook was a blessed individual whom we shall all miss tremendously." I've heard this story about a hundred times, and I mean to nip it in the bud. Besides, we're approaching the Rip and I have to get myself in shape for playing the role of the dutiful, attentive wife.

"No, as a matter of fact, he said, 'whom we shall all miss greatly,' Miss Smarty. Well. Here we are. You sure you don't want me to pick you up later?"

"No, thanks. Shirleen's coming." I get out of the car slowly, wanting to postpone my entrance. I also want Vinnie to get an eyeful of the new, svelte me. God, that stuff tasted awful! Moldred's got another beauty preparation, bubble bath that takes off pounds and rejuvenates skin. I'm trying that next time.

"Irene! You've been slimming behind my back! You naughty girl. Have you been working out at the gym? Come on, now. It's that new instructor, right? All the girls say he's fantastic."

I turn and give her my most enigmatic smile.

"Well, then, don't tell me how you did it. But you did it. And, my dear, you look ab-solutely fabulous."

"Why, thanks, Vinnie." Jealous, you old bat? "Coming from you, that's a real compliment." I slam the door hard, knowing this act of violence perpetrated against her shiny new toy will make her wince.

★ ★ ★

"Geh me ow heah!" Teddy yells as soon as he sees me. No "Hello, sweetheart, it's nice to see you," just some back-from-the-brink gibberish. I understand him perfectly. Now that he's rejoined the living, he sees that this place is a loony bin, and he wants out. "Wah go home!"

Lily, the aide, is standing beside me, so I'm sweeter than pie. "Sugar, there is no home. Remember what I told you? I'm living with Shirleen and Deke, in a little room across the hall from Junior. That's home, now. Our house has been sold, sugar."

"Buy ih bah!"

"I can't buy it back, darling."

"Why noh?"

"Because I can't. There's a young couple living in it now, and they won't want to move out, because they just moved in. So, you can forget that scheme."

"Geh anuh pla."

"Why, sugar, you talk as though we're made of money! How can I get another place?"

"We hah enuh."

"Not any more we don't! You've been private pay here, sugar.

Your comfort is the most important thing to me." I practically gag on
that one.

"Don bleeh yuh."

"Well, you should believe me." Just because he can't talk doesn't
mean the wheels up there aren't turning. He's smart as a whip, but
not smart enough for me. "Ask Shirleen." I know he will, and I know
she'll tell him the truth. I look at my watch. It's eleven, almost time
for dinner. "Lily, isn't this the day you work in the kitchen?" I can't
think of any other way to get rid of her.

"Why, sure it is, Ms. Richards. I almos' forgot."

Lucky guess. I wait for her to leave the room before I move closer
to Teddy. He has to lean forward to do his arm exercises. Maybe if I
don't lift a finger to help him he'll fall out of bed. He's looking at me,
wanting the solution my voice seemed to promise when I was putting
on my little act for Lily. "Look, you bastard," I whisper. "If you think
I'm going to set up housekeeping with you, forget it."

Hurt clouds his face and tears spill onto the sheet that's tucked
under his chin.

"Oh, for God's sake, Teddy, get real."

"Hah pih! I'muh meh."

"You want me to pity you because you're a mess? No problem. I
do feel sorry for you, asshole, but there isn't a thing I can do."

"I wah go home."

"I've told you: there is no home sweet home."

Just then Lily appears with his tray. "Lookee here! Your favorite.
Meat loaf, mashed potatoes and peas! Mmm-mm!"

Teddy eyes the unappetizing palate of grey, grey, and green. He
makes a face to match, then pushes the tray away.

"How you gonna get your strength back? Come on. Just a little."
Lily tries to push a spoon past his clenched teeth. She shoots me a
look. "What'd you do to him to make him so feisty?" I shrug my shoulders and play the wide-eyed, despairing innocent. Finally, she picks up
the tray. "He never gives me any trouble. I don't get it."

"Goh weh," he says to me when she leaves.

"Why, Teddy, I'm surprised at you." I back away, knowing what will happen next, wanting it to happen. *"Tipsibus, flipsibus, wobbledy woo,"* I chant, and watch him pitch forward, his still-useless legs buckling, onto the floor. A distinct crunch should signal the hip fracture, but all I hear is a muffled thud. Although I could have pulled it off without the spell—he was so angry he was bound to get at me in any way he could, and if I taunted him more he would have leaned forward just enough in his attempt to get at me—the words were my insurance that my scheme would work. Now, with any luck, he'll be back in bed where I want him, but not before he has surgery to pin that hip, and with surgery comes the risk of anesthesia. Ooh. This is delicious.

He moans, and points to the cord. Slowly, very slowly, I walk over to the bed and pull ever so gently, not quite hard enough to flick on the light and summon help. "Sorry," I say. "My fingers are so weak. Arthritis, you know." He pulls himself along the floor until he reaches the bed, then extends one arm. I dangle the cord just out of his reach. "I know I should call for help, but something's holding me back. I'll just sit down on the bed for a minute until my thoughts clear." He's looking very pale. I figure, in another minute or two, he'll pass out. Then I'll go for help.

Teddy cries, big sloppy tears which puddle on the floor and in whose slick surface I can see my angry face. I do pity him. After all, this is the man to whom I once gave my heart and soul (which he proceeded to throw in the trash.)

Just to prove I'm part human I decree, "Nullify all.

"All right, Teddy. Here's your fucking lifeline." I put the end of the cord into his hand but it's too late, he's already losing consciousness. His head hits the floor with a thump. Lord of Darkness, what have I done? I pull the cord, the light flashes. "Thank God you're here!" I say to Earl, and my panic is genuine. "He fell out of bed! I think he's broken his hip! Oh, suddenly I feel all woozy. Thank you, dear. I'll just lie down here for a minute or two until I get my sea legs. He's just fainted, right? He's not…oh, thank goodness for that. I couldn't stand to lose him now, after all we've been through." At times like this my training in the theater serves me well, as does the makeup: dark circles under the eyes, pale cheeks, lined brow. I only hope I got the nullify part right.

They've got him on a gurney. The charge nurse says, "You can ride with him in the ambulance, if you like, Mrs. Richards. I'm so sorry. I can't think how this could have happened, although Lily did say he seemed sort of agitated when she was in with his lunch. Did you notice anything in particular?"

"Well, maybe one thing. He seemed awfully anxious to get to the bathroom on his own. You know, not waiting for someone to come get him and not wanting my help. You know how men are. And doctors make the worst patients, don't you think?"

"Not Dr. Richards." She blushes. "He was always a love. So caring and gentle. That was before his stroke, of course."

"Of course." How can I shut her up? If only I could remember the spell for that. How useful. I'd use it ten times a day. People are always running off at the mouth, driving me crazy.

"Anything I can get you? Some dinner, maybe?"

That pig slop? No thank you. "Thanks, but no. Seeing him like that…" I give her a look which says it all.

"Of course. Uh, maybe it's best you don't ride with him. I'll send one of our nurses to check on his vitals, make sure his pressure doesn't dip."

"You're so kind." And such a royal pain in the ass.

"Dr. Richards is very special to us." Again that blush. What, pray tell, has Teddy been up to?

"I think I'll pass on the ambulance ride, dear. I've had quite enough excitement for one day." Just in case I didn't undo the curse and Teddy really needs surgery, I wouldn't want him ending up better than before. I'm cataloguing disasters in my head. There's a sleep disorder called apnea that causes people to stop breathing. A healthy person might get struck by lightning while sitting on the toilet. Well-meaning nurses give patients the wrong drugs—it happens all the time. Then, should a person recover his ambulation, there's always the chance he'd wander outside the Rip, stroll onto the highway and get creamed by a truck. According to the Rip Van Winkle staff, it was hard for anyone to believe how or why the accident had taken place. The night orderly, who found Dr. Richards on the road, was interviewed. "Flatter than a pancake," were the words he used to describe the doctor's condition. The truck driver swore he hadn't felt a thing. "I'd know if I hit someone," he claimed, "even a skinny little critter like the Doc." The driver continued: "I musta just missed him with my tires." Of course, the tire marks on Dr. Richards' pajamas contradict the driver's statement.

Ah. The ambulance is here. They're loading Teddy. Good riddance, my dear, and don't worry; I didn't use my full powers on you after all. In fact, I'm wondering if I had anything to do with your misfortune. Maybe you did simply fall out of bed.

★ ★ ★

It seems that while I've been napping, Bingo's been going on right under my nose. "B thirty-three," yells the Dear Volunteer, a sweet-faced young woman who wears her hair pulled back in a ponytail. "I twenty-one." This is the group from Teddy's wing: one catatonic, two hard of hearing, and the man who keeps yelling "Marsha!" The volunteer keeps trying to get them to cover their numbers. "N eleven," she barks. "G fourteen, O six." I have to hand it to her: she could be shopping with the girls or cheating on her husband but here she is, twice a week, talking to herself. "Somebody must have Bingo by now," she says.

"Ma, what's happened here?" Shirleen shakes me from my nap and pulls me to my feet. "They told me Pop had an accident."

"Hard to believe, isn't it? And just when he was doing so well. But sometimes, honey," and here I pause for effect and raise my voice a few decibels so the nurses can hear as we pass by their station, "bad things happen to good people." We float out to Shirleen's car on a wave of sympathy: As if they haven't been through enough.

* * *

Finally, it is evening, the end of one of the sorriest days in my life.

While I'm grateful that Teddy's hip is only bruised, I wish I'd been able to delay his recovery. As it is, in a day or two he'll bounce back to the Rip, they'll start physical therapy, and, in a week or two, he'll be where he was before he fell out of bed. Shirleen is beside herself with glee. "Just a teensy setback, the doctor said."

Moldred would say I'm a wimp.

I think I'm ready for the next phase of my tutorial. I've dialed 1-800-Witches. Now I'm listening for the phone, hoping to get there before anyone else does. This is the first month I've subscribed to Dial-a-Spell, and I want to be sure I get my money's worth. I'll never know whether I could've really broken Teddy's hip. If only Teddy hadn't cried! Can witches have soft hearts? Is it possible to be mildly mischievous? What do I want from my powers, anyway?

Right now, Junior is trying to reach Antoinette, so I'll probably never get my call. When we got home there was a message saying she needed to talk to him right away. He was supposed to call her at her school. I wonder what it's about? If I concentrate, I can hear what he's saying, since the walls in this house are so thin (cheap construction—the builder was Deke's friend). That reminds me: I've gotta talk to Shirleen about getting my own phone. Junior has his. I don't see why I shouldn't, also. I really should get a separate number, too. Then I could be listed in the *Sorcerer's Directory*, which would be handy for networking.

The other bad thing that happened to me today is that the diuretic effects of the potion wore off, and I'm a blimp again. I had to get out of my slacks as soon as we got home—they were so tight they were impeding my circulation. Once again, my upper arms are quivering masses, my boobs watery as melons. I believe it's worse than before. Maybe I can find a longer-lasting recipe that tastes better. Come to think of it, I'm going to mix up a batch of bubble bath. If it works, I could market the product and make a million bucks. I could retire to Florida, leave Teddy in the Rip, start that new life I've been dreaming about. Vinnie would bless me. She could certainly stand to lose thirty or forty pounds herself. Will you listen to me! Pandering to fatties! This is what got Teddy in trouble, and I want to do the same thing? I must be crazy.

Don't shut your door completely, Junior. Atta boy, crack it for air. All those pent-up hormones steam up the place. Okay. I'm listening.

"Antoinette? Jesus. It's hard getting through to you. Hey, baby. I can't wait 'til Wednesday."

Give me a break, Junior. At this rate we'll be here all night.

"What? I can hardly hear you. Oh. You're in gym class. Cool. Basketball practice? You wear those cute little shorts that show your ass when you bend over?"

Get on with it, buddy. I'm expecting a call of my own.

"Yeah, the purple ones. Ooh, baby. I'm getting hard just thinking about your buns. Hey. Miss me?"

She's going on and on about something, and I can't hear a word. There should be a way. Yakety-yak, Antoinette. Let's not go overboard. Remember, you're supposed to be shooting baskets, not gabbing on your cell phone. Junior, you could at least grunt to give me a hint of what's going on, here.

"But I don't understand. How can she stop you from seeing me?"

Pay dirt!

"My grandfather? Christ, he's practically eighty. And your mother..."

Well, well. Rosalie finally figured out that Junior is my grandson!

"She was nineteen? She was his nurse? I don't believe it."

Believe it, sweetie. Just ask me. I was there.

"Okay, I will ask her. But I know Gram. She'd never hurt us."

Come to me, chickens. I'll tell you the whole truth. Then you'll understand.

"You can't let your mother keep us apart. I won't let her."

You don't know who you're up against, Junior.

"Did you mean what you said about loving me? Well, then, I'm gonna think of something. Honey, don't worry. Baby, don't cry. For now, tell her anything. Tell her okay, you won't see me anymore. Anything to get her off your case. I'll call you…Okay, you call me. Before Thanksgiving. Call me collect. Yeah. Wednesday night. I'll be here. God, I love you so much. Mm, me too. Bye."

Next, he'll be in here wanting to know the truth about everything, and I'll have to tell him about the affair, and the trial—the whole goddamn mess. I'll also have to tell him that I suspect Antoinette is Teddy's daughter, conceived when he was supposed to be in San Francisco at a medical supplier's conference. It'll break Junior's heart. Moldred, I wish you could get me out of this one.

I'll lie down here, pretend I've been napping. "Yes? Oh, come in, Junior. I was just resting. It's been a difficult day."

* * *

He took it well. I tried to tell him I knew that Antoinette was nothing like her mother, that she was a sweet innocent little thing who would never deceive him the way Rosalie had deceived Teddy into having an affair with her. I had to say this. How could I admit that she was sexier and lovelier than me? I told him I bet that Antoinette took after her father. Of course, I've never even met the man, but it seemed to make sense to Junior, who hasn't met him either. One of these days, he will; and he'll remember what I said.

About Teddy being her father: I never said a word. I just couldn't.

* * *

Shirleen wants to bring Teddy home for Thanksgiving. "Deke and I really want to have him with us, now that he's back to his old self.

Well, almost. Actually, I can understand him pretty well, now that I'm used to his speech patterns. So, what do you say, Mom? How about burying the hatchet?"

In his skull? "I don't know if I can do that." This calls for a little stalling, a pretense of heavy soul-searching. I figure if I say okay right away, she'll suspect something.

"It'll only be for a couple of hours. Deke can take him back to the hospital whenever you say."

"Well…" I can't resist teasing her a little. "Okay." Bring the bastard here. A turkey for a turkey. Stuff the old bird. Truss him. Carve him. Give me some privacy, my own phone, and a gift certificate for ten hours of Dial-a-Spell, and then we'll see who gets the wishbone!

"Oh, Ma, I knew you could do it! I'm so proud of you." She hugs me, presses me close, overwhelms me with lilacs. When she was little, she'd always give me the same kind of cologne for Christmas. Teddy helped her pick it out: lilacs. And here I am, pretending to be the all-forgiving wife, but I don't know what else I can do. I need Teddy here, close.

Junior mopes around the house acting like it's his last day on earth. Shirleen knows something happened between him and Antoinette, but she doesn't know what, and Junior asked me not to tell. I love being his confidante, and I wouldn't betray that trust. I know he's cooking up a plan, though I don't know the details.

"It doesn't make sense," he told me the other day when we were having our little chat about his grandpa's checkered past. "If Mrs. Bixby hates us so, why did she call Ma to ask about Gramps?"

"She hates me," I explained. "She didn't realize I was living with your mother until, well, I guess until just the other day, when Antoinette must have told her." It's also occurred to me that Rosalie could never sanction a romance between Antoinette and Junior if Teddy is Antoinette's father, but of course, I won't mention this to Junior.

"You know, I just figured out something. When Gramps woke up that time we were all at the nursing home, he thought Antoinette was her mother. Don't you remember he called her Rosalie?"

"Really? I didn't notice," I lie. "But then, I was in shock."

"You didn't seem too happy. I remember that. We wondered why. Now I guess I know why. You hate him, don't you? You probably made him fall out of bed! You probably wanted him to die! You and your witch crap!"

Perceptive kid. "Oh, Junior. I should be able to forgive. I'm going to try. Did your mother tell you that your grandpa is coming here for Thanksgiving?"

"Yeah. That's great," he says flatly.

"I hope you're not going to let this color your feelings for him." As if I haven't secretly wished for this to happen. I admit I've always been jealous of my rivals, but I've got to keep playing my part.

"I can't help it. How could he have hurt you like that?"

Okay, here goes. "I think…no, I know that he let his feelings get out of control. He couldn't help himself. You know how you feel about Antoinette. And then when the trial came up and everything got all mixed in together, it was as if some giant wave was carrying us away. We were powerless. That sometimes happens in life. You'll learn."

"Yeah. Like with me and Antoinette, right? We have to be together or we'll die. But nobody seems to understand that. It's like we're swept away by the tide of our feelings, but somebody's trying to pull us back to the shore. Does that make sense?"

"Of course it does, darling." He looks so sad I want to take him in my arms and cradle him, but he's too big for that, so all I can do is reach over and touch his face. "There, there. Things will improve. You'll see. You know me. I have ways."

"Gram! No! I don't want any of that! And Mom would kill me if she thought I encouraged you in any way. You've got to let go of that stuff. It's creepy, and it can hurt people. Look what almost happened to Antoinette. And to Gramps."

He looks at me and I can see Teddy and Deke and Deke's father and all the men in both families from eons ago, faces I've known only through photographs. Junior has their dark eyes and full lips and chiseled features, but then there's that surprising Teutonic hair: white-blond, like his mother's when she was young, hair that resists being slicked down, hair that sticks up and looks best when cropped short. Hair soft to the touch. I reach out now and stroke it. "Don't you worry," I tell him. "Everything will work out. Trust me." I only hope I'm wrong about Teddy being Antoinette's father. That I certainly couldn't undo with a spell.

"Everything's changed."

"Well, honey, that's life. You wouldn't want everything to stay the same, would you? That would mean no surprises, and surprises are nice."

"That depends on who's being surprised and what the surprise is," he says solemnly, getting up from the couch and looking at his watch. "You'd think she'd have called by now."

Beep!

Hello? This message is for Irene Witchards.

(Interesting Freudian slip, there. Might work well, if I go into the bubble bath business.)

Concerning your spell for fractures, we can find no record of the rhyme you quoted. Where did you get that nursery-school wording? From Moldred? Not a good source. Highly unreliable. Could get you into trouble. We suggest that in the future, you consult Dial-a-Spell using the directory we mailed you last month. If for some reason you never received this directory, call us again at our toll-free number and place another order. That's 1-800-Witches.

A directory? First I've heard. Well. That explains it. You just can't rely on the mails these days. Or could someone be keeping it from me? Moldred?

A Plan Hatches

Shirleen

Something's going on with Junior and Antoinette. "I need to know for sure if she's coming for Thanksgiving," I tell him, hoping to elicit the truth. "If she's coming, I have to set up the cot in your grandmother's room."

"Jeez, Mom. I'll set up the cot. I'll get it out of the closet, put it in Gram's room, slap some sheets on it. No big deal."

"Then she's coming."

"Did I say that? I don't know if she's coming. I think she's coming."

"You don't have to be so testy. What's the problem, anyway?"

"Did I say there was a problem?"

"Do you think I'm stupid?"

He sits down on the kitchen chair, his chair, the one he's sat in ever since he grew tall enough to reach the table. There's a scar on the seat of the chair from the time he was doing a wood-burning project for Scouts. He puts his head in his hands. He's Deke all over, this son of mine: same figures of speech, same mannerisms. When Deke's worried, he puts his head in his hands. "No, Mom, I don't think you're stupid."

"Well, then. Out with it. Is something wrong between you?"

"We're fine. It's just that...she's got to take PSATs the day after Thanksgiving. Yeah, that's it. And, uh, her parents want her to stay home to study."

I give him a look. Nice try, Junior.

"You know what PSATs are, right? Those practice tests for college entrance."

I give him another look.

"Ma, could you please just get off my case? I told you she's gonna call me tomorrow night."

"All right." I'm tired of being jerked around, but what can I do? Deke says relax. He thinks I'm nervous because Pop is coming for Thanksgiving dinner. And why shouldn't I be? Will Ma behave? "You've got to promise you'll be nice," I tell her, treating her like a child. "You're not to say anything mean. Promise."

★ ★ ★

The night before Thanksgiving I'm in the kitchen peeling potatoes, Deke is bowling, Junior is sitting by the phone waiting for Antoinette's call, Ma is hanging around waiting for Lavinia to pick her up for their weekly trip to Bugsy's. "Will you at least let me make the pies?" she pleads.

As if I'm going to let her prepare anything to be served to Antoinette or Pop. "No, Ma. We've been over this a hundred times. I want you out of the kitchen."

"I'm still being punished, then."

"Let's say you're on probation. Anyway, it's not punishment. It's prevention."

She mumbles something.

"I beg your pardon?"

"Oops, that's Vinnie. Gotta go." She grabs her coat and races to the door, my second teenager who can't wait to get away from Mother.

"Don't get snockered!" I yelled after her. "And no barfights." It's gotten to be such a joke, the two of them off on a toot in that fancy car, though when I think of the damage they did that first time, I stop laughing. We got a bill for $548. I shudder to think what Barclay Donderhook got socked with. In all the years Junior's been raising hell with his buddies, we've never once had to pay any damage. My mother the juvenile offender. At least she's got spunk; my friends tell me I should be glad for that.

The phone rings. I can tell from the way Junior hushes his voice that it's Antoinette. I hate to do it, but I'll put a Kleenex over the mouthpiece so he doesn't hear me breathing.

She's doing all the talking, about Rosalie and her dad not wanting her to see Junior. Well. That was in the cards. I know it'll be tough on him, but there are other fish in the sea, right? Christ, I don't believe I said that. Ma and Pop used to console me with that phrase in high school until I met Deke, that is, and then I knew he was the only fish for me. It won't be like that for Junior. He's got his college years ahead, getting away from here, having chances we never had. Now he's telling her he can't accept her parents' decision. She's starting to cry. He's starting to cry.

The potatoes are boiling over. I'll have to hang up.

Too bad she won't be coming for the weekend. Too bad. I was getting to like her, though I could tell Junior was getting more involved than he should. Probably it's just as well they're breaking up now, except there's nothing like a miserable lovesick teenager to sabotage a holiday. And I suppose I really was looking forward to some time for the family to be together. Of course, I'm always hoping that Ma will let go of her anger.

I even saw a sweater I thought would look beautiful on Antoinette. I was going to put it on lay-away next time I went to the mall. It was part angora, so soft, the prettiest shade of pink. Just the thing to set off her dark hair.

Junior streaks past me down the hall, into his room where he slams the door.

I'll wait a while. Then I'll go down and knock on his door.

I know. I'll bake something. Who am I kidding? It takes more than brownies to mend a broken heart.

All evening Junior stays locked tight in his room. No music. No TV.

Ma's in a mood when she gets home, so I don't tell her about the breakup.

About 10:30 Deke comes in, happy because his team has moved up in the league standings and he bowled two hundred for the very first time. "Sorry to burst your bubble," I say, "but Junior and Antoinette have broken up. Her parents don't want them seeing each other." I slide into bed beside him. I can smell what's on tap at Jordan's Lanes. If there's anything that'll dampen my ardor besides just plain not wanting sex it's the smell of Miller. "Yech. Brush your teeth."

Like an obedient dog he pads into the bathroom, runs the water, shoves the toothbrush in his mouth, forgets the toothpaste, starts all over again, spits. I don't have to be in there with him, I know the drill. He comes back to bed, leans over and breathes in my face. "Better? Do I pass the test? Will you kiss me now or do I have to gargle with Listerine?"

I give him a chaste peck on the cheek hoping to avoid a prolonged encounter. Deke loves to French kiss. His tongue is the hottest part of him, not including his you-know-what. "Junior's heartbroken," I say, hoping to bring him back to the subject of our son. I turn over so my back's toward him, but his friskiness won't be denied. "Hey, honey. No. I mean it. No means no. Remember Marriage Encounter?"

"Fuck marriage encounter. Fuck you instead," he slurs, still buzzed from the beer and his bowling score. He reaches around and grabs my tits. "Tweak. Time to turn on the love machine."

I try to escape his reach by sitting on the edge of the bed, but he slides after me and pulls me back. At first the Cave Man approach freezes me up, but then I swing from my own vine, discover fire, don't let myself douse it, and before I know what's happened, bingo. I'm not suggesting this is the way to go. I like to think I'm raising my son to be higher than Mr. Cro-Magnon. I hope I am, at least. Antoinette was a good, refining influence. That's another reason I'm sorry to see her go.

Later, when Deke is snoring, I get up to use the bathroom and notice Junior's light. It's 2:30. Poor kid. I wish there was something I could do. In the sink the toothpaste clings like a snail then slides slowly towards the drain where it waits to be dislodged. How wide awake I am. Thanksgiving. I don't know what to do with myself this early on a holiday. Give thanks? For what? Squinting at my reflection I see a face marred by little bits of food that we've dislodged with our dental floss and flicked against the mirror. I see yesterday's beef stew and tuna salad; this morning's waffles, tonight's fried chicken. I can be thankful for Windex. Christ, look at me. Almost thirty-six years old— young by today's standards, most women my age aren't even having their first babies yet—but I look forty, easy. Ma's right. I am a mess. And Deke, with his gut hanging out and his thinning hair and his this and his that. Imagine the two of us going to college football games looking like Fred and Wilma Flintstone! At least with Antoinette out of the picture Junior will get that scholarship. I know he will. And Deke and I will have an incentive to shape up.

★ ★ ★

"Deke. I think I hear a car backing up."

"Yeah," he says sleepily. "It's coming from across the street." Our neighbor Bev Anderssen has a job delivering papers. She has to pick them up in the middle of the night.

"No. That's our garage door going down. The china's wiggling in the cabinet."

"I'm telling you, it's Bev. Their garage door is heavy as lead. When Gunnar threw his back out, I had to go over there to close it every night. Remember? They didn't want Frisky raiding their garbage."

"Frisky never raided anyone's garbage! It was raccoons."

"Whatever. Hey. It's almost morning. Get some shut-eye. Today's your big cooking day. You'll need your strength."

"Junior's light's still on."

"So? Maybe he's reading *Penthouse*, getting over his loss. Nothing like a good pair of jugs to give a guy some perspective."

"Deke. He's suffering."

"Not for long. Trust me. The phone will start ringing tomorrow night. 'Is Junior there? Lemme speak to Junior.'" Deke does Junior's formed girlfriend's squeaky little voice. "'Wasn't Junior just awesome in the game today, Mr. McClure?'"

"Shh."

"Roll over. I'll rub your back. Hey. Did you come last night? You were wild, babe."

And I didn't think he'd noticed.

★ ★ ★

Morning breaks too early, as always when I've been awake half the night. Deke is dead to the world. I get up quietly and go to the window to see what kind of tidings the day will bring. So far the sky is clear, though they've forecasted snow—typical for an upstate New York, Thanksgiving Day.

In the kitchen, I find Ma with her *Byblle* in one hand and a cup of steaming coffee in the other. For a moment I don't see the cup, only the cloud rising from her fingers. "You're up early," I remark. Usually she stays in bed until eight o'clock.

She doesn't look up. "Mm, yes."

"Something fascinating?" I reach for the book, but she's got a firm grip.

"I'm looking up something."

"It better not be pumpkin pie. I already made one."

Now she looks up. "You told me in no uncertain terms that I was not to cook, so I'm not cooking. This has to do with matters of health."

"You sick? Because if you're relying on Moldred for old-world remedies, I can tell you now I'm not gonna stand for it. You'll go to see a regular doctor, that what's-his-name who took care of your flu last year. This is the twentieth century, not the Middle Ages."

"Oh, stop your fussing, Shirleen This is not about me. It's about a...product that Vinnie and I want to manufacture and sell to women everywhere. It's something we all can use at one time or another. It's a weight loss aid and skin renewer rolled into one. We're gonna call it 'Forever Young.' Of course, we haven't quite worked out the 'Forever' part yet, but it'll come."

I take a deep breath, pour myself a cup of coffee, dump in a little more cream and sugar than usual, and sit down across from Ma.

She slides the book in front of me. "There. Read for yourself."

I peer at the little script. "A Cure for Fatte," I read. "To be prepared as needed and employde by womman fully grownne." I skim the list of ingredients: powdered this and slivered that, nothing really out of the ordinary. Wait a minute. "Lark's tongues and beetle's wings? They don't have those in the Grand Union."

"You import them from China. Or you substitute."

"You've tested this?"

"Of course. Remember when I wore that pantsuit you like and you noticed how thin I looked? I drank a potion with the same ingredients. Only thing, by nightfall I was back to my usual size. I told you we had a few kinks to work out."

"My God, Ma! You're a human guinea pig."

"Well, would you rather I used you to test our product?"

"Whoa. Hold on. What's this 'our?' Am I included in this crazy scheme?"

"As if I'd even ask you! Vinnie's my partner. She sold her Mercedes, traded it in for a Ford Escort. We're using the proceeds to set up our factory. Barclay's gonna help us find a place."

"My old classmate Barclay? Stuffed-shirt Barclay, voted Most Likely Not to Make Waves? That Barclay?"

"The very same. Vinnie showed him what our product could do, and he thinks there should be one for men."

"He'd use the stuff? He'd actually swallow it?"

"Shirleen. Did I say anything about swallowing? You bathe in this. Then you wrap yourself in warm leaves."

"Leaves?"

"Okay, you can use towels. Vinnie prefers to marinate in her terry robe from Saks."

"And what does this stuff do to your skin?"

"See for yourself." She shows me her arms—firm and white. "No more age spots. And I haven't bathed in the stuff since that day Teddy went to the hospital."

I have to take a couple of minutes to let it all sink in: a twelfth-century witch invents an on-again, off-again cure for obesity which, coincidentally, revitalizes aging skin, and my mother, a recent graduate of the School for Sorcerers (correspondence division), is going to be a millionaire. Well, well.

"That part's a keeper, the de-aging factor," Ma says proudly. "Now, if we can only figure out how to make the slimness last…"

"Oh, I'm sure you'll find a way." Secretly, I see a future filled with injury lawsuits. How will Ma look in stripes, I wonder? But nowadays incarcerated women probably wear Donna Karan and do needlepoint. Prison will be much too tame for Ma and Vinnie.

"Look, Shirleen. I hate to change the subject since you seem so interested in what we're doing, but I need to tell you…"

"Not now, Ma. I've got to get breakfast out of the way so I can stuff the turkey, do the vegetables, make the dip, mash the potatoes, you know."

"I hope you'll let me do something."

You can thaw the turkey. Just glare at it a minute. "Set the table. We'll be five for dinner."

"Five?"

"Yeah. You, Pop, Deke, Me and Junior. Antoinette isn't coming."

"No? What a shame. We'll be four, then."

"Five. You, Pop, Junior, Deke and me."

"Whatever."

"Ma." Don't tell me we're gonna have one of those days.

Deke pokes his stubbled face in the kitchen. "After breakfast I'm gonna run some errands. You need anything?"

"Ten 48-ounce boxes of baking soda," chimes Ma.

Did they have baking soda in the twelfth-century? Is this a substitution? If so, for what? "Just milk," I tell him.

"About Junior," Ma says while I'm stuffing the turkey.

"What about him?"

"Shirleen!" Deke yells from the garage. "My truck!"

My hands are full of stuffing and the turkey, propped against the toaster, is about to slide sideways into the sink. "Can you see what that's about, Ma?" I ask her.

"I know what it's about. Junior took Deke's truck."

Without asking? He knows better. And where would he be going? There's no football practice today, it's...Ma put him up to this! I can tell just by looking at her. Suddenly it dawns on me. "Oh, my God. He's gone to kidnap Antoinette!"

The turkey bounces into the sink, spraying stuffing all over the counter.

"That," Ma says, "Is what I've been trying to tell you all morning."

★ ★ ★

When Deke gets back from the grocery store, we go to get Pop. At the last minute, Ma decides to come with us. She sits hunched in the back seat, disgraced. Deke is furious at her for not waking us in the middle of the night when Junior was getting ready to leave. I'm furious at Deke because it was our truck I heard backing out. If only I'd trusted my instincts. En route to the Rip the atmosphere in the car is one of stony silence.

★ ★ ★

Here's what's on the machine when we get home:

> This message is for the McClure family, from Maxwell
> Bixby calling from our home in Short Hills, New Jersey.
> If our daughter is with you, we want to speak with her. I
> hope to settle this calmly, but if I have to, I'm driving up
> there today and bringing her back with me. Apparently, her
> mother didn't make our position clear enough to Antoi-
> nette. She's not to see your son—Junior? That his name?—
> under any circumstances. I've already talked to our lawyer
> about a restraining order. Just so you know we mean busi-
> ness. Now. I'll expect to hear from my daughter or from one
> of you as soon as possible. We'll be waiting for your call.
> Your son has our number.

We settle Pop on the couch with Ma, who acts as though he has
leprosy. We serve them dip and chips, martinis, *TV Guide*, and the
remote. Then we make our escape into Junior's room. As Maxwell
Bixby has suggested, I find their number scrawled on a yellow post-it
that says "Antoinette's folks." When Deke dials, I notice his hand is
shaking. I wrap my arms around him to say we're in this together,
babe.

"Bixby? This is McClure. For starters, your daughter isn't here…"

★ ★ ★

When I check on my folks, I find Pop napping chin on chest, Ma
pretending to read *Sports Illustrated*. Back in Junior's room, Deke is
still hunched over the receiver, taking a swig from his beer every now
and then. I stand in the doorway and let my eyes take in the contents
of that room. Every inch reflects some stage of Junior's evolution
from toddler to lovestruck runaway. There are: yearbook photos of
the football and track teams with Junior, a kneeling, smiling hunk,
always in the front row, center; an enlarged head-and-shoulders photo
of Antoinette covers one-third of another wall. His sporting awards

crowd the top shelf of his bookcase. On his desk, propped up between the Syracuse beer mug from a friend's older brother and a little bust of JFK he'd bought on a junior-high know-your-government tour, is his teddy bear, mangy and missing one eye. The corner usually occupied by his football gear bag is empty. Not much is missing from his closet or his bureau. I take this to be a hopeful sign, like maybe they're just planning on getting a motel room for the weekend.

"Well," Deke says finally as he hangs up the phone. "There's one mad son of a bitch. He's threatening to charge Junior with kidnapping, even though I told him Junior's just barely turned seventeen. Christ. I tried to tell him Antoinette's not a baby. She's sixteen going on thirty, wouldn't you say? Been around a bit. But that only made him madder."

"What're we gonna to do? He have any ideas?"

"I gave him the information about the truck. He's calling the state police in New Jersey, New York, Pennsylvania, and Connecticut. There's really not much else we can do. Except to pray the kids'll call, just to let us know they're okay." He comes over and hugs me and I start to cry. "I know, hon. It was supposed to be a nice day, with your father here and all. Well, hell. I say, let's make the best of it. Let's enjoy that wonderful meal you've been preparing. Let's pop open a couple beers."

When Deke delivers the prayer of thanks with his eyes shut, we stretch out our arms to touch hands. Pop's skin is smooth and cool, and he moves his lips when we get to "Amen."

"How ya doing?" Deke asks as he piles Pop's plate high with food.

"Pehie Dah Goo," Pop answers, forcing a smile.

"That's pretty damned good," Ma translates. Pop mumbles something else. "You'll have to speak up, Teddy." She's being her usual frozen self, the way she always is around Pop, but somehow today it isn't getting to me. I have other things to contend with. When we say our prayer about the bounty that the Lord hath given us, all I can think is "The Lord giveth and the Lord taketh away." Why hath he taken away my son? I want to know. And I pray silently that Junior and Antoinette will be protected from harm. I eat mechanically, hardly tasting anything but the metal of my fork. Deke puts up a good show, but I know his heart isn't in it. Ma eats only the things she really likes—the turkey and the stuffing—and Pop eats only the potatoes.

"The therapist says he's lost his will," Ma points out matter-of-factly. "She says he has to be reminded to put on his clothes. Teddy, wipe your mouth. No, not like that. Oh, here, I'll do it." With the harsh hands of an impatient mother she pokes a corner of his napkin at a splotch of gravy.

"More wine?" Deke asks. In deference to my upcoming trip he's chosen a French rosé. "Nice bow-kay," he jokes. He doesn't know squat about wine protocol. There's a man in my French class who's toured the vineyards of Burgundy. He knows all about the famous reds—which to choose, which to avoid. I love to hear him go on in his snobby way about this or that vintage year. Sometimes I wonder if it's just a pose. He refuses to go to Montréal with the class. He says the Canadians don't speak real French. Our teacher, who's from Québec City, hates him. "Earth to Shirleen. I asked if you wanted more wine. Your glass is half empty. Madame. Ah, that reminds me. Knock knock…"

"Who's there?" Ma says.

Deke grins. "Madame."

"Madame who?"

"Madame foot's caught in the door!"

"Haw!" hoots Pop.

We all jerk our heads up, surprised. We haven't heard him laugh in ages. This isn't like his old laugh, so warm and hiccoughy. This is staccato. But we all join in anyway. In fact, I laugh so hard I nearly wet my pants.

Dessert goes better. There's something so soothing about pumpkin pie, so appealing. Pop asks for seconds, and for a moment or two I forget my troubles.

Afterwards we watch the news, and the rerun clips from the Macy's Parade. "Remember when we took you there?" Ma asks. "You were nine. It was the year after we moved up from Florida."

Pop reaches over to pat my hands. "You lih paraye. Shirlee. Sush a goo girh."

"You were such a good girl, Shirleen, and you liked parades," Ma enunciates. "Look, Teddy. Watch my lips: such a good girl."

Pop gives her a dark look. "Piss awf," he says.

At 8:30 Deke loads Pop in the car and heads back to the Rip. I decide to stay in case there's a call from Junior, though how I'd get it I don't know. Ma's been on the phone with Vinnie, catching her up on our day's events, discussing manufacturing techniques.

I finish cleaning up the kitchen, put the turkey carcass in a large pot with vegetables and stock, and settle down in the living room to read *Les Misérables*, which I'm supposed to report on next week in class.

"I'm having dinner with Vinnie tomorrow," Ma says. "We're going to meet with the real estate agent in the afternoon. Barclay thinks we can get a good deal on some property his bank foreclosed on. So. What're you reading? 'Less Miserable,' we used to call it. What a bore. Anything good on television?"

I turn on the classic movie channel, Ma's favorite. Clifton Webb has just dumped porridge on a baby's head. It's gotta be the tenth time I've seen this scene, but who cares, as long as it'll keep her happy.

"Did Junior call?"

"How could he get through? You've been on the phone for an hour."

"Well, excuse me."

"You know I've been waiting for his call. How could you be so thoughtless?" I look at her. My own mother. In her face I see a reason for everything that's ever gone wrong in my life. I want to strangle her. "All you can think about is yourself. You didn't even say goodbye to Pop. You selfish bitch!"

"Oh, nice. My daughter calls me names on Thanksgiving! I stick out my neck to help my grandson, and his mother calls me a bitch. Well, maybe I'll just take Vinnie up on her offer, and live with her. There, at least, I'll be appreciated."

"Wait a minute." I get up, stomp around the couch and grab Ma's shoulders. "Wait just a damn minute! You stuck out your neck to help Junior? In what way? Come on, I want to know. I deserve to know." Suddenly I realize I'm shaking her as hard as I can.

She's stronger than I am. Stronger than anyone in her mid-sixties should be. She pulls my grip loose like she's picking lint off a sweater. "I gave him some money."

"How much?"

"Not much. A couple hundred. It was all the cash I had."

"You knew he was planning to run away."

"Yes," she says proudly. "Yes. I encouraged him."

Before I can even think about what I'm doing my arm shoots forward and I slap Ma across the face. She stands unmoved, as shocked by the force of my blow as by her own resistance to it. Then she smiles triumphantly. "You see? I knew I'd get a rise outta you. I'm fucking glad!"

"You did this to hurt Rosalie!" I scream. "This isn't even about me!"

"So? I have a right to get even. Get outta my way, Shirleen."

She's into her room before I can count to five, slamming the door not once but twice. Good. Let her move out. I don't care if I never see her again. I'm so happy I can hardly breathe.

Part 2

Five Months Later

A New Beginning

Irene

Whoopee! Now that I'm famously out of the closet I've even changed my name to Witchards. A year ago, if anyone predicted I'd take up witchcraft I'd've said "pshaw," which is a corruption of the Middle English "pssawf." Now that's a good example of the fine art of bullshitting I've perfected these past three months, blabbing endlessly and authoritatively about anything to Oprah and Sally Jessy Raphael. I guess I've always wanted to be center stage. Forever Young has made that possible. Forget Mary Kay and her pink cars; my salespeople don't need incentives. We're in the revival business. Just looking at our born-again customers is reward enough. These women have been baptized in the Fountain of Youth!

The basic formula consists of milk and honey, olive oil, and hyper-sudsing bath soap with other fragrant oils stirred into it. Irene Witchards' secret ingredient is then compounded, allowing the product to permeate the epidermis, removing cellulite, and restoring elasticity. The woman who emerges from her bath will be younger looking or she'll get her money back. An eight-ounce simulated crystal imitation gold-filigreed container of Forever Young costs fifty bucks, a small price to pay for a dip in the Fountain of Youth. This infomercial will be aired on all the major networks this spring, to spark sales in time for bathing suit season.

My ad agency—Flimsee, Blatt, and Bombaste, who designed the packaging and promotion—also hired a handler. Soignée Charmante is an overly fussy young twit who selects my wardrobe and schedules my appointments. Last week I found myself feeling mawkish, and no wonder—I was overbooked: Monday, LA; Tuesday, Denver; Wednesday, Chicago; Thursday, Pittsburgh; Friday, Dubuque. Where the fuck is Dubuque, and who can spell it?

I'm doing Sally next month. Oprah wants me for June. I suppose they'll want samples, though I frown on freebies. The one exception I'd make is Queen Elizabeth, poor lady, a really deserving woman whose dowdy demeanor demands relief. A big sack of Forever Young for Her Majesty!

Of course, when I'm not on the road, it's business as usual.

Last week I ran into Teddy in the supermarket. Literally. I was rounding the corner where they pile the toilet paper, heading towards Baked Goods, when the corner of my basket caught him in the hip. Ouch! That's the left hip, the one he hurt falling out of bed. (Sorry, Teddy.) At first, I didn't recognize him with a jelly-belly and a beard, his cart filled with frozen entrées and cream pies. He needs a trainer—maybe I'll lend him mine. And lose the whiskers, Teddo! Facial hair reminds me of pubises. Anyway, when he recovered (it was an accident, I swear!) we lingered between the Depends and the Polident, blocking the aisle.

"You're looking fine, Irene. Notoriety agrees with you."

"You're looking fine, too," I lied. "Still at the Rip?"

"I've been promoted. Assistant Living Division, apartment 3-C. Moved last month. Come visit. It'd be a treat. My wife the witch." He rubs his hip as a reminder of what dark powers can accomplish. "Of course, you probably don't want to waste your time on me when you could be whooping it up with a matinee idol."

"Don't be silly. I'd love to see your place." Yeah, right.

"Shirleen tells me you and Lavinia have a regular palace."

"It's comfortable enough. Actually, we're thinking of adding an extra wing to accommodate our home spa. You've no idea how complicated my life has gotten, Teddy. Listen to this: Vinnie wants to hire a chauffeur! She traded her Escort back in for the Mercedes and says it doesn't look right for her to be doing the driving. But hey. I'm probably boring you with all my little troubles."

"I only wish I could still drive," Teddy said wistfully. "Remember our old Buick?"

"Yeah. What a gas guzzler."

"But oh, that baby could purr! On camping trips we'd load 'er down with everything, and she'd still ride high. Not like these low-slung foreign jobs." He shifted his weight and scratched his crotch, thinking, no doubt, of the diminutive bikinied Québecoises we'd seen in Orchard Beach, Maine, the last summer we camped with Shirleen. "Those were the days," he sighed. "Now Shirleen has to drive me everywhere. She's my chauffeur."

I didn't want to admit how long it's been since I've talked to Shirleen. What's the point of talking? She and I have so little to say to each other. Vinnie sees them at church and gives me a weekly report. She says Shirleen and Deke have joined the Couples' Club. How cozy! Vinnie tried to get me to join the choir—I have a splendid contralto, just a bit uncertain on the higher notes—but now my life is so crowded with events, I'm relieved if I can even find time to pee. Face it, I said to myself in the mirror the other morning. My life is an event. I'm an event. My pinkie is an event. I thought about my pinkie and how it extended so gracefully during tea time on Sally Jessy. I love to fast-forward my souvenir tape so I can savor my crooking digit peeking over the rim of the cup, announcing my arrival in Upper-Crustland.

Assessing Teddy, I saw a tired old man in rumpled clothing, pants too short, jacket frayed at the cuffs. Eight years separate us in age; more like thirty. Just then a pretty girl squeezed past, her tits brushing his chest. He straightened up, clicked his heels together, sucked in his gut as those hormones kicked him in it. Moldred has a recipe for molasses ginger cakes that'll gum up his insides like cement.

Then, to get things moving again, there's always Licorice Sweetmeats, just the trick to keep him glued to the throne for a day or two. If only it were as easy to dent his libido! "I don't suppose I'll ever get to see your place," Teddy said.

I watched his eyes follow the girl's twitching behind. Randy old bastard! "Maybe Shirleen will bring you over," I said. "But not this month. This month is crazy. Maybe May. Yeah, end of May. We can have a picnic on Memorial Day."

"That'd be nice, Irene. Well, gotta go. There's a Bingo game at two, and I'm calling the numbers today."

I smiled sweetly and blew him a kiss. Give my best to buffalo-butt, the night nurse. "You take care, dearest," I called as I headed towards Day Old. I reminded myself I could afford Freshly Baked, but some habits are hard to break.

* * *

Vinnie is itching to get her mitts on *The Cooke's Byblle*, but I keep telling her she can't just pop in and out of sorcery. If she wants to dive into the seething cauldron, I'll be her coach. I'll send her off the springboard. I'll watch her jack-knife into the pool. Then I'll see how quickly she surfaces! The company I used isn't sending out kits anymore, but I'm sure there are other correspondence courses. In fact, just the other day on Oprah we got a telephone call from a witch over in Rhode Island who'd like to start a mail-order business. I told her to go online, find a Chat Room. Networking (in our field we call it newtworking) is big in Cyberspace.

I'm doing my best to keep Vinnie in the background, where she's needed. As Vice President in charge of Manufacturing, she has the responsibility of seeing that our orders are filled. Right now, we're trying to upscale—Estée Lauder and Ralph Lauren instead of Walmart and Sears. In the works is a rejuvenating spray for men, something they can spritz on their privates, something that'll take the sag out of those testicles. God knows, men are as vain as women. Of course, it'll take more than spritz to put the bounce back in Teddy's balls.

* * *

"Irene. Wake up. You're supposed to be at the airport in two hours." Vinnie shakes me, plucks off my eye shades and flips back the covers.

"Where the fuck is Soignée? She was supposed to pack my bag, see that my notes were ready for *60 Minutes*. Why didn't someone set my alarm?" I roll out of bed, stiff as a board—too many abdominal crunches. My new trainer is merciless, a real Schwarzenegger. Polyester-panted Vinnie is running around like crazy, flapping the sleeves of her heavily-embroidered smock. She reminds me of the chickens. If only my mother the poultry farmer could see me counting my eggs now!

"Isn't today Soignée's day off?"

"What day is today?"

"Monday. Remember? You're supposed to be at CBS by noon. Andy Rooney and Molly Ivins are taking you out to lunch."

"Shit. I wanted P. J. O'Rourke to wine and dine me."

"Well, Irene, it's time you learned you can't have everything you want."

"Ha! And why not? When you're top of the heap…Wait a minute. Where are my Birkenstocks? You know I don't go anywhere without my lucky shoes."

"Soignée threw them out."

"They were my favorite shoes! Who gave her permission?"

Vinnie starts to tremble, and I know what's coming: the truth. She threw them out. "I…didn't think you'd really miss them, since they were so cruddy. You'd stapled the straps, remember? And they smelled awful. Pew. Like you'd stepped in something. Dog poop. No, rotten eggs."

Sulphur. I was fooling around with spells one day, and the pot boiled over. Shit. I'm gonna miss those hippie clodhoppers.

★ ★ ★

Two hours later I'm at the Albany airport waiting for the shuttle to Manhattan. I'm wearing my haggish getup: black jumpsuit, purple jacket, orange cape. Flamboyance is my trademark, but I hide from my public in oversized Foster Grants with little pointed hats on the temples. The lenses are so dark it's impossible to see whether I'm winking or blinking, so I'll just nod. I used that line on Leno and they loved it. "Sign your little autograph book? Why sure, honey. There. Why don't I travel by broomstick? Because it's faster by plane, sugar. Does your mommy use Forever Young, sweetums? She needs to. Give her a big bottle for Christmas. If you start saving now...sorry, dear, that's my flight they're announcing. Watch me on the tube!"

★ ★ ★

"Look, Ms. Whatever your name is, I'm supposed to be lunching with Lesley and Anderson. Oh. On location where? Iran? And they couldn't get back for lunch? I see. Well. How about Scott? I see. In conference. Well. Bob, then. Not available? NOT AVAILABLE? I'll show you who's not available. Wait 'til Willie Morris hears about this. Well, of course I know he's dead. I mean his agency, butthead. I'm outta here. No, you do not have to call me a cab—I have my broom. That's a joke, sweetie.

★ ★ ★

"Tell him that Irene Witchards is here. The developer of Forever Young. No, it's not a movie, it's a revolutionary new beauty soak. Not soap, soak. You put these lavender-scented swift-dissolving granules in your bath and in ten minutes, voilà! you emerge years younger and your skin never shrivels. References? Try Oprah, Sally Jessy, *Entertainment Tonight*, *Hard Copy*, the *National Enquirer*, *Star*. I was scheduled for *60 Minutes* next Sunday but there's been a wrinkle, something you can avoid if you bathe in Forever Young." What do I have to do to see the buyer at Saks? At Lord and Taylor?

I've walked miles and my feet are killing me. If I only had my broken-in Birkenstocks instead of these fucking Manolo Blahniks! My sample case weighs a ton. Unseasonably warm? Compared to this, Hell is a vacation. I stashed my cape in the trash. This lycra bodysuit is sticking to crevices I didn't know I had. Now I have smelly wet splotches under my arms and at my crotch. This trip, the only impression I'm going to make is the imprint of my sweaty ass on Naugahyde.

"Finally! You must be...Oh. Well, I guess a secretary could... You're not a secretary? You're Security? I beg your pardon, you don't seem to know I'm Irene Witchards. All right, all right. You've made your point. I'm outta here. Somebody's gonna regret it. But would you just do me this teeny-weeny favor? Would you give Luigi this brochure? Ciao, bambina."

★ ★ ★

Vinnie meets me at the airport. "God, you look awful," she says.

"Right back at you, babe."

"I mean, you look as though you've...had a stressful day. Wasn't Bob as charming as we thought he'd be? Didn't you have crab souffle at Lutèce?"

"Put a lid on it, Vin. It was a disaster. I'll tell you about it later. How did things go at the factory?"

She winces. Damn! In Vinnie, wincing is always a bad sign.

"N-nothing really bad happened. N-nothing that can't be fixed, I mean."

As we get into her car, I notice the big yellow letters on the side: CRONE ZONE. "What's this shit?"

"J-just some silly prank."

"Mm." Oprah warned me I might be the target for some mild attacks by vandals. 'No 'count mischief-makers,' she called them. "I'm sorry, Vin. Maybe it'll come off. Or we can have it repainted."

"They'll only do it again," she sniffles.

"Hey, watch it! You're doing sixty in a forty zone!"

"You didn't s-see the other side. It says LESBO LAIR," she sobs.

"Oh, for purgatory's sake! Here. Pull over. You'd better calm down."

"See? If we had a chauffeur, I could sit in the back seat and cry all I want." I give her my little packet of Kleenex. She peels it open, lifts out a tissue and dabs at her eyes. "You want to know what went wrong at the factory, or c-can it wait 'til later?"

"Later. Look at me! I need a soak! I need a martini! Step on it, Vin, but be sure the fuzzbuster's working."

★ ★ ★

Fuck the bird lovers of Asia! My shipment of larks' tongues has been delayed by Audubon Society protesters. "This isn't good," I mumble, downing the dregs of my second martini. "Not good at all. We're behind schedule as is."

"Do you think you could substitute frogs' tongues? Those Budweiser frogs have humongous tongues. You'd get a lot of compound from a frog like that."

"Vinnie. Those are cartoon frogs. Attributes are always exaggerated in cartoons. Think of Ross Perot's ears or Nixon's nose. Besides, there might be a couple of flies rolled up in those tongues. You never know where a fly has been."

"All right, I get your point. But what about synthetic larks' tongues?"

"No such thing."

"Don't be silly. There's a synthetic everything. I'll do a search on the Net."

Maybe she has something. "Go to it, girl." I'll say this for Vinnie: she's gotten to be a computer wiz in no time at all. I'll scour the pages of my *Byblle* to see if Moldred has a solution. Meanwhile, I'll pour us another drink.

"These olives are terrific. Where'd you get them, Irene?"

"I found them in the freezer."

"Oh," Vinnie says. She fishes one out and examines it. "Oh!"

When it comes to sorcery, some things are best left sleeping in the dark. "Put a lid on those olives," I say.

* * *

"Lark's tongue, substitute for," I read in my appendix. "Occasionally it's possible to approximate these hard-to-come-by items, but don't count on the results being the same as with the real thing." Now that's a red flag if ever I've seen one, but I read on, undaunted: "The best results are obtained by using an amalgam of beetle wings and bee thoraxes ground to a fine consistency and mixed with the saliva from a frog which has just laid its eggs in pond scum." Yech. Years ago, Junior would have waded into the water to scoop up anything I wanted. That's it! I'll call the junior-high-school biology teacher. What a project that'll make for his classes. I'll tell him I'll make a donation to the science lab if he'll help me out. Whoa, Bessie! I'm cookin' tonight.

* * *

"What did you say you needed these things for?" Mr. Glopfer teaches eighth-grade science at the Riverton Middle School. From the rows of desks in his classroom a horde of pimply brats are staring at me, their eyes riveted on my face. I've stuck a few extra warts on my chin, added some whiskers, and elongated my nose, just for effect. Ya gotta play the part.

I explain to him that the specimens will be key ingredients in a cosmetics formula. "I can't really tell you any more than that, because the actual formula is a secret. My secret. Forever Young is a concept I developed myself, with Lavinia Donderhook's support. Her son Barclay is my business manager. You know Barclay? Of course, you do. Everybody knows Barclay."

"He and I went to school together."

"Then you must know my daughter, Shirleen."

"Married to Deke McClure the football player, helluva athlete? Sure do."

"Well, then. We're practically old friends. Do you think your students will help me gather specimens, Mr. Glopfer?"

"Call me Arnold. You know, I think you really oughtta try Ellen Chinney, who teaches zoology at Washington Irving Community College. I just don't feel real easy about turning my bunch of eighth graders loose in a swamp."

"Pond, Mr. Glopfer. Oh, I agree with you. Swamps are much too sinister for eighth graders. But ponds. Ponds are so…innocent. Ponds are perfect for these youngsters." The recess bell rings. Suddenly I'm surrounded by pubescent monsters—Frankenstein, whose genitals threaten to leap out of his jeans, and Morticia, a buxom teaser who'd better be on the pill.

"Mrs. Witchards, I…"

"Call me Irene."

"Irene." Glopfer stares down at his shoes, sturdy shit-kickers he probably uses on field trips. I can tell he's feeling uneasy with me. It could be my getup, or the fact that I'm in cosmetics. "I think adult learners would be a better group for you to be working with. Call Ellen. Daytimes she's in her store, The Knitting Needle. Evenings she teaches at the college. Tell her you and I have talked. She and I are old friends."

Do I detect a blush? Has the science teach scored with the zoology prof? This guy's a real nerd. I can't wait to meet her. "You've been such a help, Arnold." A big help. Now I have to spend all day trying to recruit this Chinney broad.

Fuck those Audubon twits, anyway.

* * *

The Knitting Needle is a store I've never patronized, a place where earnest-looking housewives exchange gossip behind the yarn bins. One such patron looks up from her afghan, a nauseous display of conflicting colors that would give even a vampire nightmares. "Ellen Chinney?" I say to a mousy maiden with Coke-bottle glasses who's hiding behind the register.

"Yes?"

"Arnold Glopfer sent me."

"Oh." Beet-red splotches dot her cheeks as she reacts to her dear nerd's name. "Mrs. Witchards. Arnie...Mr. Glopfer called me. He said you seem to think my students could help you with a...project. Just exactly what do you have in mind?"

I tell her as much as I told Arnold, but she doesn't seem intrigued, so I decide to sweeten the pot. I offer her a sample of Forever Young. "Of course, dear, it may take a couple of soaks before you notice a real difference. And be sure to read the cautionary statement on the label. My, this print is fine, isn't it? Here."

She reads: "Manufacturer is not responsible for the furrows and glitches that may infrequently follow prolonged soaks, nor do we promise any long-lasting results. Furrows and glitches?" queries Ms. Chinney, obviously a woman of scientific exactitude. "Just what, precisely, does that mean?"

"Your guess is as good as mine. But I think it has something to do with the spaces where wrinkles used to be. Let me just say that one of our volunteer testers experienced a little gapping on her forehead."

"Gapping on her forehead? But you don't soak your forehead. You soak your...body." She blushes again.

"Yes! That's why we say infrequently."

"Oh." She gets up to help a doddering grandma with her knitting and holds up a tiny garment that looks like a doll's sweater, but with four armholes instead of two. "Isn't this just too precious? It's for Woofie." Right on cue a chihuahua peeks out of the woman's knitting bag, fixes me with its marble-eyed stare, and starts to yap. "He doesn't usually bark at strangers, does he, Sarah?" Ellen yells at the woman who's obviously deaf. I wait patiently for her to finish casting on. "Look," she says finally. "I'll have to think about this. Exams are coming up, and I…just don't know if we can manage a field trip right now."

"Well, you take all the time you need. Take years," I say, to send her a message: Have you looked in the mirror lately, Toots? You haven't a minute to spare. Why, right now, as we speak, you could be soaking. Your prince could be riding up in his white Audi. "Here. Take my card. If I'm not in the office, Ms. Charmante will take the message. Or you can FAX me."

"Oh, what the heck! I'll do it. I'll tell the students I'll give them extra credit. You can count on us, Mrs. Witchards."

Now that's what I like to hear! "Call me Irene." On my way out, I stop to pet Woofie, who shrinks at my touch, snarls, and yaps louder than ever.

"He never does this," his owner says. "I just can't understand it."

I send Woofie a message: what a nice little addition to my soup cauldron you'll be. He stops barking.

★ ★ ★

"Irene!" Soignée wails. "You've got to stand still! How'm I supposed to get this hem pinned up if you keep jumping around like that?"

She's fixing my new robe, the one I ordered from *Powers 'n' Potions*, the sorcerer's catalogue. I was going to wear it on *60 Minutes*. Oh, well. Now I'll have something to wear for the Barbara Walters interview.

"Ouch! Look what you've done, Irene. I've pricked my finger and it's bleeding all over your robe."

Clumsy bitch. "I'm sorry, dear. Get a Band-aid from the bathroom cabinet, but watch out—the tub is full of frogs and they tend to hop out."

★ ★ ★

"Nobody told me I'd be doing this." Soignée is crouching in the lab, massaging a croaker's epiglottis. "I hate frogs. They give you warts."

"Toads, dear. Toads give you warts. Or so they say."

"I should get paid extra for this."

You wish. "You think I like doing this? I've been working on this one for ten minutes, and he refuses to spit! Remind me to kill myself before I give another penny to the Audubon Society. Finally! Okay, buster, into the bucket you go. Ellen's doing a pickup later this afternoon, and before nightfall you'll be back with your brothers and sisters."

"At least the Frog People can't accuse us of cruelty."

"It's bad enough we have Ralph Nader on our backs. And all because one sniveling wimp had to complain about gapping."

"Is Ellen bringing in the bees tomorrow?"

"I'm counting on it."

"The beetles, too?"

"Yup."

"You promise me they won't feel anything."

"Hey. Have I ever lied to you, Soignée?"

"No, but…"

"No buts. There! I never thought I'd be glad to see frog spittle."

"I never liked impaling moths in biology."

"Who said anything about impaling? We're using chloroform."

"We?"

"I mean Ellen and her students. You and I are going shopping, remember? I need a new pair of Birkenstocks."

"I give up. This one won't spit. Here, you try. I'm going to get a cup of coffee."

★ ★ ★

All in a dither, Vinnie comes running in to my office. "Ralph Nader is threatening a class action suit if you don't retract some of the promises! I just heard it on the Albany news. Irene! What're we going to do?"

"We're going to grind bee thoraxes, that's what we're going to do. Did you look up royal jelly like I told you?"

"Yeah. Honeybees feed it to their queens in the larval stage. So?"

"If it's good enough for a queen bee...yada yada yada. I want to be able to capitalize on that connection."

"What connection? We don't use royal jelly in our formula."

"But we use bee thoraxes. And any bee can become a queen if it's fed royal jelly."

"Oh, I give up. Stop changing the subject, Irene. We've got Nader breathing down our necks, and you're blabbing about bees."

"Fuck Nader. Get me Mattel on the phone. I haven't received the prototype of the witch doll yet, and it was supposed to be here by Friday. And tell Soignée to type that letter to Simon & Schuster. The latest draft of my autobiography is gonna be late. What's new with the protesters in Shanghai? Are they still guarding the nests? Any minute I expect to hear they've given up, and my tongues will be on their way."

"But Ralph Nader!"

I get on the intercom. "Soignée. Will you call Barclay? Tell him his mother is freaking again. Have him take her somewhere. Anywhere. We've got thoraxes to grind, and wings to clip, and miles to go before we slip."

"Very funny, Irene. Soignée went to lunch a half hour ago. And speaking of that dear girl, you should know that she's on the verge of quitting. That frog episode just about sent her over the edge."

★ ★ ★

"Yes, Barclay. I understand. The next batch will have a warning in big red letters: Persons allergic to bee stings may not use this product under any circumstances period. There. That oughtta do it. Yes. I know the woman almost died. But she didn't die, Barclay. She's still kicking. And we can thank Lucifer for that. Well, you can thank whomever. If that's all, I've got to get back to ABC. That Nader shit, and now this bee stuff, is making me hotter than ever. They want to move up the date of my appearance. Well, sure, I'm a little nervous, but Barbara's a sweetheart and I understand, from Oprah, that she puts you right at ease. By the way, thanks for calming Vinnie down the other day. Nader sent her into a spin, all right. She was convinced we were going to jail. But we're not. Are we? Ha ha, Barclay, only kidding. Stay cool.

★ ★ ★

"Shirleen? Well, yes, it has been a while. How are you? And Deke? Hear anything from Junior? Oh, give him time. Yes, I know how you worry. I worry, too. Well, I know you didn't call to chitchat. What's up? Did you use the samples I sent you? It didn't work? Nonsense. I've used it myself. You have to follow the directions. Try it again, and call me back. What? You tried it a second time and it still didn't work? Well, I can only say it must have something to do with your water. Ah, that's it. If the water's too hard—or too soft, for that matter...Who? Mabel Gallagher? My God, the woman's got skin like a shar-pei. No wonder it didn't work. What? I'm not cheating anybody. I resent that. How can you even think I'd...Wait a minute. Does this have anything to do with the fact that I kept Junior's plans a secret from you? Are you trying to get back at me for that? Because if you are, Shirleen... Well. You can't blame me for thinking that. All I can say is, Forever Young works for most people. Honey, I wish we could go on forever, but I just got beeped."

★ ★ ★

There are times when I yearn—yearn—for the simpler times when Teddy and I were in our little house yelling at each other. I can't help it if I get nostalgic for those bad old days; I'm really a softy at heart. Beneath this flinty businesslike exterior lies the soul of a homebody— the woman I once was, a loving wife and mother.

I miss that woman, but I don't know how to get her back.

I want to be soft and hard. That way, I won't get hurt.

And what about Shirleen calling to discuss Forever Young? I know that was an excuse. She wanted to hear my voice as much as

I wanted to hear hers, yet she called to complain and I cut her off. Why? I felt no rancor. My palms didn't perspire. I didn't want to wring her neck. Let's not be strangers, I could have said. Let's be friends.

Escape

Shirleen

I write in my diary: "April 21, tomorrow, is the day of my dreams, *le jour où je prends le bus pour Montréal. Je n'ai pas besoin du réveil.* No alarm clock needed..."

I've Ziplocked five nights' worth of labelled packages in the freezer, dinners for Deke: Macaroni and Cheese, Beef Stew, American Chop Suey, Chewy Gooey Pasta, Barbeque Pork, and Chowdown Chile—his favorite meals, oven-ready. If only Ma hadn't ruined our microwave by melting Moldred knows what! I've promised him I'll call every afternoon around 6:00 when he usually gets home from work and talk him through the heating-up stage. Of course, he'll have to remember to take his dinner out of the freezer in the morning...He's such a baby, depending on me for everything. I offered to show him how to use the washer, but then I forgot. Too late now! Oh, well. If he runs out of underwear, he can always go to Penney's and buy some more.

The next morning I'm up by 5:30—no alarm clock needed, I'm too excited—taking a shower and dressing in my easy-care pantsuit and sensible walking shoes. I've checked my purse for essentials: wallet, passport, itinerary, lipstick, blush, mirror, comb. The discount coupons I'll leave here. Five days without setting foot in a grocery store! I can hardly believe it. Last thing I do is pin on the badge that says, "Shirleen McClure, Membre, Cercle Français de Riverton."

Summer camp was the last time I travelled any distance from home. How I loved sleeping in that wreck of a cabin! My bunk was way at the back, next to a window. At night I could hear all this rustle and bustle—nocturnal critters, counselors sneaking back from dates with the boys' camp staff across the lake. The summer I turned twelve, I too had a boyfriend, Ronald Webster, a pimply gap-toothed four-teen-year-old from Ohio. I let him touch my breasts. He let me touch his penis, which soon grew stiff. I did a lot of petting that summer and afterwards, but I was a still a virgin when I started going with Deke. Ma made a convincing case for chastity: once you start, you won't be able to stop. Prick teaser, the boys called me. I didn't care. I didn't want to turn into a sex machine.

I've been faithful to Deke all these years, and he says he's been faithful to me. I believe him. Anyway, for my part, I haven't really been tempted. Well, okay, there was this French Canadian who painted my kitchen last year and sang love songs on his break. Jeez. Nobody's perfect. But nothing happened, and that's what counts, isn't it?

When you've been married for a long time, boredom sets in. You have to work to keep up the interest. You have to add spice. I suppose that's one of the reasons I joined the French club. I thought it would make me a more interesting person, and therefore more desirable. This doesn't necessarily jibe with Deke's idea of spice, which is a triple-X movie on cable.

I decided a little separation couldn't hurt. I decided nobody would stop me from going on this trip. Not my son the fugitive who's holed up with his newfound sweetie, hiding from a tri-state search instituted by her father. Not my husband the helpless homemaker who worries he'll run out of clean underwear before I return. Not my mother the manipulator who juggles bogus bubble bath and celeb-rity status with equal aplomb. I did worry about my trip when Ma was accused of causing that woman's skin damage, but the grand jury refused to indict on the basis that Forever Young is labelled with precautions. As Ma testified, the woman clearly oversoaked and now she looks like a turnip; whose fault is that? Now Ma needs to figure out how to prevent a recurrence. She says she's faxed Moldred on the InterNewt. As if. Lord knows, I need a vacation!

★ ★ ★

At the bus station he hugs me so tight my ribs ache. "Hey, hon, you be good, you hear? If any of them kaybeckwahs come sniffing around, tell them you're taken."

"Deke. Come on."

He turns away from me. "Sorry."

"Honey. You crying? Aw. It's only gonna be five days. And look," I indicate the others in my group, all involved in goodbyes of their own. "We'll all take care of each other." I realize I must seem more like a pilgrim in search of pleasure than a student of French. There was a woman in the next town who went to visit her sister in Buffalo and never returned. Just up and left her family, bam, to start a new life. In the back of Deke's mind, he's still taking a razzing from his buddies: class trip, hell, she's only going up there to get laid by some Canuck.

"I don't see what's so exciting about going to Montréal with a bunch of old biddies," he says, wiping his eyes with the sleeve of his jacket, leaving little dark splotches, tear stains he hopes nobody but me will notice. It's not like Deke to blubber. He makes me want to cry, but the truth is, I'm too happy; I can't even shed a drop. When I stand on tiptoes to kiss him one last time, his skin smells fresh and wonderful, good enough to lick and nibble. He must have forgotten to splash on his smelly cologne. I like him better au naturel, I discover, glad to find there are still things to discover about him, and me. "*Je t'aime*," I whisper. Spice.

I wait for him to respond in kind, to sweep me off my feet in a wild embrace, but no, he only backs away slightly, leaving a small space between us. "Say what?"

We board the bus. I watch my big bear lope away, shoulders sagging, and feel a tinge of regret that's gone in an instant.

★ ★ ★

"Well, hi. Shirleen, isn't it?" I squeeze past a small, plump woman with short-cropped, carefully curled greying hair, Ellen Chinney, I remember, and claim my window seat.

"You remember me?"

"Oh, yes! You're Irene's daughter."

Here's trouble, I think.

"Did your mother ever tell you I helped her out of a jam? She needed pond specimens, and I had my students collect them. Oops, I guess I'm not supposed to divulge any secrets of the Forever Young formula, am I? Well, I didn't tell you what kind of specimens."

I'm not going to admit I know nothing about this little scheme. "Oh, yes. She did mention it," I fib. "She was very grateful."

"Well, she made it worth my while. Oh, look! You've got a tote just like mine! It came with my fifty-dollar purchase of bubble bath."

My God. Ma made her pay? After mucking around in pond scum I'd have demanded a lifetime supply. My mother the cheapskate. I check Ellen's skin for any resemblance to turnip. I'd like to trust Ma, believe in her product. If only I hadn't soaked, I could have gone on believing in miracles. Ma says I didn't follow the instructions. She says I might have gotten a defective batch. Quality control, I tell her. You've got to pay more attention to quality control. Before I know it, we're fighting again. Over bubble bath! Then you take Ellen, here. She looks pretty good, actually better than I remember her. Except for the whiskers, but Forever Young can't do anything about testosterone.

"We could have been twins with our matching totes! Instead, I brought this old thing," Ellen chirps, holding up a battered string bag. "I bought it in Paris, years ago, and I always use it when I travel. It's my good luck charm. You must have lots of those around, with a famous sorceress for a mother."

Is Ellen going to yakity yak her way to Montréal? Deke was an eager lover last night, storing up gratification for these lean nights ahead. Consequently, I'm sleepy. And I'm beginning to get carsick. Buses do that to me. The smell of my tuna sandwich doesn't help, either. Just when I'd like to indulge in memories of last night while the tingle's still there.

Ellen shoves a thermos under my nose. "Coffee? I brought an extra cup, just in case. It's half milk, *à la française. Café au lait. Alors. Prenez-le, m'amie.*" Without waiting for a nod from me she pours and I watch the coffee spill over its paper dam and onto my pants. "Oh, damn! Look what I've done! I'm really sorry, Shirleen. Those look like new slacks, too."

I spit on my finger and rub. The stain darkens. Damn. I drink the coffee. It's awful. I'll probably have to use the toilet. Yech. I hate toilets on buses, and I hate people who think that just because you're stuck sitting next to them they have to tell you their whole life story. Maybe if I close my eyes, she'll get the hint. At this moment, I wish I'd stayed home in bed with my lover boy.

* * *

When I wake up it's tuna-sandwich-time at a rest stop in the middle of nowhere. Le Cercle Français de Riverton has paused to picnic. When I emerge from my stale bus-cocoon into the brisk North Country air, Al Smathers, Deke's bowling buddy, offers a greeting. "Hey. It's sleeping beauty," he hoots. "You musta needed your sleep. That Deke's a tiger after dark, eh, Shirleen?" Al, who bowls with Deke even though he's a senior citizen and should be in the Old Farts League, is married to Lisette, the Québecoise, who organized our tour. I like her, can't stand him.

"Shut up, Al-baire," Lisette says, poking him in the ribs with her omnipresent clipboard.

I send her a silent message of thanks.

"How could you sleep through that racket?" Ellen asks. We're balancing on bench-ends, facing each other. "Lisette dragged us through all the verses of Alouette." Lisette has a high, thin soprano that reminds me of some of Ma's quavery 78s she brought with her from the farm when she married Pop. The old records were part of her meager dowry. "And don't you just hate Al? He pinched my bottom when we boarded the bus." She laughs. "If it'd been anybody else, I might have enjoyed it." Well, I think, hallelujah. Maybe she's got a sense of humor, after all.

Tuna fish and mayo is just fine, washed down with enough Diet Coke to drown the flavor. I feel virtuous and cleansed while eating my apple, watching the others peel the wrappers from their Ring Dings.

★ ★ ★

A fresh-faced young customs inspector boards the bus to ask one question: "Everybody born in the States?" Lisette's the only one who doesn't raise her hand. "Een 'bout wan ower we're gonna be dere," she says. "Moanrayall. Byooteeful citay."

"I can't wait," Ellen sighs. "I love to travel, don't you?"

"Sure." Well, maybe, if I had the opportunity. There are a million places I'd like to see.

"Tell me. Oh, you don't have to if you don't want to. But I'm dying to know. Was your mother always, well, different? I mean, did you always know she was a witch?"

"She wasn't always a witch."

"But..."

"She likes people to think she always had powers, but truth is, she's only had them since last year, when she took a correspondence course."

"I never heard of such a thing!"

"Saw an ad in Ladies' Own Journal, sent away for a packet, and *pouf.*"

Ellen's eyes blur wide behind her coke-bottle lenses. "My goodness."

It seems I've given her some food for thought, because she shuts up and pretends to study her phrase book, flipping through the same pages again and again. I concentrate on the landscape. The towns we pass have musical names—La Prairie and Longueuil, and the flat farmland stretches before us, promising nothing but more of itself, a beautiful sight if you believe in eternity. Then, in the distance, the blurred outline of the city appears. "Look!" I shout. "Montréal!"

Ellen leans into the aisle, then turns and grabs my hand. Her skin is surprisingly smooth and firm. Could it be Forever Young? "We're rooming together, you know," she says. "Won't that be fun? I hope you don't snore." I want to tell her there's a trick you can do to stop yourself from snoring. You put a tennis ball under your nightie so when you roll over, it wakes you up. There's also a gadget you can buy that fits behind your ear, sort of like a hearing aid, that sounds an alarm when you start in. But I'm hoping we won't need such drastic measures. "Do you sleep with the window open? I like it cracked. Any more than that, this time of year, I get chilly. Of course, some hotels don't let you open the window. I hope this one does. I tend to be claustrophobic if I can't at least crack the window. What about you?"

I think of Deke sleeping in the nude on the coldest winter nights with the windows open. I think of me, burrowed beneath flannel sheets, cocooned in my granny gown. He and I have made our adjustments. "Oh, I'm easy," I blurt. "You just do how you like, Ellen." She wants the window open, she can sleep next to it. I don't give a shit, just as long as she shuts up.

Mercifully, Lisette shifts into the role of tour guide, using a microphone to announce several landmarks we'll pass as we enter the city. As she mentions each one Ellen says, "Ooh, a must-see!" It seems she's memorized the guidebook. I want to strangle her. God. Roommates. How will I ever survive? Is this trip going to be worth the aggravation? Why am I here?

Why am I here? What do I want?

An adventure. Let something happen to me in the next five days. Is that what the woman in Buffalo wanted? Was she disappointed? Is that why she stayed on and on, hoping for something new in her life?

I remember our hotel is located within walking distance of Le Vieux-Montréal, the old quarter. If there's time after check-in, I want to wander off by myself. My plan is to unpack quickly and scoot. I'll say I'm going downstairs to the lobby to look around. I can't wait.

*   *   *

Our hotel room is on the eighth floor, facing the Boulevard. I look down on the busy thoroughfare, the glassy blur of traffic and pedestrians scampering this way and that. In Riverton, we take our time. In the fall and spring, when I take my mid-afternoon walk, I pass the houses of people I've known since I grew up. I hear the soft chirp of their phones. The ringing goes on, uninterrupted by answering machines. I imagine them rising slowly from their sofas to pick up. In the summer, when windows are open wide to encourage eavesdropping, I can hear the lazy lilt in their hellos, the lingering fondness of their goodbyes. Then when it's really hot, in late July and early August, it seems the whole neighborhood takes a nap.

What must it be like here when the temperature soars? Weekends, they probably escape to the Laurentians. An apartment in the city and a house in the mountains, the perfect way to move from fast to slow. It's Friday afternoon, and I'm driving out of the city in my little sports car, thinking about the events of the week, the business deals I've made. Of course, I'm only twenty-five, but already I've made a name for myself in international finance. I have a lover—no two lovers—and there'll be a made-for-TV movie about me starring Jaclyn Smith...

"Shirleen! Are you dreaming?" Ellen's voice pulls me back into the reality of our shared room with the cracks in the plaster and the window that won't quite open and the incessant, insistent whine of her voice. "I need to know: Would you mind if I took the bed on the left? I'm used to sleeping on that side of the room. And it's nearer the bathroom. I'm afraid I have to tinkle in the middle of the night," she says, giggling. "T.B. That stands for Tiny Bladder. Oh. That's okay. You take the top two drawers. I don't mind bending over. That little bit of straining won't bother my arthritis, not in the least! And the towels? Why don't I take the ones next to the shower? Look. I'll just put my cosmetics case underneath them, so you'll remember."

It could be worse, I suppose. I could be rooming with Edna Feingold, who clears her throat and spits, or Doris Needham, who passes foul-smelling gas. At least Ellen is tidy.

"I'll hang my things here," she says, indicating the left side of the closet. "Oh, what a pretty dress, Shirleen! My, how fancy. I didn't bring anything nearly that elegant. Too bad it's wrinkled. Maybe you can get an iron from the concierge. I know! Want me to dial housekeeping and ask? Oh, I don't mind at all. *Allo. Allo. Ici chambre numéro—*"

I grab my shoulder bag and tiptoe out of the room. "An iron. Hell, I don't know the French for iron. *La chose pour presser les clothes. Oui. C'est ça. Merci.*' Shirleen! Oh, for God's sake, she's gone out."

Her voice trails out into the hall and disappears. I take a deep breath, push the elevator button, and hope there's nobody I know inside.

★ ★ ★

"*Là bas,*" says the older woman I've asked for directions. "*Pour trouver le Vieux-Montréal, vous allez là bas.*" She points down the street. "*Et puis, à droite. Prenez votre premier gauche. C'est peut-etre dix minutes, pas loin d'ici.*" A bus pulls up and she starts to get on it. "*Merci!*" I yell, realizing I actually understood her! She spoke so fast! Lisette warned us about that. We're supposed to say, "*Plus lentement, s'il vous plaît.*" Slower, please. Shit! Where did she say to turn?

I watch the bus pull away. Schoolgirls in uniforms approach. "*Pardon, Mademoiselle...*" I address one, but her teacher plucks her away before I can finish. Finally, I remember I have a map in my purse.

★ ★ ★

Ten minutes later I'm teetering on the lumpy cobblestones of Old Montréal, the late-afternoon chill cutting through to my bones. God,

I'm cold. You'd think Lisette might have warned us that spring comes late to the Province of Québeque. I button my sweater and pull the sleeves down over my hands.

When I turn the corner I recognize the wide street lined with cafés, where flowers are sold and songs are sung, where lovers stroll on a sunny day, pausing to sip a beer or swirl a glass of wine, and maybe nibble some cheese or paté...Like Ellen, I've memorized the guidebook, at least the parts that appeal to me. But where are the musicians? The mimes? The awning-covered patios with the miniature wrought iron tables? The myriad blooms gathered in pastel tissue-paper cones, tied with pink ribbons to please milady? It's clear the author of our guidebook wasn't here in mid-April.

I walk over to a restaurant and read the sign: Le Petit Navire, The Little Ship, *ouvert 17:30 jusqu'à Minuit*. I count back from 24:00, which would be midnight, and realize they don't open until an hour from now. There's a café next door, open in mid-May. My fingers are frozen, and so are my toes. I long for mittens and heavy woolen socks, maybe a blanket from the hotel. Those sweet young things in soft summer dresses should be glad they live in the forever-warm pages of my guidebook. They wouldn't last five minutes in this icy blast.

A man wearing a Navy jacket and cap brushes past me. *"Pardon, Monsieur, ici...ouvert...*now?" I stammer.

"No, but you can come in," he says in English. "I'm the bartender."

"Je suis une Américaine. From New York State."

He tells me he's from New Jersey, then leads me inside and offers me a stool. When he turns on the lights, I can see the bar is designed to look like a ship's hold. There are several small tables with barrels for chairs. A larger room set up for diners features a huge stone fireplace. "I'll build a fire," he says, and in a few minutes flames appear. Some have the knack, some don't, Pop used to say.

"Where you from? Southern New York?" He laughs. "Only kidding. It's just that you look so frozen. You want something to drink? I'll make you a toddy. That'll warm you up." He's wearing a leather vest and tight-fitting jeans, very macho, and I'm almost sorry when he dons his apron. When I was younger, I used to watch for signs of an erection to know if I was making an impression.

"Red wine, maybe." I think of Mr. Know-it-all in our class, Beaujolais, 1985. "Any red'll do." The bartender's hair is greying. He has nice eyes—brown I think, though it's hard to tell in the murky light of this mock-ship. A beard makes him look seaworthy. "You know, I didn't realize it'd be this cool up here. I didn't even bring a jacket. Just a raincoat. Is that stupid, or what?"

He laughs. "Hey. You can buy something. There are lots of pretty shops downtown. Don't look in this neighborhood, you'll get ripped off. Here. My wife works in a nice place. I'll give you a card." He fishes in his pocket and brings up a small business card on which is scripted the words Boutique Mireille, an address and a phone number. "Tell Pauline—she's the young one with the red hair—I said you should go there. My name's Burt, by the way." When he stretches to shake my hand the leather buttons on his vest squeak against the surface of the bar. His skin feels dry and warm, and I welcome his firm, Deke-like grasp. I've always been proud of Deke's strong handshake. If there's anything that puts me off, it's a wimpy greeting from guys who think you don't know the difference, who act as though your hand is poison.

The wine burns at first, then goes down easy. Before I realize it, I've drained every drop. But I've stop shivering. Burt pours me another glass. I get out my wallet. He puts up his hand. "On the house. I insist." I watch him arrange skinny knots of lemon peel in one bowl, shiny maraschino cherries in another, and small, dry wedges of lime in a third. He unloads the dishwasher, blots the bottoms of the glasses and sets them upright on the counter. "The food's good here, too," he says. "If you like fish stew, there's none better in Montréal."

"I'm with a tour. We're staying at the Majestic, not far from here. I'm supposed to be back in the lobby by six, to go to dinner at some bistro on the other side of town. We're taking the Métro. Part of our Montréal experience. The world is our classroom, that sort of thing."

I laugh self-consciously, aware that I'm talking too much and too fast.

While Burt goes about his business, I watch the waiters set up their stations and listen to the kitchen noise. I notice a small stage, and a microphone. "You have entertainment?"

"Folksingers. Mostly awful. Not tonight, though. You should stay." He smiles. "Hey. Here he is now, our troubadour du jour, M'sieur Lambert, or Rolfe, as he prefers to be called."

A common name, yet I look up with interest. A man enters the bar, backlit by the fading afternoon that filters through the bubbled panes. He takes off his coat, opens his case, removes his guitar. Burt flips a switch and light spills on the singer's head and shoulders. This Rolfe is my Rolfe, for sure.

I remember how I discovered him in Riverton. Expert indoor/outdoor painting done to your specification, read the formal hand-written notice posted on the Grand Union bulletin board. Modest rates. He listed the phone number of the local Y. When I called, the girl at the desk said, "Oh, Rolfe," in a breathless way that should have told me he was in demand.

His hair's longer now. He wears it pulled back and braided, a look that's popular with the girls. Long tresses or short, I'm reminded that he's one sexy piece of work. Although nothing actually happened while he painted my kitchen, he certainly got my juices flowing. I smile, remembering Deke's astonished reaction to my lovemaking during those days.

Now I watch him shrug off his coat and flex his muscles casually as if he doesn't know there's someone around to appreciate the goods. He sets up, does a sound check, runs through a couple numbers—softly at first, then a little louder, to get a feel of the room and how the music will play out to the crowd. I'm flushed from the wine and from the exhilaration of seeing him again. His voice is warm and compelling, just as I remember it. He'd paint a little, strum a little. Deke did wonder why it took so long to finish the job. "*Toi, toi qui m'aime*" is the simple refrain, but he caresses the lyrics with his slightly throbbing voice until they take on much more meaning than the simple chant between verses. In the song the girl who leaves him comes back, and he rejects her, as far as I can tell.

Burt jumps in, breaking the mood. "Didn't you say you had to meet your tour at six?"

"Uh huh," I say dreamily.

"Well, you'd better go, 'cause you're five minutes from being late."

"I know this guy, Burt."

"You and half the female population of Montréal."

"No. I mean, he did some work for me. Painted my kitchen. Last year."

"Oh, yeah? Hey, Rolfe. *Viens ici, mon ami.* This lady says she knows you."

Rolfe slides over to the bar, sits down beside me, looks me up and down. "*Vraiment,*" he purrs. Really. "From where?"

"Don't you remember?"

"Forgive me. I don't."

At least he's honest. "Riverton, New York."

Still a blank. He shrugs his shoulders, looks at Burt. Burt looks at me. See? This is what happens when you try to pick up a sleazeball in a bar.

"You painted my kitchen. I fed you beef stew. I wanted you to stay and paint another room, but you said you had to get back…"

"Again your name?"

"Shirleen McClure."

"And where was this…kitchen?"

"Riverton, New York. Near Rhinebeck. On the Hudson."

"They're not gonna wait for you," Burt says, tapping his watch.

"Ah, yes. Now I remember. Well. I must have been a fool to leave."

Burt rolls his eyes. Even I know Rolfe's used that line before. I imagine a trail of broken hearts stretching from east coast to west and back again, but who cares?

★ ★ ★

The evening passes in a blur of wine and conversation, some English, mostly French. In other words, Rolfe does most of the talking. He whispers to one of the waiters, we get a cozy table in the corner, and he orders us dinner. At the end of the meal he takes a piece of bread and wipes his plate, the way he did in my kitchen. I don't eat much; I'm too busy consuming him. It's a replay of the late eighties and I'm a teenager again and he's Deke, only Deke wouldn't be caught dead in a bistro listening to folk music.

From time to time we're visited by *jolies jeunes filles*, pretty young girls who keep flipping their straight blonde hair over their shoulders. They come to flirt with Rolfe, who turns them on like crazy. I can see their nipples pressing against the thin fabric of their dresses. I remember what it's like to go braless and have everybody see how aroused you are.

Burt, trying to be discreet, comes over to remind me that I'm breaking the tourist code. Thou shalt not mess around with the Natives, his eyes say. My eyes say, buzz off. Actually, I say, "Thanks. I called to tell them I'd met a friend," but Burt knows I haven't used the phone. So what? Ellen will be so happy organizing her underwear she won't miss me at all.

I drink more wine. Rolfe's first set is at nine, and the next at ten, then it's midnight and Burt is handing me a check. The dinner I haven't eaten, the wine we drank, and the several shots that Rolfe tossed back between sets cost me over seventy dollars. I give the guy my Visa. Simple.

"Want me to call you a cab?" Burt asks.

"Well…" I look at Rolfe. "I guess that would be a good idea."

"I'll call you one," Rolfe says. He's finished packing up his things and has his guitar slung over his back. "Or you can come to my place." I nod. He drapes his coat on my shoulders. It smells sour, of beer and brine. I can picture him hopping a freighter, sailing around the world, breaking more hearts. "I don't live far," he promises.

"You sure about this?" Burt, my protector, asks.

Rolfe laughs. "Burt here, he don't trust nobody."

* * *

It must be the cold that's making me tremble. The cold, or my nerves. What's the difference when you're shaking so hard your teeth are rattling? We walk a number of blocks with our hips bumping. I can feel his sinewy body moving through the layers of our clothing. I know what's ahead. Or do I?

When we reach his building, my heart is slamming inside my rib cage and my mouth is so dry I can hardly swallow. Rolfe pulls me into the doorway and kisses me hard, not a first-time fool-around soft meeting of lips, but a no-nonsense fierce grinding of teeth, not fun. When he stops, I run my tongue across my lips, testing for blood.

He wants more kisses. At first, because he's so rough, I resist; but then he turns gentle. I begin to respond. His mouth tastes sweet and sour, and he does this thing with his tongue that Deke used to do.

By the time we've groped each other up the two flights of stairs I feel receptive, yet there's an edge of anxiety as though I'd really like to put on the brakes. Now. I tell myself, kissing is one thing, fucking's another, yet I follow him into a room that smells of beer and shit. "Home sweet home," he says. "*Bienvenue.*" He turns on the ceiling light. Cockroaches skitter across the floor. I shudder. What was I expecting? In French Canada, it's the same: guys who live alone are slobs. "You want to use the can?" he asks, pointing to a doorless cubicle. I can see a toilet without a lid. Brown stains darken the bowl.

"I think maybe I'd better leave. Can you call me a cab, Rolfe?" I say, trying to sound grown up and businesslike even though I feel like a fifteen-year-old who's just decided she wants to remain a virgin, after all. Once you start. I can hear Ma's voice warning me about sex.

"No phone," he grins. "Besides, no cabs this time of night. So, you're stuck." He shoves me towards the couch, a worn pullout whose upholstery is soiled and torn. "Hey, don't worry, Shirley. I'll make you glad you came home with me." He fumbles with my blouse. He has dirty fingernails and his clothes stink of sweat.

I'm scared. He's drunk, but suppose he's wired? He could have done drugs at the restaurant any of the times he went to the bathroom, or he could be just naturally violent and mean. I should have listened to Burt. "My name is Shirleen, you bastard!" I yell, pushing him away.

It works. He loses interest. "Who the fuck cares? I have to piss" he moans, and staggers towards the toilet. Now. Leave now, I tell myself, but at the sound of his urine hitting the water I freeze, fascinated by the sight of his buttocks tensing up at the end of the stream to force the last drops. Even Deke closes the door when he pees, but of course here, there is no door. And of course, Rolfe doesn't flush.

"She's going back to her hotel!" he squeals, mocking me. A bottle falls from his hands. Yellow liquid washes the floor with foul-smelling foam—if not Quebec's best brew, certainly her cheapest. Rolfe's laughter follows me down the stairs and into the cold, black night.

* * *

Three blocks up there's a cab, but when I tell the driver where I want to go, he makes a fuss. "Too near," he grumbles. "Too little money to go so near."

I shove a ten-dollar bill at him. "This enough?" I just want to get back to the hotel, to the safety of Ellen and her underwear.

"Crazy American bitch," he yells.

* * *

Ellen wears black lace-trimmed eyeshades to bed.

"I'm sorry. I'll try to be quiet," I whisper, tiptoeing around her bed.

"Where the hell have you been? Lisette called the police. They're looking for you. And your husband called three times."

"I ran into somebody I knew from home." Not a lie.

"Remember: the towels next to the shower are mine."

I undress in a hurry, throw my clothes in a pile, brush the taste of Rolfe's mouth out of mine, turn out the light and sink into bed.

"We had a good dinner in a kind of pub, but Al got drunk and we had to leave."

I should call Deke, but it's so late.

"We were really worried about you. That was very thoughtless, going off like that without telling anybody." She turns on the overhead light, blinding me. "You really should call Lisette. And the police. My God, Shirleen. You've made an awful mess." I turn on my stomach and put my head underneath the pillow. I hide from the light, from the punishing tenor of Ellen's voice, from the tawdry aspects of my misadventure. I have a headache and heartburn. I can't sleep. How could I have been so stupid? What did I think would really happen? Did I think we'd fall in love, be star-crossed forever?

How will I explain the Visa bill?

In the bathroom, in Ellen's neatly-overstuffed, extra-large cosmetics case, I see an envelope of Forever Young Bubble Bath. I turn on the water full-force and watch the small blue and green granules, colors chosen for their soothing association to the ocean and the land, dissolve into bubbles. Slowly I lower myself into the tub, entrusting body and soul to this baptism, expecting to be made new again.

Rendezvous

Irene

Although Deke is handsome in a beefy sort of way and sweet-natured if you like affectionate goofballs, he's never been a big favorite of mine. And vice versa, I suppose. Is it the dream of most mothers-of-only-daughters that someday they'll have a son-in-law who's Best Pal in addition to Good Provider? Deke does okay in the latter category. I suppose you could say he's successful in the business he inherited from his father—his employees like him, and he makes a profit. What else can a mother-in-law ask for? As I say, we've never been tight, so it's a surprise when he calls me, all out of sorts because he can't reach Shirleen in Montréal.

"Are you sure they gave you the right room number? Did you ask if she left any messages for you? Maybe the plans changed, and they went out to dinner earlier. I bet that's what happened. Relax. She'll call you when she gets back to the hotel."

"But it's after ten now. She was supposed to call me at six. She promised."

He sounds like a man who's learned to distrust his wife, and yet Shirleen's such a straight arrow I can't imagine her fooling around. Certainly not with a complete stranger, someone she's picked up in Montréal. Lordy, no. Not this day and age! And it couldn't be anybody in her French Class. I know who went on that trip and there's not a fledgling lothario in the bunch. "Come on, now, Deke. Pull yourself together. Did you eat the dinner she cooked for you?"

"No," he says forlornly. "I forgot to defrost it this morning."

"Well, no wonder you're in such a state! Your blood sugar is low. Hey. I have an idea. Take a meal out of the freezer now."

"What?"

"Just do as I say: take it out and put it on the kitchen counter." I wait for him to plod over to the refrigerator, follow my instructions, and come back to the phone. "Now back off. Get out of the way."

"Why?"

"Just do it. Or picture yourself as a pile of warm goo. Your choice."

"Christ, Irene, I…"

"Hush. I gotta concentrate. *Swiftily, giftily, I ply my skills, niftily, shiftily, causing no ills.* Well? Did I do it?"

"I'd say so. The food's sitting in a puddle of water."

"Well, now, all you have to do is heat it up. Unless you want me to."

"Uh, no thanks, Irene."

"Trust me, Deke. You'll feel better with something in your stomach. Have a beer. Have two. Want me to come over and hold your hand?"

"Nah. I'll be okay. It's just that…we've never been apart."

Oh, now we have it. The truth comes out. He misses her! What a softy. It's touching, really. I can almost say I like the guy. "I know, honey. But look at it this way: You can leave the toilet seat up the whole week and nobody'll yell at you."

"Yeah."

"Call me anytime," I say warmly, meaning it. It's nice to be needed.

After I hang up, I think, he coulda used the microwave—no defrosting needed there—but then I remember I destroyed it making

my bat-wing souffle. This way, I know I haven't lost my touch. Teleki-
netically speaking.

★ ★ ★

"Who was that?" Vinnie asks when I come back to the living room.
She and I have been going over the designs for the new packaging.
Forever Young's sales are beginning to soar again, a pleasant surprise
after that little Nader-inspired setback. I'm sending every member of
the jury a complimentary gift set with a personal note of infinite gratitude. I coulda hugged each and every one. When I think how close
we came to losing everything! "Was that Shirleen? Is she having fun?"

"Deke hopes not."

"Excuse me?"

"That was Deke. He's in a panic because Shirleen forgot to check
in with him at the appointed hour. Honestly. What a baby!"

"I think it's sweet. Hendrik was like that, too. So…dependent."

"Hm." I remember Hendrik. He was a big lump of clay with a
personality to match. Bored the hell outta most people, including me.
"Do you like the blue and gray, or the aqua and yellow?" I ask, getting
back to business. At least I harbor no illusions about Teddy. He always
went his own way, never relied on me for anything he could get from
somebody else. Until his strokes, of course.

Vinnie peers at the sketches. The woman has no artistic sense,
but I feel obliged to consult her. "What happened to black? I thought
we were going to stay with chic and mysterious."

"The agency ruled out black, remember? Too common. Everybody does black. Midnight this and mysterious that."

"Really. Well. What time is it? Oh, I've got to go soak, then get
my rest. Tomorrow the choir's singing for the governor at Hyde Park.
We'll miss Shirleen. She has such a warm soprano!"

The choir from the Dutch Reformed church? I hope Pataki has
earplugs. Thank God Shirleen has the sense to steer clear. I can see
them now, that bunch of biddies, lining up neck to neck to deliver

God's message. The last director had a nervous breakdown. Now they've got some young thing from the conservatory who doesn't know the difference between "more feeling" and "shut up."

"Should I wear my new pink linen with the navy trim, or that polyester polka-dot vest and white pleated skirt you like so much?"

"I don't know. Which is more slimming?"

"It won't matter, because I'm soaking, remember?"

I'm thinking it'll take a lot of tub-time to make a significant difference, these days. Vinnie's really let herself slide. Too many crêpes with cream sauce followed by chocolate éclairs. "That's true, dear. Well. Whatever happened to your navy shirt-dress with the red piping? It looks so...patriotic. Just the ticket for the governor, don't you think? And it's that flattering middy style, not clingy around what used to be the waist, if you know what I mean."

"Oh, Irene. That's inspired. You always know how to advise me. And with so much tact. Whatever did I do before I met you?"

Beats me. "Run along now, dear. I'll just go over these sketches one more time, and then I'll turn in, too." I'm going to visit Teddy in his new apartment tomorrow. I'll have to be strong. If I expect the worst, from him, from myself, will I be pleasantly surprised? I've been invited for lunch. Lunch! I picture Meals on Wheels: melted cheese, cold, with the cheese bonded to the bread, and a soggy side of fries. Yech.

★ ★ ★

This is my first visit to his new apartment. Teddy loves Macadamia nuts, so I'm bringing him a jar as a house gift. Soignée's my chauffeur. "Thanks, darling, I'll call you when I'm ready to escape. Five minutes from now. Ha ha. Only joking. I hope." Vinnie swears Soignée is ready to quit, but she hasn't said anything to me, and I'm not asking. Pretty soon I'll be driving again. It seems like forever since I've been behind the wheel. Looking back, I don't know what got into me, taking Mabel's car. Six months' suspended license! Come on, Teddy, answer the door. Six months is nothing compared to six minutes, sometimes. Oops. Maybe he's dead. Shit, no such luck.

"Irene! What a pleasant surprise!"

You invited me, you nincompoop. "Teddy. You look wonderful!" The Devil take me if I'm lying. He looks fantastic! What a difference from the last time I saw him with his gut hanging over his groceries.

"No more therapy! I've graduated to powerlifting. Wish they could do something about my memory, though."

"Don't we all! I can't remember from one minute to the next." That's a fucking lie. I'm sharp as a tack.

"Shirleen has to make notes for me. It's really odd. Some things I remember."

"Yes. Well. Aren't you going to invite me in?"

"Where are my manners? Sorry." He ushers me in to the apartment, which is boringly beige—so like Shirleen. She always had a taste for blah. "Here, you sit there, in the comfy chair. I'll take the rocker."

"Thanks." All this politeness is giving me a headache. "Here, I brought you a little something. Macadamias." Five bucks for a teeny jar. He used to gobble them up, forgetting they made him constipated. With any luck, these expensive little buggers will still cause him trouble. I wonder, does he remember we're married or is that little fact tucked away in some inaccessible area of his brain? Even in the darkest days he knew Shirleen was his daughter. Who else, besides Rosalie, has been so favored? Junior? "You have a grandson who's practically all grown up, you know."

"Junior? But I haven't seen him for a long time. How's he doing?"

"Who knows? He ran off with his girlfriend, Antoinette Bixby." Takes after you, Teddy. One whiff of pussy and he's gone.

"Wait a minute. Don't I know a Bixby? First name begins with Ro something. Oh, damn it. I'm supposed to relax, count to ten slowly, and the name will just float to the surface…"

In my sweetest dreams Rosalie doesn't surface, she sleeps with the fishes. "Let me help you out here, Teddy. Her name is Rosalie."

"You're a wonder, Irene. Now, why couldn't I...? I can see her face now, clearly as if it was yesterday. I can see her sweet little..."

Spare me. I interrupt. "Say, this is a nice little place you've got." It must have cost a bundle to fix up. Shirleen would never tell. But this is nicely furnished with upscale goods—all this oak and linen didn't come from K-mart. "You used a decorator?"

"Nope. Took a course at Community College. See the drapes? I sponge printed the fabric in textile class."

"Very attractive." I hate to admit it, but the drapes are splendid. "And the rug in the entryway? I suppose you..."

"Hooked it in Rehab. Yup. Oops. There goes the timer. We're having Quiche Lorraine. Hope you like it."

"Something smells delicious." Of course, these days anybody can serve gourmet, with a little help from Stouffer's. "That looks scrumptious, Ted. Lean Cuisine?"

He shakes his head. "Guess again."

"Scratch?" Here is a man whose idea of cooking was a melted cheese sandwich.

He nods his head. "They send instructors over from the Culinary Institute. Last week we did lobster soufflé." He places the quiche in the center of the table and pulls out my chair. "Madame."

Blue cloth napkins compliment the grey pottery plates. The goblets are blue. The placemats are blue. There are blue candles and holders. Everything matches; Martha Stewart, take notice. "My, my. It's all so...blue. Who did your coordinating?"

"Well," he blushes, "I'll admit I chose everything. Shirleen took me shopping, but I'd already worked out the color scheme." How too, too precious. "We went to a craft fair up the mountain, in Hunter. We used to take Shirleen up there when she was little, remember? You were doing ceramics then. You had a booth. Did pretty well, I recall."

He's the one with the stroke, but I don't remember any craft fair. Still, best to play along. "Yes. It was a nice craft fair."

"Well, it was pretty tacky back then. But you should see it today. People come from all over."

Crap Fairs we used to call them. Little old ladies pushing ceramic ash trays in our faces. Twelve-year-olds hawking balsam-stuffed pillows. I had enough of Rip Van Winkle's bearded mug on mugs to last a lifetime. I dig into my quiche. "Delicious! Compliments to the chef!"

Once again, he blushes. His once-sallow skin has regained its healthy luster. He seems much younger than I remember. Could someone be slipping him Forever Young Bubble Bath? Of course. Shirleen. Why hadn't I guessed? Well. If my product can breathe life into an old fart like Teddy, what won't it do? I'm a genius, that's all there is to it. Fess up, Teddy. You've been soaking.

"Damn! I forgot the salad, and the wine. Just a minute." He hops up with the agility of a thirty-year-old and plucks a bottle of Chardonnay and a bowl of salad from the fridge. He decants the bottle and ties a napkin around its neck. "They taught us all this," he said. "Would you believe I'm thinking of working part-time in a restaurant? Waiting tables during lunch. There's a place in Rhinebeck that hires seniors."

The good news: Teddy's made a complete recovery; in fact, he's quite a bit improved. The bad news: in making the transition from homewrecker to homemaker, he's become rather a bore. Good intentions don't seem to suit either of us.

* * *

After lunch we take a little stroll around the neighborhood. The assisted living apartments are clustered around a dining hall/recreation center, with craft rooms, a bowling alley and a swimming pool. Teddy says he goes swimming three times a week. "Keeps me limber," he says, patting his no-longer-existent belly. "I ride the Life Cycle, too." So, he's a fitness freak. He eyeballs my figure, hidden under a long cape. "You ought to try exercising."

Mind your own business, muscle brain. "What a good idea. Of course, I'm sooo busy these days. Personal appearances, lectures, talk shows…"

"I know. I was very proud of you on Oprah."

"Why, thank you, Teddy." My giddiness surprises me. The sun, the wine, the compliments. Too much in one day, or too little too late. I'm not sure which. "Do you think we could go back, now?"

"I usually walk for an hour, but, sure, we can go back. Here. Take my hand. You seem a little…unsteady on your feet."

I put my hand in his. How long has it been? His skin feels warm and dry, and his grasp is firm. He puts his arm around my waist and we walk back to his unit in this manner, masquerading as a devoted couple on their afternoon stroll.

★ ★ ★

"Cream and sugar?" he asks, handing me a small cup of decaf. "I can't remember if you take either, neither, or both."

I steady my cup hand on my knee. "Both. Two sugars, please." You used to say it was bad for me, all the sugar I put in my coffee. You used to say I was sweet enough.

"So, Irene, where are Junior and Antoinette? I'm assuming you know."

Ah. Thank you. Here's my opening. Can he tell how nervous I am? "I don't know," I lie. "But he called last week to say that everything was okay." Junior's sworn me to secrecy, but this much I've told Shirleen. No point in having her worried sick. "Teddy. There's something I have to ask you."

He looks up from his coffee, his gaze guileless.

I set my cup on the coffee table next to a copy of *Life Anew*, the residents' newsletter. "Did you see Rosalie again? I mean, after the trial?" I realize this is a gamble, that he may not remember the trial and all the anguish that ensued, but I have my reasons for needing to know. "I mean, after you said goodbye to her."

He pauses long enough to invent another cockamamie story. "No," he answers firmly. Can I believe him? "I remember the trial—don't ask me why, since there are so many other things I don't remember about that time in our lives. But I remember the courtroom, and the lawyers, and the way the press hounded us. And I remember that she and I said our goodbyes in a little room off the main hall. We had to run in there to escape the reporters."

So far, he's sticking to the facts, as I recall them. I can feel my face heating up. "And where was I?"

"With the lawyers. With Shirleen. I don't know, exactly. I only know where I was, in a little room saying goodbye to Rosalie. You see, she and I agreed we'd never meet again, and we didn't. Oh, I don't deny it tore me apart, the thought of our affair ending so abruptly. But I knew it had to be done. For Shirleen's sake. And...I know you're not going to believe me...for us. You see, I knew if we were ever going to put our marriage back together, I had to swear off Rosalie. For good. But why are you asking this now?"

Because, you shit, I suspect you did meet her. And I worry that Junior's got his arms wrapped around the result. "No particular reason. Just curious."

"I don't believe you."

"That makes two of us."

"What do I have to say to convince you? And why is it so fucking important? What if I did see her again?"

"There! You admit it!"

"But I didn't see her. I'm only saying, what if I had? Aside from the fact I would have been compounding my sins. In your eyes, I mean."

I ponder this a minute. Is he saying he wouldn't have been doing anything wrong, that it was all in my perception? The bastard. Okay, no more Ms. Nice Gal. The gloves are off. Here goes. "All right! I'll tell you why it's so important. If you took up with her again, and if she became pregnant and bore your child, that child could be Antoinette!"

"My God." He drops his saucer and it clatters to the table, sending small gray chips sailing across the smoothly-waxed surface. "Antoinette is Rosalie's daughter?"

"Now do you see why I have to know?"

"What I see is that you've been torturing yourself over nothing. There was no post-trial assignation. There was no baby. There couldn't have been."

"You expect me to believe you didn't fuck her anymore? How could you even be in the same room with that whore and not fuck her!"

Teddy puts up his hands. "Enough."

"Don't you see, Teddy? If you're Antoinette's father, then she would be Junior's aunt. Aside from pregnancy, there are other risks, here. They deserve to be told. So, I beg you, please, the truth!" I reach for his hands, those well-worn paws that he now holds up in a gesture of what? Surrender? Those hands that caressed me and Rosalie, that pinched the fat women and decided which of them should take drugs to get skinny. Those hands that held Shirleen so tenderly after she was born. "Teddy, we have to figure out a way to break the news to Junior."

"I have told you the truth!" he yells. "God damn you! You'll never believe me! Why do you think I slept with Rosalie in the first place? What did I have to lose? You wouldn't have believed in my fidelity anyway. No matter what! So, I figured, why shouldn't I sneak around?" He hits the table so hard that coffee sloshes out of his saucerless cup and splashes across *Life Anew's* Guy of the Month—Teddy, captured in all his latent glory: new dentures gleaming, golf cap perched jauntily on his Rogaine-enhanced head of hair. He starts to cry, a small child's whimper that barely produces tears. An act. I'm not convinced. "Irene, I couldn't have fathered a child. Don't you remember? I had a vasectomy right after the trial. I remember that. Don't you?"

I jump. The truth? I don't remember.

Fallout

Irene

"**A**re you sure you don't want me to stay with you for a while?" Soignée asks, her small, ferret-like face close to mine, forehead creased with worry over me. She's a sweet girl, wanting to help, but nobody can help me; I have to be alone in order to sort out my feelings. The visit with Teddy addled my brain. I want to believe him, I really do, but his track record...his past denials...I just don't know. "You look as though you've been through a real rough time," she croons. I think, bravo, it doesn't take a genius.

I started out fine, determined to make the best of my luncheon date with Teddy. But once I arrived at his place my mood barometer started to plummet, and by the time Soignée arrived to pick me up, it had bottomed out. I'd forgotten how deadly-dull spousal conversation can be. Once you've asked each other what kind of day it's been, once you've discussed the front-page headlines and tomorrow's weather and the price of groceries, there isn't much to talk about, is there? And now that Teddy's turned into The Perfect Homemaker, he's become a heavy-duty bore. When I complimented him on the quiche, he actually wrote out the recipe for me! Why, two months ago he couldn't even sign his name on a hospital release form. The miracles of modern science! "You should treat yourself to a nice soak. Let me run a bath for you, Irene. Let me brew you a cup of chamomile tea. Mix a pitcher of martinis. Something. I just feel so...helpless," Soignée moans.

Honey, I'd like to tell her, you wanna do me a favor? Leave me alone! How am I gonna get rid of her? I know: I'll just come out with the truth. She'll understand. You're getting to be a pain in the neck, Soignée. No, that's too harsh; I have to acknowledge that she means well. I've got it! You're kind, sweetie, I'll say, but I need to be by myself. There. Just the right touch of familiarity.

"Of course. I understand completely," she acquiesces when I tell her. There's just a hint of hurt in her voice. "And Vinnie should be here soon. She'll cheer you up. She always does." Just a touch of jealousy, perhaps. "You will call if there's anything..."

I nod, then mwah, mwah, mwah, I plant continental air-kisses to seal the sendoff. When I hear the front door close, I think, finally.

★ ★ ★

Now where was I in my reflecting? Oh, yes. If Teddy's lying, he's doing a good job. And those tears. He's gone soft on me! Now that I think of it, he's always been a sentimental slob. He even brought flowers the first time he took me out. Oh, I see him so clearly on that summer day, standing on our threshold with a bouquet of wildflowers in his hands. He was so handsome! Resembled Alan Ladd, only taller. My girlfriends even said so. Of course, to hear Poppa talk, you'd have thought he was a bum. "You seen that new young upstart calls hisself a doctor? Why he don't look any older than Irene. What kinda medical school he go to? Why, if I was dyin' I wouldn't let him near me! No, sir." And then when he found out we were dating! The scolding I got from Poppa! Even a slap. But Teddy's kisses made up for everything.

We were passionate lovers. It was like that for years, even after Shirleen was born. He had a way of arousing me by just a look or a touch. Once, when we were making love in the kitchen, Shirleen wandered in. I was so embarrassed. I was sitting on the kitchen counter, fully dressed but without my panties. Teddy's shorts were down around his ankles. He believed in spontaneity. Obviously. Look what he got away with when he was fucking Rosalie in his office, with the maintenance staff hovering in the hallway!

I hafta admit, after the trial, I do remember I wanted to have my tubes tied. I was well into my forties and I knew I didn't want any more children. And I remember Teddy saying no, he'd have a vasectomy. He said I'd been through enough already, with the scandal and all. He said he'd have an associate of his, a urologist, do it, but what I can't remember is if he actually went through with it. I guess I could always look up the urologist, if he's still practicing. That'd be one sure way to settle the issue.

Of course, I've heard of guys having the procedure reversed, and somebody we know said his didn't take...

Oh, this is ridiculous! Why shouldn't I believe him? Today, for the first time in years, I felt a thaw, a spot of warmth creeping into the corners of my heart. Would forgiveness be so bad? Oh, I'm not saying I'd take him back. Only put an end to the animosity.

Soignée's right—a soak would be good. A warm jacuzzi'll make me relax, clear the cobwebs. And a frosty pitcher of martinis will blunt the pain of having to make up my mind, finally, on the matter of trusting Teddy.

★ ★ ★

Soignée, bless her heart, rigged up a writing board that fits across the tub so I could jot down any inspiration during my soaks. "Dear Teddy. Thanks for lunch, and for showing me your new place, which is lovely." The words flow from my brain through my Bic, as if I knew all along what I'd say to him. I take another sip of my second drink. My secret? All Vodka, a kiss of Vermouth, mammoth olives with no stuffing. I'm on my way to numb. "I should apologize, I guess, for the way I acted. I know I said I didn't believe you about Rosalie. But when I got home and had a chance to think, I changed my mind. I do believe you, T. Why the change of heart? Because, I guess, I have to let this all drop. I have to trust you to do the right thing. I know, Teddy, that if there was even the slightest chance you fathered A. that you would admit it, for Junior's sake, for her sake, for the sake of their children. You're not an evil person. What's more, you're a man of science, and you know how important genetics is. Although they're not closely related…"

I've gotten this far without dropping the stationery in the water.

Assuming they are related, I don't really know their chances of producing a defective offspring, given the remote nature of their blood ties. I only know that I wouldn't want to marry my grandfather's son. The thought makes me nauseous.

Mm. Nothing like B 'n' B—bubbles 'n' booze. Shit! I smudged. I shoulda typed this on my laptop, but that would have meant getting out of the tub, drying off, being sober and sensible. Besides, email didn't seem proper. This is personal stuff. Should be in longhand, the old-fashioned way. Pitcher too far away, have to get up. Oops, slippery! Better hang onto the towel rack while I—

★ ★ ★

How long have I been lying here? I musta passed out. Now I'm a seal stranded on an Italian marble rock, this floor so fucking slippery I can't get up. Plus, I'm wounded. Been harpooned. All of me hurts. "Vinnie?"

"I'm here, love. Ambulance on its way. Look at you! Your leg looks broken, your lip is split. Oh, God, Irene, I feel responsible! Soignée called to tell me you were in a bad way, but I figured she was exaggerating. Oh, I should have rushed right over! Can you ever forgive me?

"Shut up and get my robe. Can't have them see me like this. Oh, shit! Everything hurts."

"Here. This'll cover you up."

"A blanket? I'm not a horse. I want my silk robe!"

"Don't be ridiculous. You're going to the hospital, not the Ritz."

Besides, they'll only take it off in x-ray. You'll have to wear a paper johnny like everybody else."

"Damn! The letter. I was writing a letter to Teddy. Where is it?"

"I don't see any letter. Wait. Something's floating in the tub. Ick! What a mess. You can forget about sending this one. The ink's all blurred. Good God, what's keeping that ambulance? I called 911 ages ago. How much did you drink, anyway? The pitcher is almost empty, and there's an olive stuck in your navel."

"Give me that letter!"

"It's ruined."

"I don't care. It's my letter, and I want it!"

Vinnie wrings it out and hands it to me.

Blue smudges are all that remain of my effort to make peace. "So much for good intentions. Toss it, will you?"

"You're going to be all puffy and bruised, you know. Pull that blanket around your shoulders. There. I think I hear them pulling into the driveway. Thank God you didn't leave the water running or we'd be floating down the Hudson. Oh, Irene! You're not going to faint again, are you?

⋆ ⋆ ⋆

I'm in a jungle. The grass is ten feet high. Lions and tigers are chasing me. I try to climb a tree, but I can't. They're getting closer. Does it hurt to be eaten? I don't want to find out. What's that noise? A roaring, like the ocean. Like a wild animal.

"Mrs. Richards. Can you hear me?"

Do lions behave this way before they eat people? What am I doing here? Why is the first branch of that tree so high? I'll never get my foot up. Forget my foot—I can't move it.

"Don't try to move, dear. Do you know where you are?"

In the jungle.

"You're in the ER. You fell in your bathtub. My, it's not every day we have a celebrity! You just rest easy. I'm here if you need me."

"Gimme a boost. Gotta get up in that tree!"

"Hey, Clara. We got a tree-climber here."

Senile dementia. I can see it in her eyes. She thinks I'm crazy. Well, I'll dementia you, you bitch. "Sorry. Musta been dreaming. It's Wednesday, April 23, and Bill Clinton is President. My name is Irene Richards, and I'm sixty-four years old." There. Satisfied?

Florence Nightingale makes some notes in my chart: Patient appears gonzo but isn't. "You have a visitor," she says.

The curtain opens and in walks Deke, carrying a bouquet of roses. "Jesus, Irene. I heard it on the scanner. Look at you! Hey. I brought you these flowers..."

The big lug! Did I say I wasn't fond of him? I lied. Look at him: Mr. Beefcake offering roses, which cost a pretty penny, to his mother-in-law. "Thanks, hon."

"They say you bruised yourself up pretty bad, but nothing's broken. You're gonna have to take it easy for a week or so, is all."

"You talk to Shirleen?"

"She called first thing this morning and apologized for last night. Said she'd run into somebody she knew and lost track of time."

A likely story, but he seems to buy it. "Well, then. Feel better?"

"Uh-huh. But I'll be glad when she's home. Oh. Should I call her? She doesn't know about your accident. 'Course, she'll be home day after tomorrow."

"Well, tell her not to rush right over here. She'll have plenty to do without spending her time visiting me." I figure the last thing I need is a lecture on temperance, delivered by my goody-two-shoes daughter. "Hey. You run along, now. Thanks for coming, hon." Poor guy. He looks exhausted. Probably hasn't been sleeping well, with Shirleen gone. Ran into someone she knew. Well, we'll see about that.

Deke bends to kiss me, and I smell Junior's Christmas standby, the aftershave he always used to give Teddy. Old Spice. Doesn't Teddy just wish! "Mom, I told Vinnie to call me when you're ready to leave. I'll come and get you."

In all these years, Deke's never called me Mom. What a good boy. A perfect son-in-law. "You take care," I tell him. "Don't worry about Shirleen." I watch him lope out of the room like a big ole moose.

★ ★ ★

Back in the jungle. No, on safari. A native bearer pokes his head in my tent and croons, "Irene, Irene." Shit! It's Teddy. With tears in his eyes. Gimme a break! An act for the nurses? "Vinnie called me. She said you'd had an accident."

Might as well tell him the truth. "I fell in—or outta—the tub," I giggle. Me in all my naked glory—musta made a splendid sight! Good thing Vinnie arrived on the scene in time to make me decent. "I wrote you a letter, a thank-you note, but it fell in the water and got ruined." This, too, makes me laugh. Must be the painkillers.

He squeezes my good hand. "A nice thought, anyway. I hear they're going to keep you overnight. VIP treatment."

"I'd rather go home."

"Here they can give you shots for your pain. You got pretty banged up, old girl."

I wish he wouldn't call me that. "I do feel kinda floaty."

I watch him pick up my chart and read it. Hard to break old habits, I guess, but I wish he wouldn't snoop. There's probably a blood alcohol level recorded in there. Bathing while intoxicated. Serious stuff. "I had a crazy nightmare from the drugs," I confess. "Lions were chasing me." I catch Mother Theresa eavesdropping. She makes eye contact with Teddy and that doctor-nurse thing passes between them: We're in on this secret together. "She thinks I'm mushbrained," I whisper.

Teddy smiles. What a difference those dentures make! "Well," he says. "We'll just have to set her straight, won't we?"

A Little Night Music

Shirleen

No, on the morning after my fiasco with Rolfe I do not want to go traipsing through Le Jardin Botanique. What will be blooming there, anyway? It's too damn cold. Oh. Okay. Tulips, hyacinths, daffodils, crocuses. Bulbs that have been forced. Thank you, dear Ellen. The very term "forced" hits a nerve today. I'm lucky I escaped with my—well, what do you call it when you've been married for eighteen years?—with my dignity intact. Oh, God, am I hung over! My head feels like a bruised melon. After the Jardin we're supposed to visit some famous shrine. There's a lot of walking involved, Lisette says. I'll never make it.

Ellen has been scolding me because I used up her last packet of Forever Young without first getting her permission. I tell her why: it was past midnight, she was sound asleep, I didn't even think straight. All I wanted was a soothing soak in the tub. I've said I'm sorry, but it isn't good enough. Plus, I've promised to get her a whole package of bubble bath, free of cost, from Ma. But nothing will make her forget that I stole from her. "Look at me!" she cries. "My skin's a mess! I was counting on a soak to rejuvenate. It isn't that I wouldn't have let you use it. The point is, you didn't even ask!"

I peer at her face, which looks perfectly normal to me. Ellen's no beauty, but there's a freshness about her that some, like Arnold

163

Glopfer, might find pleasant. I have to laugh when I think of Junior's eighth-grade science teacher mooning over Ms. Chinney, but as they say, love is blind; besides, Arnold's no prize. He has a pot belly and his ears stick out, and Junior says he farts a lot. Uck. And Ellen's worried about her appearance? "You look very nice," I say. "Besides, I think all this stuff about Forever Young's ability to alter one's appearance is a crock of shit."

"Oh, I know what you think," Ellen sniffs. "Soignée told me. We both think it's perfectly horrible for you to go around undermining Irene's product. Besides. How can you even say it doesn't work when you yourself have undergone such a change? You look years younger! And you're not even old to begin with. It's not even fair!"

I'm amazed at Ellen. She's supposed to be an educated woman, yet she's as gullible as the rest of mother's followers. Le culte d'Irene, I call them. "I look the same," I insist. If anything, last night's little adventure with Rolfe has aged me, but I'm certainly not going to go into that with Ellen.

"No, no. Look!" She pulls me into the bathroom and shoves my face in the mirror. "Those puffy places that used to be under your eyes are gone!"

"But I soaked my body, not my head."

She sighs. "That's the beauty of Forever Young."

Poor Ellen. She's lost it! I pity those earnest adult learners who sign up for her biology course. My mother has succeeded in turning her brain to mush. "Oh yes, now I see it," I pretend, knowing this is the only way I'll get her to drop the subject of my rejuvenation.

* * *

Later, in the metro station named for a pope, Ellen has her nose in the guidebook and almost walks into a passerby. Lisette is herding the flock, counting heads. Nobody has mentioned my absence at dinner last night. I'm suffering from lack of sleep and a guilty conscience. Good thing I didn't have sex with Rolfe; I'd be a total wreck.

"Did the concierge give you your phone message?" Lisette asks.

Message? I'd better think quick. "Oh, yes. My husband called. I tried to reach him this morning, but he'd already left for work."

"The call was from someone named Rolfe," Ellen snaps. "I just happened to notice the message. It was just sitting there on the front desk, Shirleen. Anyone could have read it."

Why, the little snoop! I count to ten. "Well, thanks for bringing it to my attention, but there's obviously some mistake. I don't know anyone named Rolfe." Jesus. Why am I such a bad liar? And what's wrong with me? I feel all hot and sweaty at the mention of his name. I can't believe it. I still have a crush on the jerk in spite of the way he behaved last night!

"He said he's sorry about last night." Ellen's voice carries throughout the metro station. The grey heads of the Cercle Français snap to; nothing like a little gossip.

"I said it was a mistake," I stage-whisper. "Now shut up."

But Ellen is determined to humiliate me, and presses on. "He wants to know if you're all right. Now what could he mean by that? Oh, and he left his phone number at work, in case you want to call. Oh, here," she says, shoving a folded piece of paper into my hand. "Take your damned message!"

"*Faites attention, mes amis!* We will now ascend to the street!" Lisette barks. "*Suivez-moi!*"

We do as we're told. We stick close together, we cradle our purses, we don't dawdle. Single file, we march up the stairs towards daylight. I shove the piece of paper in my pocket. Ellen, engaged at last in the spirit of adventure, is silent, and I don't want to give her any reason to start up again. Besides, Pope Pius IX is watching me from his portrait-perch on the subway wall.

★ ★ ★

Six hours later, back at the hotel, I take a couple of Excedrin and soak my feet. Then I make two long-distance calls, the first one to Deke at his office. "He's not here," the secretary tells me—aging, chatty Elspeth, first woman in the county to graduate from secretarial school. No cause, ever, for jealousy there! "He's gone to pick up your mother at the hospital. Lucky, eh? She could have broken her neck, falling in the bathroom like that. Mr. McClure says she's bruised up pretty bad. No use you rushing home, though. Mrs. Donderhook has every-thing under control. Say, what's the weather like up there? Weather Channel's saying we're gonna get some snow. Can you believe that? In April?"

Alarmed by the news about Ma, I call Vinnie. "Oh, Shirleen, don't you fret! She's feisty as ever. Wants to go ahead with her western promotional tour, as scheduled. I told her you can't cover bruises like those with makeup, but you know how vain she is! She's napping now, but I'll tell her you called."

So much for my fearing I'd have to rush home. Now. Should I call Rolfe? Ellen's off at an art gallery, and won't be back until 6:00. My hands are shaking as I unravel the piece of paper.

"*Le Petit Navire. Bon soir.*" Burt's familiar voice does nothing to calm me.

"Hey. This is Shirleen McClure. Remember me?" I stutter. Well, duh. Of course, he remembers me.

"Lemme guess. You're calling to book a table for your tour group! Only kidding. Wait a sec, I'll get Rolfe." There's a click, then silence, then I'm listening to a recording of Rolfe singing "*Toi, toi qui m'aime.*" How embarrassing! I didn't even have to ask for him. Burt knew. The waiters must be having a good laugh at my expense.

"I was afraid you wouldn't call." Rolfe's real voice, breathless and low, is enough to set my heart racing. "Is it enough to tell you I'm sorry for acting like a jerk? I had a big head the next morning. I must have been really drunk. The last thing I remember is kissing you on the stairs. What else did I do? Wait. Don't tell me. You have every right to call me a prick."

Sober, he speaks English well. I listen carefully, enchanted by the sound of his voice.

"Would you let me take you to dinner? My way of saying sorry. Not here, though. Burt doesn't approve. He thinks you're much too nice for me."

Imagine that.

Tomorrow night, our last night in Montréal, Lisette has arranged for us to attend a big tourist attraction, Le Festin du Gouverneur, a medieval feast. I figure I'd probably get stuck sitting next to Al, who behaves like Henry the Eighth, and all that burping and pinching would drive me crazy. Of course, I'd rather be with Rolfe! "All right," I say. "I'd like to have dinner with you." Like is much too mild for what I'm feeling, but he doesn't have to know that. Not yet.

"I know a little place in the country, maybe an hour, an hour and a half from here," Rolfe says. "I'll pick you up at your hotel at six."

"That sounds wonderful."

Have I forgotten how he behaved last night?

Do I need to have my head examined?

Don't all seductions begin this way?

★ ★ ★

The next morning, as we tour Île Ste-Hélène, I keep dreaming of a new, well-groomed Rolfe and imagining his long, slender guitar-playing fingers caressing my body, playing me like an instrument.

"Shir-leen!" hoots Edna the spitter. "What is the matter with you? Ever since yesterday you've been off in another world. Oh, I know. You're missing Deke. How sweet. But just think how grand it will be to see him again. You know what they say: Absence makes the heart grow fonder."

"For somebody else," Ellen mumbles.

Edna clears her throat and deposits some mucous in a napkin before addressing the dilemma at hand. "What are you going to have? The Big Mac or a Filet-o-Fish?" We're standing in line at Mickey D's.

Here we are in the eating capital of North America, and we're having junk food for lunch! I have to laugh.

"I thought Lisette was going to bust a gut when you told her you'd lost your badge," Ellen says. "What did happen to it, Shirleen?"

"Well, if I knew, it wouldn't be lost now, would it?" I snap. I know the badge is someplace in Rolfe's apartment, ripped off my blouse in the heat of groping. I shudder to remember. Why am I assuming this night will be different?

We find a table for three. "Tonight will be fun, won't it?" trills Edna, setting her tray down in a pool of ketchup. "Don't they wipe the tables here? Oh, well. Lisette says at the Festin you have to eat with your hands and the actors call you up on stage to participate in a skit. Well, they'd better not call me! I'd just plain faint away!" She crams half a cheeseburger into her cavernous mouth.

"Don't worry. They only call plants," Ellen says.

Edna swallows a huge chunk of beef. "Plants?" she gulps. "What d'you mean?"

"You know. People they've set up ahead of time. Volunteers. They'll probably get Al. He's such a dweeb!" Ellen giggles.

Edna has a milkshake moustache so I show her, in pantomime, that she needs to wipe her face. She does. Then she asks, "What's a dweeb?"

"A good actor," I say. I pick at my fish filet and wonder, does a halibut know it's going to end up like this?

★ ★ ★

Here's how I get out of going to the Festin: an hour before we're supposed to leave, I develop a crushing headache and send Ellen to get ice. "I read somewhere you're supposed to use heat," she says. "Do you want me to call down to the front desk? What's French for heating pad?"

"This is fine," I say, folding a towel to make a compress and filling it with ice. I don't feel in the least guilty about fooling her. What a bitch! How can Ma stand to have her around? "I don't think I'll make it to the banquet, though. Would you tell Lisette how sorry I am?"

"I hate to leave you like this, but I'm dying to go."

"And you should." I pat her on the hand. "I'll be okay. Really I will."

"We're going to a strip club afterwards, you know. I won't be back until way past my bedtime. Oh, Shirleen. Do you think they really take off everything? I mean, is that even allowed?"

I especially hate her when she pretends to be cute. "Oh, how would I know? I've never even been to a strip show." Which is the truth. "Go on, now. You run along. Don't even think about me. I'll be fine, as long as I stay perfectly quiet." I roll my eyes for effect.

"If you're sure..."

I nod ever so gently, so as not to incur discomfort.

"It must hurt soo much."

Will she never leave?

"If you're really sure..."

"I am."

"I wish you'd let me call for a doctor."

"No need. I have these headaches often. I know just what to do."

"Well, then, if you insist..."

"I do."

"Kiss, kiss!"

"Mm." Finally!

* * *

A half-hour later, I meet Rolfe in the lobby.

He's borrowed a friend's compact American car, a two-year-old Escort, aptly named. He's wearing a suit. His hair, shiny-clean, is tied back. And he smells delicious—some wonderful spicy *cologne pour hommes*. He takes my hand and leads me around to the passenger side. "Please," he says, and guides me into the seat. Then he walks around to the driver's side, gets in the car, and takes a moment to size me up. He grins. "You look lovely."

I believe him. I'm wearing my best dress, the one Ellen admired, and there is a glow about me, I finally saw it in the bathroom mirror. I applied two tiny dabs of perfume, my only purchase in Montréal, behind my ears, at the base of my throat, and on the insides of each wrist. Make him desire you, the ads say. No doubt Ma can bring this about by reciting a chant, but who cares how it's done as long as it works? And it's working. I see desire flaming up in Rolfe's baby-blues.

We drive out of the city under a sky that promises snow, just as Elspeth predicted.

★ ★ ★

I discover that lust makes time pass quickly.

Before long we reach our destination, Val David, which Rolfe assures me isn't far from Mont Tremblant. En route we passed a trio of towns named for female saints: Agathe, Adèle, Thérèse. I hope they're watching over me. "I hope you like this very charming inn," Rolfe says. I do. The dining room, decorated to look like a country farmhouse with wide-board floors, low-beamed ceilings, and kerosene chandeliers, is empty except for us. It's between seasons, too early for spring and too late for winter, although, the owner assures us, stubborn snow will cap the peaks through June.

When we first taste the Châteauneuf du Pape, it is 9:30. Even without alcohol to relax me I feel mellow and supple. Rolfe is very attentive. He asks my permission to order, and I give it. We dine on roast duck, and for dessert there are crêpes, my first flambé. Oh, if the wine snob could only be here, he'd faint with ecstasy over the process! I'll never forget it: the oval copper pan shining in the candlelight; the half-orange squeezed so deftly; the Cointreau and Triple-sec splashed into the pan with such abandon; the tender crêpes, folded like little napkins, then laid in a sizzling bath of butter and sugar, engulfed in flames. Afterwards, tiny gem-colored vials of cordial reflect the candles' glow.

"It's snowing," Rolfe says. "The roads are slick. I think we should stay here tonight. Do you mind, chérie?"

Desire is making a lump in my throat. I shake my head, no.

* * *

Upstairs, there's a canopy over the bed, and a puffy down quilt to ward off the chill. Rolfe lights a fire. Hearth and heart seem one. When he undresses me, I'm shaking. Cold and eager to explore this new experience, I welcome the softness of the bed and the insistence of his embrace. "Don't worry," he smiles, holding up a condom. "I am always prepared."

Always. I try not to think of the others. In a few minutes, I don't.

* * *

In the middle of the night when I wake to use the bathroom, I notice the snow is still falling heavily, and I think, good, we had to stay. There is just enough moonlight to guide my way to the w.c., where a small dish of dried lavender gives off a heady perfume. The seat is cold beneath my still-warm flesh, and there's a chain with a wooden handle that I pull to flush. I think, before tonight, I'd only had one lover.

Rolfe sleeps quietly, on his side, with his arms bent and his hands crossed loosely. I climb back into bed and face him. Now we are two separate beings, but for the instant we climaxed, we were one. I've never known it was possible to come at the same time. Hours later, my naked skin still feels like velvet.

I wonder, did Irene and Teddy ever come together? I saw them once in the kitchen, so absorbed in their lovemaking they didn't even hear me enter the room.

Rolfe licked my breasts. He wanted to consume me. When Deke sucks my nipples, I know he does it to provoke a response. One of the guys must have told him, "They love it when you suck their tits." And I do respond. But nothing like this. I was not me.

★ ★ ★

At breakfast Rolfe asks, "What time does your bus leave?"

We have been holding each other's left hands, leaving the other free to stir our café-au-lait and feed each other pieces of croissant so light and flaky they must have been baked by angels.

"Twelve-thirty." I have no sense of time. We woke early, as the sun was rising, and made love again, then slept until almost 9:00. The snow has stopped, and the roads are clear. I put on the same panties I'd worn yesterday, the first time I'd ever done so in my life. What would Ma think?

"Good. We have just enough time to get back to Montréal."

★ ★ ★

He pulls into a no-parking zone in front of the hotel and starts to get out of the car. I grab his arm. "Don't, please. I want to say goodbye here, in the shelter of the car." I'm crying. Tears are running down my cheeks and into the bodice of my dress. I'm wearing only a thin jacket, and I'm shivering. I can see members of the group standing with their suitcases in the lobby. I know I have to hurry. I wait for his kiss. "I'll never forget you," I say.

He reaches for my hand and kisses it. "I am coming to see you in Riverton, Shirley."

"Oh, no you're not. This is goodbye. Really. You have to promise me." I say this knowing he'd never come. I lean over, as far as the seat and the steering wheel will let me, and brush his cheek with my lips. "Thank you."

I run into the lobby, head down, hugging myself to keep warm, not looking back to see if Rolfe's friend's car is still there. "What the hell..." is all I hear somebody say as I pass the group.

* * *

Up in the room I see that Ellen has packed my things. "Well," she says. "I hope you had a good time. A really good time. Because you scared me to death, Shirleen. I got in at three-something and your bed was empty. No note. Nothing. Jesus! What was I to think?"

"I hadn't planned on spending the night. It was snowing, and I...we..."

"Spare me the details. Come on, we're due to load in five minutes. Do me a favor. Splash some water on your face. You're a mess. Oh. I should tell you I covered for you, big time, at breakfast. Said you were feeling better, but not up to eating. Honey, do you ever owe me one."

* * *

On the way back to Riverton, although my Walkman provides a welcome escape from the busy chatter in the bus, I can't stop thinking about Rolfe. Was the word love ever uttered by either of us? I don't think so. Neither he nor I were looking for a confession of that sort. Besides, he knows better than to risk commitment.

I know I'd never leave Deke. I'll tell him I was unfaithful. Perhaps not right away, but eventually. I don't know what the consequences will be, but I know I can't lie. My father did, and look what happened.

I've always thought Pop and I were alike. Physically, we resemble each other. We've always liked the same books, laughed at the same jokes. Ma was always the heavy. Until recently. Now she's turned into a wit, of sorts. Life of the party. She's come out of her shell. Maybe, if she'd always been as free, Dad wouldn't have fallen for Rosalie. Who knows? Speaking of falling, I hope Ma is okay. I just know she was drinking. There. I'm already worrying about my mother. Reality testing. A good sign. Means I'm getting ready for re-entry.

I'll find the right time to tell Deke.

Saying love and not meaning it. Would that have been so awful?

In the Flesh

Irene

The Palenville Mountain is a pimple by Alpine standards, but it used to seem like Everest, back in the days when my parents climbed it in their old Hudson. That jalopy would rumble and stumble its way around the hairpin curves until, inevitably, I'd get carsick. No matter how hard Ma scrubbed and sprayed, the back seat still smelled sour! We'd scale the Palenville twice a year: once when Pop took his summer vacation, and then again in the fall, for a long weekend, to see the blaze of autumn colors. Ma would get the neighbor to feed the chickens, Pop would put away his salesman's sample cases, and we'd pack the car. On these sojourns my parents stopped their fighting and acted like newlyweds, cuddling and joking and hugging and kissing, pretending to hide their affection from me. I ate it up. I'd seen enough of their brawling, heard enough of my father yelling, my mother sobbing. Pop had plenty of women on the side, which caused Ma grief. Maybe that's why I reacted so strongly to the news of Teddy and Rosalie; I'd grown up with that kind of hurt. I'd watched Ma slide into a pit of self-deprecation. Not that she was a beauty by today's standards—thin, with classic features and an air of self-assurance. She was a farm woman, tall and broad-hipped, overtly sensual; even I, a child, could feel her animal heat. But when she started comparing herself to the skimpily-clad chippies Pop picked up in bars, all she could see was that they were petite and helpless, qualities he seemed to prefer. I understand, because I've felt like that myself—clumsy, inadequate, unworthy in the face of an adversary who seems ultimately more desirable.

In recent years I've stayed away from the old haunts, the mountain-top resorts with the rolling Italian names, the Villas and the Villaggios, resort hotels my parents used to frequent. I've preferred to remember these places as they were, with a shuffleboard court on the front lawn and a big concrete swimming pool with a lifeguard who looked like Hulk Hogan. The wide, wraparound verandahs held rocking chairs that were always in motion. It seemed to me the older guests sat out there from early morning until dusk, moving only to go to the bathroom and attend meals. Sunday mornings buses would come and take the Catholics to Haines Falls, the Protestants to Tannersville. I don't remember where the Jews went on the Sabbath. Most of them probably stayed at Rosenfeld's Guest House on the Notch road, where the atmosphere was glatt Kosher.

These days on the mountain top, the villas crumble and peel and wait for the wrecker's ball to bash in their sides. I used to dream about buying one, fixing it up, filling it with the hoi polloi from the city, like in the postwar heydays. I always knew I didn't want to be a chicken rancher. The idea of being a resort owner appealed to me. I'd move all the old fogies off the porch and put them in the back where people wouldn't see them right away and think it was a rest home. I'd build a bubble to enclose the pool. That way the skiers could enjoy a dip after the slopes. I'd have Theme Nights, with costumes for rent and food to match. Even now, I get all excited when I think of it. Hey. I still could do it. Teddy could be in charge of the kitchen. Shirleen could be Hostess. Deke could keep the place looking spiffy. Junior could be the recreation director. Antoinette could plan the special events. And me? Leona Helmsley, the wealthy hôtelière they called the Queen of Mean, slide your funky prison butt over to make room for Irene.

What am I thinking? I've got a career. Shit, I've got more than I can handle keeping women across America wrinkle-free! That's my karma, baby. And I've got my mentor to thank for it: Moldred the miracle-worker. When she faxes, I jump. Which is why I'm driving up the Palenville in Vinnie's Mercedes. The car leaps ahead like a buck in rutting season, eager to reach its destination. Moldred and I agreed on a meeting place, a spot I knew would be deserted at this time of year. Just beyond Tannersville and before Hunter is a road which veers to the left, goes over a bridge that spans the Schoharie Creek, and meanders its way through the Notch; the spot where two mountain peaks dip and form a V. There, at the public campground known as Devil's Hump, Moldred and I will rendezvous.

★ ★ ★

As I pull into the now-deserted parking area I'm conscious of a nagging pain in my hip. I should be home recuperating, preparing for another marketing blitz on behalf of Forever Young. In my haste to leave I forgot to quaff my Ibuprofen. Well, Moldred'll have something that'll mask the pain. She has a bag of tricks bigger than California. I can't wait to see what she looks like! I've tried to imagine—I guess the term nowadays is visualize—a sorceress, but all I come up with is a little person with whiskers on her chin, a sort of hairy Dr. Ruth.

When was I last here? Now, in the cold, murky stillness of an early-spring afternoon, the ghosts return. I watch Shirleen blow out her birthday candles, then join her pals in a game of hide-and-seek behind the playground, in the heavily-forested area where perverts sometimes lurk. Teddy watches over his little angel while I gather the party supplies. It's a warm summer day and grownup laughter filters down from the main lodge, where somebody's celebrating an anniversary. Here, in the shelter of a gently sloping hill wrongly named for Hizzoner, warm family dramas play out each weekend.

So many years have passed. I recall when Shirleen's Brownie troop had a sleepover at the campground. One of the chaperones rolled over on a hairbrush and thought it was a porcupine. How those girls squealed! In recent months, Junior's Senior Class Picnic was held here, minus Junior. I wonder how many cherries were busted down by the pond while Ranger Rick was rounding up stragglers. Last fall Vinnie's niece married her best girlfriend on the hiking trail. Lem Stuart, the gay undertaker and Justice of the Peace, did the honors. Vinnie's sister slipped and broke her ankle and had to be carried down in a canvas sling.

It was behind Kissing Rock that Teddy proposed to me.

Sometimes it seems my whole life has been measured in outings to Devil's Hump.

And now, another milestone—my encounter with Moldred. A little woman as wide as she is tall, wearing a coarsely woven gown the color of mulberries, toddles toward me and comes to a halt several inches from the car. From beneath the hem of her heavily-petticoated skirt poke black shoes with big metal buckles. She has an enormous head topped by an unruly mass of grey hair (a wig?) on which is perched a squashed velvet cap of the type that Rembrandt's subjects wore. This style of hat seems appropriate since Moldred looks more Renaissance than twelfth century. I have to say, given her wobbly gait, she strikes me as a cross between a Russian nesting doll and a bag lady. "Hullo, Moldred of Brest!" I shout, climbing out from behind the wheel and sticking out my hand in greeting. "It's Irene of Riverton."

A paw creeps out of a sleeve to clamp my flesh. She presses. Her skin feels dry and warm and her grip is firm. "Know you!" she snaps. I expect her to speak the way she writes, mellifluously. Instead, her voice is low pitched and growly. Our hands touch, she's wearing leather gloves with little buttons. Her forearms are plump and the fabric barely stretches enough to cover her skin.

"You look wonderful, for someone who's...come such a long distance," I say, wanting to break the ice. "Not a bit wrinkled."

She bows, lowering her big head and pushing her right leg out in a curtsy. "Compliment! Thanks. Can't return it. You look kinda banged up. On the sauce? Fell in—or was it out—of a bathtub? How ordinary."

I should have guessed she'd have the ability to see and know everything. Unless Shirleen has been in contact, which I doubt. Whenever I mention Moldred, she rolls her eyes. "Ma, don't start," she says. I know she thinks I'm crazy. "Twelfth-century people do not tell twentieth-century people what to do. That's plain ridiculous." I just wish she could be here now, to see what I'm seeing.

"Learned your lesson?"

Spare me another lecture about temperance! While I was hospitalized, I thought the social worker would never shut up about my drinking. I practically had to take the pledge in order to get discharged. Of course, I know who's behind all that. My darling daughter is determined to reform me. Kids. When they're born you struggle to push them out and then they return to give you an even bigger pain!

Moldred gurgles on. "S'pose you're curious. Splendid voyage! Skipped the wars. Tiresome! Better things, like this." She reaches in her knapsack and pulls out an Italian meatball sandwich dripping with marinara. "And this!" She brandishes a dill pickle. "Absolute inspiration! Beats cucumbers. Never know what to do with 'em all. Useless in potions. Seeds make you burp."

Her syntax is clipped, as though someone had taken lawn shears and pared her sentences. I think, she didn't come all the way to make small talk about fast food, and neither did I. "So, Moldred," I say casually, like I'm talking to Soignée or Vinnie instead of the Titan of Time Travel. "You had something important to tell me? Something you had to say face to face?"

Moldred hefts her significantly squishy butt onto a picnic bench and pats a place for me to sit. "Take a load off. There. Better." She holds something up in her pudgy fingers. "Want a cupcake?"

"No, thanks." Who knows how many centuries it's flown through? We sit in silence, siblings of sorts. She swings her feet back and forth—they don't reach the ground, so what else can she do? I'm reminded of Shirleen, age six, sitting with her pals on this very same bench. Moldred seems to be enjoying the moment. She takes my hands and squeezes them, giving me no choice but to stay and listen to whatever she wants to tell me.

"So. Been having fun with Forever Young?"

I nod, wondering what she's got up her flowing sleeve. All I can see is a knobby wrist.

"But at the Craft's expense, eh? The stuff you've been doing! Cartoons and broomsticks. Plotting to get rid of the cleaning lady and the FedEx man, not to mention that poor cat. And poisoning that sweet young girl! Casting spells on Teddy! Shame on you! We don't even call that witchcraft. We don't even mention the word witchcraft because of what people will think. Witches have such a bad rep. People have turned us into caricatures that have nothing to do with our real purpose, to create harmony in ourselves and our surroundings. Have you ever heard the term Wicca?"

I notice her syntax has loosened; she's picking up momentum as she scolds, and she's stopped swinging her feet, which tells me she's absolutely serious about this. "Wicca?" I repeat. "As in furniture?" Bad pun, but I'm hoping she'll lighten up.

"Don't toy with me, Irene," she scowls. "I'm here to lecture you in earnest. You're a disgrace to the trade. Look at you. Hair all frizzed out, pointed cap, shopworn cape. Product spokesperson? Don't make me laugh. You're in your sixty-fourth year, well into your crone stage. You should be revered for your wisdom, not ridiculed for your appearance. Why, I saw you on Oprah and cringed! Sometimes I think I made an error in giving you my formula. I thought you wanted it for yourself. I never dreamed you'd share it with half the planet! And pocket the profits, to boot. Tsch, tsch. I am truly disappointed in you, Irene Richards."

I'm beginning to think I'm dealing with a Moldred impersonator. Can I ask for credentials? This is beginning to take on the characteristics of a bad dream. And to think I was looking forward to this encounter.

"Listen up, Irene. I've decided to divest Forever Young of its powers."

Now I know it's a bad dream.

"From now on, it'll be just your average bath preparation—a water softener, maybe also an emollient. In other words, a grossly overpriced, useless product, the kind that consumers spend millions on each year. You dig?"

I don't like what I'm hearing, but I dig. "So," I fume. "Is this some kind of punishment for letting things get out of hand?"

Moldred tilts back her head and laughs, revealing teeth that could do with a good cleaning. Apparently, they don't provide time-travelers with dental hygiene kits. "Punishment? No! More like a rescue. We want to get you back on track."

"We?"

"Oh, I couldn't possibly make a decision like this without support from the Grand Coven."

"Hm." I wonder, has she been brainwashed? Born again? This smacks of evangelism. "But my powers. You'll leave them intact. Right?"

"Oh, don't worry your frizzy little head. Your powers will remain essentially the same, with one exception: no dissing your fellow man and womyn. Do what ye will, an' ye harm no living thing. From now on, this will be your creed, as it is mine. You dig?"

I dig, but again, I don't like it. "I can't even get back at my enemies?"

"Evil intentions beget evil consequences. Haven't you learned this by now? In your new state, you'll achieve harmony in all phases of your life. Now isn't that better than revenge which leaves such a nasty taste in the mouth? You'll have a wonderful life."

"But I don't want a wonderful life. Not in the goody-goody sense. I want to be rich and famous. You don't get that way without being a little nasty."

"Well, from now on, you'll have to settle for being benign and blessed. And I'm talking Teddy and Rosalie here, Irene. The days of retribution are over. Oh, look at you. Pouting! Don't be glum! You'll be one with the universe! That's a kick, baby. A blast. A trip. Talk about rejuvenation. You won't need any bath crap to keep you young. Look at me. I'm seven hundred if I'm a day, but you'd never guess."

One with the universe, eh? Bullshit. All this proselytizing sounds like dull old preaching to me. And I thought Moldred was a fun, mischievous kind of person! What a downer. I hope I'm dreaming. The first pay phone I hit I'm calling Soignée, just to make sure everything is all right. Bogus bubble bath will mean lost revenue: customers will demand refunds, they'll threaten lawsuits. Of course, Moldred doesn't give a shit about that. In the twelfth century, justice was delivered by an axe.

"...and then when you've proven your worth in the service of the goddess, when you've reached the high estate of Third Degree, you'll be known as the Lady Irene. Or you can pick any name from mythology or legend. Won't that be a trip?"

Big fucking deal! The lands of Zeus and Wotan. I can think of other destinations I'd prefer. As it is, I'll probably end up in bankruptcy court. Woe is me.

I keep waiting for her to make her exit, to fade or whatever it is she does. I don't see any sign of a time coach. Should I call a taxi? Shit, I can't. Off-season, the buildings are locked. There's no access to a pay phone, and no flush toilets. The poor perverts are forced to cuddle in the woods. It's a bit cool for al fresco fondling, but I suppose they make do.

"Irene! How can you even think of buggery at a time like this?"

She reads minds! I give up. If she won't leave, I will. "Have a nice day!" I mutter, and walk away. What did I expect? You don't strike up a business arrangement with a seven-hundred-year-old kook and hope to emerge unscathed. I was naive. Damn! I locked my keys in my car!

"Irene. Look over there, at the base of the hiking trail. Isn't that your grandson with his girlfriend?"

My eyes follow Moldred's. Sure enough, Junior and Antoinette have paused to adjust their knapsacks. I'm saved! "Junior! Antoinette! Over here! It's Gram!" I yell at the top of my lungs, but they've started walking towards the parking lot. Funny, I didn't notice the truck before. Musta been too focused on Moldred. I can see Deke's gun rack through the front windshield. There's a .22 at the ready. During hunting season, he and Junior stalk small game. I useta try to snatch the entrails for my brew. Of course, that's all history. "Hey! Kids! It's me, Irene."

Moldred grabs my arm and stops me from pursuing them. "Not so fast. I'm not quite finished. I want to give you the name of a coven in your area…"

"Fuck the Coven. Junior and Antoinette are headed for their truck, and if I don't catch up with them, I'll lose everything I've ever really wanted, not to mention a ride into town to borrow that gizmo to open my car door."

"Don't say fuck. It doesn't become you," Moldred admonishes primly, sounding like Shirleen. "Listen up. In the Yellow Pages under Meditation Instruction you'll find a listing for the coven in your area. The third-degree witch is a friend of mine. Lady Fortuna." Her voice fades. In an instant, she's gone, and I'm left standing in the parking lot wondering how I'm going to avoid Wicca. "I'll be watching!" she whispers from wherever. She will, too. What a *nudge*!

"Gram!" shouts Junior. "Hey, honey! It's Gram!"

* * *

"So, Mrs. Witchards." What happened to Auntie Iwene? Antoinette sits across from me, perched on a built-in sofa in their homey sectional at the Catskill Trailer Park, sedate, aproned, very much the little homemaker.

"Call me Irene, honey."

"Irene. You never did tell us how you happened to be at Devil's Hump in the middle of April."

"I was, uh, just reminiscing. I used to come up here a lot when I was little. My parents vacationed at the Villa. I've gotta lotta memories wrapped up in this area."

"You used to stay at the Villa? That old wreck?"

"It used to be a palace."

"Well, it's a dump now. Isn't that right, Junie? More tea, Irene?"

Junie? Yech. "Please, dear. Delicious! Herbal? I thought so. Soothing! Much better than caffeinated." When I hold out my cup my hand shakes. No wonder. Been an eventful day. I look around. Cozy enough. Still, Rosalie would have a bird. Her darling daughter shacking up in a trailer park!

Junior looks okay. His hair's much longer, and he dresses like a hippie—old jeans blown out at the knee and a lumberjack's shirt and shit-kickers—but he's still ruggedly handsome like his dad. Hopefully smarter, though. Certainly smarter. My genes, after all. "Look at me. Where are my manners? I wanted to take you kids out for a good meal."

Antoinette jumps up. "Oh, no, we couldn't let you…it wouldn't be…"

Junior interrupts. "There's a place we like…" he says hopefully.

He looks skinny to me, like he could use a good meal. She takes my cup and starts to put it in the sink, then suddenly turns and runs into the bathroom where she vomits.

Junior clears his throat. "They say it's normal, but it's pretty gross. She does it a lot."

"A baby!" I guess. "How wonderful! Have you told your folks?" I'm thinking, Shirleen and Deke will be happy; Antoinette's parents, less so.

"Not yet."

"You'll have to, you know."

"I know. We will. When the time is right." He fidgets, first scraping his heels against the legs of the chair, then cracking his knuckles, a habit he inherited from Deke.

"A baby will make everything all right."

"You think?"

"Sure. Babies always do."

"Well, then." For the first time, he smiles. Christ, he's beautiful! In his face I see his mother. Tears well. Time to exit?

The little mother returns, pale but smiling, and tells Junior, "Don't worry, I'm okay." To me she says, "Thanks. It'd be nice to go to dinner. We haven't been out in ages. You probably want to get down the mountain before dark, so we should go soon." She hands me my jacket and twirls a handsome cape around her shoulders, an emerald green boiled-wool circle ringed with folk-motif embroidery.

Deja vu: it's Rosalie's cape, the one Teddy brought her from Austria. "A friend bought it," Ro said demurely when I showed her the cuckoo clock he'd given me.

★ ★ ★

The restaurant is a fondue hut at the base of Hunter Mountain. Our window seat faces the slopes, where the last of the spring skiers are using up the dwindling patches of snow thrown on the slopes at midnight by gasping machines. I order a carafe of wine. "How many glasses?" asks the waitress, a plump older woman in dirndl.

"Two," says Antoinette. "Whoops. Excuse me."

While she's gone, I lean on Junior. "Don't you think it's time you made your peace with your parents?"

He shrugs, pokes his fork into the pot and winds a wand of cheese big enough to swab the throat of an ox. "What good would it do? They'd only try to break us up."

"With a baby on the way? I doubt it."

"You're not eating, Gram."

"I want to talk first."

"How's Gramps?"

"He's good. Better than good. Lives by himself, has a job. You wouldn't believe the change."

"You see him, then?"

"From time to time."

"You two make up?"

"You might say so."

"What do you say?"

"I say Yes." No point in dwelling on specifics such as how I can never really totally forgive him. Besides, now that I can't make mischief any more, what's the point in holding a grudge? An' ye harm no one. I have Moldred to thank. Antoinette returns from the bathroom, looking pale, but copacetic. "Oh, here's the little mother. Sit down, honey. Tell me, what have you two been doing with yourselves? I mean, aside from the obvious."

She blushes. "Winter, Junior worked maintenance at the Ski Bowl. Soon he'll start leading mountain bike tours. I've been waitressing. We manage okay. And you? Whatever happened with Forever Young? Somebody told Junior they saw you on television. Wow. That's awesome!"

"It has been fun. But I think I'm due for a change."

"How so?" Junior pours himself another glass of wine, offers me some, I decline. I've been on the wagon, more or less, since my, ah, episode. I just wish Moldred had given me credit for some strength of character.

"Oh, I'm not so young, you know. And beauty care products are very competitive. I've been thinking of selling the business to Soignée, my associate. She's a real go-getter." I surprise myself with this news. Not a bad idea, considering the bleak future mapped out by my mentor.

"But what would you do? After life on the fast track, you'd have to find something. Otherwise you'd die of boredom."

How wise the young. She's right, of course. It's hard for me to imagine life without entrepreneurship, though I certainly existed before. If you can call that existing. I look at my watch. "It's getting late, kids. You stay, take your time. Have dessert. Here." I hand Junior more than enough money to buy three dinners. "A little something extra."

They each hug me in turn, but it's Junior's embrace that warms me to my bones.

★ ★ ★

Fearlessly I navigate the Palenville's downslope, feeling giddy with power as I bring the road to its knees, alternately coasting and braking as I plunge back to sea level, in this case a muddy creek named for a Mohawk warrior. My heart, lighter with the news of the impending birth, would of course be even lighter if I could share the happy news with my daughter and her husband. They could use a distraction. My witch's (insert Wiccan) intuition tells me Shirleen's been up to something in Montréal, and, knowing her, she'll come right out with it and break poor ole Deke's valiant spirit. Not that it isn't good to be forthright; I raised her that way. It's all in the telling. The secret of cushioning the blow lies in the way it's delivered, in the solar plexus, where muscles have been conditioned to receive a punch. Deke, a boxing buff, told me that.

I could break a confidence and tell them where Junior and Antoinette are living. I could tell them about the baby. I'd risk losing Junior for a while, but it might be worth it.

Should I?

This is why people pray for guidance.

★ ★ ★

Moldred left me a little book, Wiccan Rituals. Following the directions, I make a shrine. I center a statue of the goddess (Minnie from Disneyworld will have to do) and surround her with candles. I sprinkle salt. I spill wine. I chant: Oh Minnie, Goddess of Family Good Times, what should I do? I smile at her. I giggle. I can't help feeling silly.

Minnie smiles back at me, her white-gloved arms akimbo, her perky polka-dotted skirt atwirl, her bulbous party shoes reflecting the white frills of her underpants.

The answer comes floating back to me: Do what ye will, an' ye harm no living thing.

★ ★ ★

The McClure household is dark, except for a light in the living room and another in the hall. Here's where it all started, the casting of dark spells, and here's where it will end, with the bringing of good news. I push the front doorbell, and wait. Nothing. In a few minutes I give up and drive home.

★ ★ ★

"Where have you been?" Vinnie meets me at the door, her eyes wide, her look wild. "All hell's been breaking loose! I've had three calls from Saks, two from Bonwit's, and Neiman Marcus is faxing like crazy. They all say their customers are claiming the bubble bath is bogus! I had to tell them we'd refund their money. What else could I do? Say something. Anything. Jesus, Irene. You weren't here. What else could I do?"

"Whoa. Slow down." I step inside, remove my jacket. I'm amazed at how calm I am. But forewarned is forearmed, as they say. Vinnie, on the other hand, is completely unprepared for disaster. "Of course, you did the right thing," I soothe. "You always do. That's why I picked you for my partner." Poor thing, she's been under such stress. I almost feel guilty.

"But what could have gone wrong?"

"A bad batch. Poor ingredients. Lack of faith. I dunno. Maybe it's time we call it quits. Get out of this crazy business."

"What? Are you sick?"

"I never felt better. It's just that, well, the pressures of running an outfit like this, they're all getting to be too much. Fess up, Vin. Haven't you ever thought of chucking it all?

"Well, I…"

"Now, a younger person could handle it. Take Soignée, for instance."

"You're not suggesting…"

"We should sleep on it, of course."

"Oh, my, I…"

"Be a love. Run me a tub. There's a box of Mr. Bubble somewhere in the closet. Use that. Just don't use…"

"Gotcha." Vinnie, glad as always to be given a chore, runs upstairs to do my bidding. Most of all, I'll miss having minions. However, I gotta admit Lady Irene has a nice ring to it.

* * *

Ten o'clock and still no word from Shirleen. Should I call? No harm in that.

"Yes?" Deke, mournful, sounds half-asleep.

"Sorry to bother. Shirleen get back?"

"She's in bed."

"I wake you?"

"Yeah. S'all right."

"Goodnight, then."

"Mm."

* * *

First thing the next morning, I pick up the receiver. "Shirleen?"

"Ma. Christ, it's only 7:00! Are you okay? Elspeth told me about your accident. Is that what this is all about?"

"I'm fine. I have to talk to you. Is later this morning okay? Say, ten? I'll bring donuts."

"No food! I musta gained five pounds on the trip."

"Okay, no food. I'll see you later."

* * *

She looks wonderful. Younger, shinier. Must be a man. I'm dying to know, yet a tad afraid, for Deke's sake. He wouldn't forgive easily. "Honey. How good to see you!"

"Yeah," she says listlessly. "Same here. Oh," her mood picks up. "I brought you something." She runs in the other room and comes back with a little box. "It's a special charm. To ward off evil. I found it in this little store near the hotel."

I open the box and pull off a small square of cotton to reveal a tiny, enameled cross on a gold chain. "How lovely!" Tears come, though I don't quite know why; religious icons have never been my style. Still, there's an endearing quality to the gesture. I can't deny I'm moved.

"Can you stay for a while?" she asks.

"Sure." I turn away and wipe my eyes. There. In control again.

"Oh, Ma! I've done something stupid!"

How long has it been since I've taken her into my arms and said the words a mother should say to her daughter? "There, there. It'll be all right. You'll see. There's no wrong that can't be undone."

"You think?" A tiny uplifting of the corners of her mouth promises a smile, Junior's smile.

"I know. Now put on some water for tea, and we'll talk this thing out. And I've got something to tell you."

Back to Basics

Shirleen

These days I sleep in Junior's old room, in his narrow bed beneath the shrine where I worship, the shelf that holds his athletic trophies. It's a far cry from a feather bed in Val David, that nest of bliss that landed me in this mess. "How was your day, hon?" I ask Deke, who slouches across from me at the kitchen table where we've eaten our weekday dinners for the past umpteen years. According to my support group, the rest of him is mired in the mud of self-pity where cuckolded husbands gather to lick their wounds. "Pardon me?" These days I invent his responses: I said, You'd like that, wouldn't you? You'd like me to pardon you. Well, fuck you, girl! My attitude is, let him say something, even if it's nasty. For weeks he's shunned me for making him the laughingstock of the town. If only I had a scarlet *A* embroidered on my sweatshirt! I'd have the benefit of being publicly humiliated for my crime. That would make us even. "Seconds, hon?" I've made his favorite, American Chop Suey. He usually cleans two heaping platefuls, but tonight that jumble of macaroni, chopped beef, and tomato sauce sits lonely in a sea of white, unforked. No thanks, bitch. I'll eat with the boys down at Bugsy's. "Chococrunch pie for dessert," I chirp, hoping to tempt him out of his slump. But how can I? His heart's been broken, and I'm to blame.

The doorbell rings. (I'll get it, honey; don't you bother your poor pussy-whipped self.) It's Biff from next door, come to pick up Deke for bowling. Biff doesn't look me in the eyes, doesn't even stare at my tits like he has for umpteen years. I can read his mind: because of what I've done to Deke, Men's League will never be the same. "He ready?" Biff grunts in Tonto-speak, the way big boys talk.

Deke is already out the door, warming up the seat in Biff's Bronco where the motor is still running. They want a fast getaway. Deke misses his truck. He used to keep his bowling stuff in a canvas case behind the driver's seat, at the ready. Now that Junior has the truck and we share a car, Deke has to remember to take gear out of the front closet each Thursday night. Bummer.

"Here, Hon." I walk out to the thrumming car, bag in hand. Neighbors flick their lights even though it's not dark. Everyone wants a good, clear view of the brazen hussy.

Later I'll dump the pie in the garbage, eat a pint of Triple Ripple Fudge, and paint my nails. TV is good on Thursdays.

★ ★ ★

The next day I visit Pop and seek solace for my sin. "Why did you tell Deke?" he wants to know. "Didn't you realize you'd be asking for trouble? I mean, the man's got his pride, honey."

"I guess I can't expect you to understand the virtue of honesty," I say bitterly, thinking, they all stick together. "Keeping secrets from Ma was your specialty."

"Ah, but that was different!" I feel funny hearing him allude to Rosalie since we've never really discussed that episode in his life. A part of me wishes we didn't have to get into it now. Still, I need to hear what he has to say. "And you only slept with this guy once? Hell, honey, nobody's perfect. Why, I bet Deke has slipped a few times." Oh, yeah. Come to think of it, there was that office temp named April, 38-17-38, who took dictation while Elspeth was out for six weeks recuperating from her hysterectomy. Bet the bowling boys had a few choice remarks to make about her. "'Course, he'd deny it." Like you did, Pop? Ma had to hire a private eye, for Chrissake. I look at it this way: I saved Deke the trouble.

"Well, if Deke ever lied about something like that, I'd know it. He's a lousy liar."

"So. You'd rather have him tell you the truth, even if it hurt you deeply."

"Yes." Would I? "Yes, I would."

"Put yourself in his shoes."

"Don't think I haven't."

"Give yourself a break, Shirleen. You've been a good wife and mother. Why, I bet in all the years you've been married, you've never even thought about having an affair."

Well, he's right, sort of. I mean, I've maybe thought about it, but I've never actually done anything. Until now. I blame the setting. Here in Riverton, I'd never have the guts. But there, in Quebec Province, with the snow falling and the crêpes flambéing and the wine flowing…

"Earth to Shirleen! I said, I'm going into the catering business and I could use an associate. Interested?"

"Ask Ma. She's the tycoon in the family. Oh, by the way. She's given up Forever Young."

"Mm-hm. Read it in the *Wall Street Journal.*"

"Ma says it's all Moldred's fault." Pop draws a blank. "Moldred. Ma's twelfth-century mentor." He still looks puzzled. "Ma's gotten very…eccentric. You musta noticed something."

"The way she dresses?" he asks innocently.

"Oh, much more than that. She thinks she's a witch! Did I ever tell you about last Halloween? Jeez. Talk about bizarre!"

Pop looks sad and reflective. "She really hasn't been the same since the trial. All my fault, y'know. I probably pushed her over the edge."

"Oh, Pop. That was so long ago. You can't blame yourself for everything that's gone wrong. What was it you told me? Forgive and forget, and if you can't forget, get on with your life anyway."

He smiles. "Did I say that? How wise. Well. Now you have to heed my advice! Get on with things!" He opens his briefcase. "Take a look at what I've planned so far." He hands me brochures, press releases, menus. "Of course, you'll have your own ideas, and I'll be receptive. We'll make a great team." He extends his hand. "How about it?"

★ ★ ★

Deke and I are trying to work things out.

Our counselor is Dr. Diaz, new to the local marriage therapy scene. At the beginning of our first session, he makes a few notes in a folder, leans back in his E-Z Exec swivel chair, tents his hands, and raises his eyebrows. Apparently, the rest is up to us. "Tell me why you're here," he prompts.

"I wish I knew," Deke says mournfully. "I didn't run away to Montréal to have fun. I stayed here and kept the ole home fires burning!" He glares at me and folds his arms, an accusing posture he's perfected.

"All right, Donald!"

"Nobody calls him Donald," I interject. "His name is Deke."

"All right, Deke! That's very good. We're here to let our feelings out! But what do you mean by having fun?"

Deke doesn't answer.

I sit here feeling raw, a cured fish deprived of my scales and rubbed with salt. Exhibit A for adulteress. After a few endless minutes I can't stand it anymore. "Go for it, Deke. Tell us. What's your idea of fun?"

He laughs, a lowdown dirty sound that cuts me to the bone and makes me dread what he's going to say. "Fucking. That's fun. Or it useta be fun. I guess for her, up there with him, it musta been fun."

My face is on fire. I think I'm gonna explode. Please, guys. Don't ask me to talk about it. I may cry, thinking I'll never know such happiness again.

"Was the fucking fun, Shirleen?" Dr. Estranged Love asks.

I tuck my chin into the loose, fuzzy neck of my sweater. If I were a turtle, I'd be inside my shell. "I don't have to answer that."

"Oh, yes you do," Deke says. "We're supposed to be completely honest in here, remember?"

"That's right!" beams Diaz, proud of his newest pupil.

All right, guys. You asked for it. I jump out of my chair and slam my fists against the desk, which startles both of them. "Oh, we're gonna play hardball, are we? Okay. You want to know if it was fun? It was more than fun. It was terrific. I've never had an orgasm like that! Rolfe really knows how to fuck!"

"Excellent!" Dr. Diaz says, leaning forward in his chair. "Here. Have a Kleenex. The both of you. Take your time." He's grinning so hard I can see his molars. I bet it usually takes three, four sessions before he sees results like this.

"I have a handkerchief," Deke says, blotting his eyes. "Wanna use it? Uh, don't worry, it's clean."

"Thanks," I say, knocking the box of tissues onto the floor. Of course, it's clean! I did the white wash yesterday. On Monday. Like always.

★ ★ ★

Forty minutes later, heading home, my head pounding from all the emoting, I still feel weighed down with guilt. I guess it'll take more than one session to purge my feelings. The problem right now is, I simply do not know what to say to Deke, who simply does not know what to say to me. In the car, the air we breathe is polluted with failed communication.

We're about a mile from our house when he pulls over to the curb in front of Junior's old school. He shuts off the ignition and leans forward, arms on the steering wheel. "He woulda graduated this June. In August, he woulda gone to State to play ball. I think about that a lot, ya know, Shirleen. Sometimes I think our troubles began that first weekend Antoinette visited."

"Yeah?"

"Yeah." Unpredictably, he laughs. "The fish. Remember how it smelled? God, I thought something had died in the kitchen."

"Well, it had!" Thinking about poor Frisky makes me laugh, then cry, then laugh again. "Poor kitty! Falling into Ma's putrid stew! Can you imagine?"

"I never could stand that cat."

"He was Junior's pet. Remember the day he brought him home? I had to say yes. Especially after Tuffy died."

"Don't remind me. I ran him over, backing up. Remember? God, it was awful. Had to take the poor mutt out in the backyard and shoot him. I tried to explain how it was an act of compassion, but Junior wouldn't talk to me for days."

"Rest in peace, Tuffy." Remembering, I cry. But black humor keeps intruding. "That dog just sat there while you mowed him down."

"Yeah. I had to prop him up to get a good shot." We both howl with laughter. Tears gush, making our faces shine in the light thrown from a lamp post in the high school parking lot. After a bit, Deke says, "Hey. Wanna go out for dinner?"

"Sure. Oh, wait. I'm a wreck. Look at me! My face's probably all swollen from crying."

"Poor baby." For the first time in weeks, he touches me, cuffs my chin with his hand, a love tap left over from the early years of our marriage. "We'll go someplace dark, where nobody'll see us." He stiffens. "Like the place you went with…" Turning ugly, he slaps me. "Cunt!" he yells, then, softening, "Oh, Christ, Shirleen. I'm sorry."

* * *

I'm not a religious person, but tonight I get down on my knees beside our bed, the way we used to teach Junior to say his prayers, and I thank God for giving me a husband like Deke. That slap was nothing. Other men might have put a gun to their wives' heads. Right after he hit me, I felt a kind of relief, almost as if I needed to be punished.

My support group would never understand.

Later, we cuddle. Sort of. Well, he puts an arm around my waist and I don't pull away. I'd say that's progress. Diaz would be proud.

★ ★ ★

Early the next morning, Ma barges into my kitchen dragging an empty large-capacity garbage sack. She dumps the leftover sludge from Deke's mug and refills it with her own favorite mix of one-third coffee, two-thirds half-and-half. "Anything for Catholic Charities?" she asks between gulps. "Salvation Army? Bundles for Bosnia? I'm cleaning out my closets. Divesting myself of my worldly goods. Starting over. Simplicity. Humility. The new watchwords." Her jacket, a wild-hued patchwork quilt that fits her like a sausage casing, gaps broadly at her chest. "Oh, by the way, speaking of new—I'm changing my name. From now on, call me just plain Cybele."

"Well," I say, sponging up the cream Ma's dribbled on my counter and thinking there's nothing plain about a name like that, "what brought this on?"

She rolls her eyes. "The coven, silly. I'm preparing to enter."

"Ah, yes. The coven." I wait for her to elucidate.

"We take vows: poverty, chastity, obedience. That sort of stuff. I told you last week. Oh, well, I guess you've had other things on your mind. How is married life, anyway? Back to normal? All kissypoo and huggums again? I hope so. Deke's a sweet man. Why you would risk your marriage for a one-night stand with some flea-bitten Canuck Casanova, I'll never understand."

"Ma. Please."

"Okay, okay. Forgive me for living!" She starts nosing around in the frig. Hey, make yourself at home, Ma. Last week's muffins catch her eye. She pops two in the toaster oven, then turns to face me. "I just had to have my little say. Now I'll shut up."

Right. "Tell me about these new friends of yours."

"My sisterhood, the Daughters of Felicity? I'm moving in with them next week. Wonderful group!"

"Does Vinnie know?"

"Of course! She's coming, too." The toaster bell rings. She halves the warm muffins, then slathers each surface with butter. Apparently, nobody's warned her about cholesterol. If they did, she probably wouldn't pay any attention.

I think of the two wealthy women shedding their possessions and going to live like monks. What will become of Vinnie's collection of furs, so un-PC yet lush, some so new their price tags are still attached? If Ma has her way, there'll be homeless people scattered across the globe who'll be mighty warm this winter, thanks to Vinnie's vow of poverty. I can't help thinking, though, that Ma and Vinnie are making a snap decision they'll regret later. The car, for instance. You just don't dump a luxury vehicle into a used clothing bin. "What about the Mercedes? Surely you're not giving that away."

"Oh, no! Well, not to just anybody. We're donating it to the coven. They can always use a second car. For occasional trips."

"I can just see the bunch of you riding around in your witches' garb in that ritzy chariot of yours."

"Very funny. I can see you don't understand." She takes a deep breath, preparing to lecture a three-year-old. "For starters," she says slowly, "we don't wear hokey outfits. We're Wiccans, members of a dignified religious order, not broom jockeys!" Got it, her eyes say. Reflexively, I nod. "We wear regular clothing, except for rituals, when we celebrate in costume," she continues. "Nothing outrageous. All very tasteful. Of course, for the summer Sabbat, some go skyclad." I gasp. "Oh, don't give me that look, Shirleen. We stay in our own backyard, which is ringed with tall shrubs so no one can see in."

"That's reassuring." I'm thinking, if Ma gets arrested this time, I'm not posting bail. Why can't my mother be like everybody else's? It seems I've been asking this question my entire life. I see she's refilled her cup. "More sugar, Ma?"

"No, thank you very much! I've given up sweets. My body is my temple."

"Of course." Harmless enough, all this. Better than before, when she got busted for stealing a neighbor's car. I can certainly live with the idea of a coven, but others may have trouble accepting her new lifestyle. Which leads me to ask, "Have you spoken with Pop recently?"

"Not since he came to visit me in the hospital. Oh! That reminds me. I should tell him I'm moving. After all, we're still married."

Minor point. "I was sort of hoping you two would get back together," I say wistfully. "I don't suppose…"

She pats my shoulder there, there. "Honey."

"Well, you can't blame a daughter for hoping…"

"You always liked happy endings, things tied up neatly."

"Even though I know that's not how life really is."

"You used to say, 'read the happy after part, Mommy.' Remember?"

"Mm. And you would."

"Again, and again."

"You were a good mother."

"I tried to be."

I reach out and draw her to me. "Give us a hug. There. Like old times."

She wipes her eyes with the back of her hand. I know better than to offer a tissue; accepting it would be an admission of vulnerability. She likes me to think she's a tough cookie, but I know better. Now she'll change the subject. "You started to say something about your father." What better way to rid the moment of sentiment than to mention Pop?

"He's starting a catering business. Manzmeals. For the guy who doesn't want to cook for himself. He showed me a menu full of clever copy. There's even a Tex-Mex casserole called Macho Nacho. Just what the *Monday Night Football* crowd needs, I told Pop."

"Well, good for him!"

"Look at the two of you. You're amazing!"

Her eyes widen. As if she doesn't know. "We are?"

"Well, sure! You with Forever Young, Pop with Manzmeals. A couple of senior entrepreneurs. I'm proud of you both."

"Well," she sighs, "that's all behind me now. I'm going to focus my energies in a new direction, one that's in harmony with my surroundings. There! How does that sound?"

Like someone else's mother. "Fine. It sounds lovely."

"You could join, too."

That would really send Deke into orbit—his wife a Wiccan. "Actually, I've been thinking of helping Pop. What do you think?"

"I think you should, if you want to. What does Deke think?"

"He says I should do whatever makes me happy."

"Within reason!"

"Ma."

"Sorry. What about the kids? Will you still have time to visit them? And when the baby comes. Won't you want to be free to help out?"

"Well, I guess Rosalie will be on first call, since she's Antoinette's mother. Did I tell you the kids want a home birth?"

"Good for them! When the time comes, we'll say prayers. Oh, that reminds me. Their handfasting is coming up next month."

"Huh?"

"Their wedding ceremony! It'll be at the coven, of course. You and Deke are invited, and Rosalie and Maxwell. Teddy, too, of course."

Rosalie and Teddy in the same room? I look at her in wonder. So. She's really let go of her anger. Hm. This...handfasting is going to be something.

"We're thinking of combining the wedding ceremony with the ritual for Hallowmas."

"Say what?"

"Sorry. Halloween."

Wonderful. Trick or treat. A different take on the wedding vows. "What do Junior and Antoinette say?"

"It was their idea."

"Well, then. A Hallowmas handfasting it will be. I wouldn't miss it for the world, Ma." I'm thinking, what a woman, this mother of mine. She's already converted the younger generation to Wicca. Does Rosalie know? There go her dreams of a big church wedding. The final round. Irene strikes a blow. Her opponent is down for the count.

★ ★ ★

Sunday. Grateful for a beautiful late-spring day when the sun is shining and the air smells sweet, we shed our church-going duds and picnic at Devil's Hump. "So," says Deke, using his pocket knife to pry the cap off a Molson, "When's this baby due?"

We're floating on a sea of blanket. Ham and cheese sandwich halves form a small deck between us while fore and aft sit Tupperware lifeboats holding chips and dip. "The end of October."

He tips a bottle into his mouth and gulps some beer. When he's had enough, there's a sucking sound to mark the separation of lip and glass. "Isn't that when this Hallo-hand business is supposed to take place?"

"Um, yes."

"Wow. What if everything comes together?"

"I think Ma's hoping it will. Full moon and all."

"Jeez." Tip, gurgle, suck, burp. He shakes his head, his way of saying he doesn't understand it all. "I guess it'll all work out, huh?"

I'm thinking, Deke's come a long way. A year ago, he'd have put a stop to all this. But now that he's mellowed, whatever the kids want is okay, and rather than interject my own doubts, I point to a land-mark, the well-trodden hump. "See that hill up there? My second-grade Brownie troop had a sleepover behind that knoll, and one of the mothers rolled over on a hairbrush and thought it was a porcupine. You shoulda heard us scream."

He rolls his eyes. "I've heard that story before, Shirleen."

"Sorry. Did I tell you the one about…"

"Hey. Wanna hike up there, to the old shelter? Grab the blanket."

"What're we going to need that for?"

"Just grab it. Hey. You're blushing. No, don't cover your face. I like it when you blush." We start up the hill. My heart pounds, pounds, pounds. I don't know what to expect. We haven't made love since the night before I left for Montréal. Will I be able to relax on the floor of the cabin where Billy Waldon and I made out during junior high school? Plus, I'm shivering. It's too cold in the mountains of New York in May for love.

The cabin smells of woodsmoke; the charred remains of a fire somebody set as an enhancement to intimacy—cross-country skiers stopping in for a quickie? Deke spreads the blanket on the floor. He looks at me. What do I see in his eyes? Hurt. Disappointment. Expectation. Love?

Help me, honey. I've forgotten. How do we begin?

Not a Moment Too Soon

Irene & Shirleen

Irene

"**W**ipe that junk off your face," Moldred commands, referring to the eye shadow, mascara, foundation, and blush smuggled into the covenhouse. Artifice isn't encouraged here; there's a little embroidered sign in the bathroom advising, "If nature didn't give it to you, it wasn't meant to be." Horse puckey. I say, if there's anything a woman can do to make herself look better, then she should do it. But who am I to argue with Lady Fortuna, the third-degree witch who's in charge? And Moldred's so much older, I figure she must know more than I. So here, with one swipe of a cold-cream-logged tissue, goes a hundred dollars' worth of makeup. "Better," she assesses, swishing her toes in my top bureau drawer where I've secreted my silken skivvies—briefs, tap pants, camisoles, the last vestiges of my lavish life with Vinnie (who by the way lasted only one week in this nunnery.) "Now you look like an initiate," Moldred croons. "Now you look like a proper witch. Let those wrinkles breathe! Be proud of those age spots. Don't hide them under a veneer of camouflage squeezed from the glands of tortured animals! Look at me: Do I try to hide so much as a second of my seven hundred and twenty years?"

I look at my mentor's face, that map of wrinkles, boils and eczematous patches. "You don't look a day over six hundred," I say brightly, stashing my Estée Lauder beauty bonus under the mattress. Impossible to tell when it'll come in handy, like prison cigarettes, for barter. Other, younger initiates find it hard to give up the old ways.

"I saw that. Give it here! And don't tell me you're saving it to give Shirleen on her birthday." She grabs the pouch and stuffs it in her knapsack. Suddenly I see the face of my kindergarten teacher. At the end of the day Miss Gimbley's purse would be bulging with lunchbox contraband—licorice laces, chocolate jelly beans, Turkish delight. We kids were smarter than she guessed. We knew she was stealing. We figured she'd get her comeuppance: teeth rotting in Hell. "Come. Let me help you with your robe," Moldred says, sweet again, no longer the classroom ogre. My beauty bonus sits on the bureau, forgotten. I guess when you're nearly a thousand years old, you don't have to account for mood swings. "It's almost time for the Ritual to begin." She hops up on the bed to smooth the folds of the gown Shirleen made for the big occasion. Not only does tonight herald my formal entry into the coven, but we're celebrating Hallowmas and Junior and Antoinette's handfasting as well. A big night! If I have any doubts about my future as a Wiccan, I have absolutely no reservations about Junior and Antoinette getting married, with her baby due any minute. "This is a lovely garment, Irene. Much too fancy, really, for an initiate." She stands on tiptoes, pulling the shimmering fabric gently over my head, smoothing the shoulders, arranging the folds. She ties the silver cord around my waist and fastens the ceremonial dagger, knotting the rope to one side. "There now. Look in the mirror. What do you see?"

"I see the goddess within," I fib, parroting our Handbook. What I really see is an old hag decked out for Halloween. "I see the one true light of the universe." If she could hear me, my mother would die. "Christ is the one true light," I'd hear her chant as she kicked manure from her boots. "He heals the sick at heart and mends the bodies of the afflicted souls." She fed the chickens to the cadence of the hymns she sang. I can still hear her voice accompanied by the chunk of the metal cup into the grain and the swish of the feed as it scattered on the shed floor. "Rock of Ages chunk cleft for me, swish let me hide chunk my flesh in thee swish..."

So, what's the daughter of a hen-householder doing in a coven of hags? My hair, which I had colored for my Forever Young personal appearance tours, is kinky and grey and sticks out all over the place, forming a devilish halo. There are hairs growing out of my chin. My nails, worn and sullied from gardening, betray my lowly status as laborer. Next month I get to work in the kitchen peeling potatoes, washing dishes—chores I thought I'd put behind me when I became an entrepreneur. In my initial interview, Lady Fortuna neglected to mention domestic servitude.

At one point my mother wanted to enter a convent, but Daddy rescued her. She once told me she didn't put up much of a struggle; maybe she figured marrying him was as good as tying the knot with God. Well, I'm taking a big step here, enlisting in Wicca, but nobody's rushing in to stop me from spending the rest of my life with a bunch of weirdos. Where is my protector? He's gone into catering. Too busy stuffing olives, carving ice. In the old days (my faux-witch foray into spell-casting, just a year ago today though so much has happened it seems like ten) I'd've conjured someone to bail me out.

"Don't even think of it," cautions Moldred, so deft at mind-reading she makes me shiver. "That's all in your past. This is your chance to make a new start. Remember?"

Shirleen

It's not at all what I imagined, this covenhouse: white clapboards, welcome sign, middle-class neighborhood, shrubs neatly trimmed and flower beds blanketed with mulch. The fleet of mid-size cars in the driveway could belong to members of the local PTO or MADD. Instead they belong to neopagan worshippers, Wiccans, and my mother's about to enter the fold. Pop keeps saying it's not too late, she could change her mind, even at the last minute—and even afterwards, she might decide to leave. Anytime she wants, he reassures me. But I wonder, if she leaves, will they return her worldly goods, or will they turn her out with just her witch's robe? And where will she go? Back to our place? Oh, God help me, I simply can't.

"What do we do now?" Deke asks. How forlornly handsome he is in his new end-of-the-season clearance suit which is really not warm enough for the end of October but which fits him so well I made him wear it anyway. I'm wearing what the fashion experts would term a casually elegant trans-seasonal outfit, a long-pleated skirt and fitted top, with short jacket to match. It is, after all, our son's wedding. We're standing in the hallway, waiting for the ceremony to begin. Somewhere inside, Junior and Antoinette are being prepared. Whoever heard of a handfasting? Ma says people get married every day in Las Vegas wedding chapels, and this is at least as legal as that, so I guess we're safe. And not a moment too soon! Antoinette is ready to burst. I can hardly believe it—I'll be a grandma when most of my friends are still having last-but-not least babies. Deke moans, "Jeez, I feel funny. Halloween, being with a bunch of Witches gives me the creeps, Shirleen."

"Shh. They're Wiccans," I remind him. "It's a religious order. Think of them as Lutherans, or Baptists. And try to think of this as All Saint's Day, not Halloween."

"Call it what you like, it's still ugga-bugga to me." He pulls a wad of Kleenex from his pocket and honks. "That incense goes straight to my sinuses."

I peer out the front windows as a black stretch limo pulls up to discharge its passenger, a very large woman leaning heavily on the chauffeur's arm as she exits. As she approaches, I begin to discern, among the various folds of her face, the smaller features of a formerly thin, former acquaintance. "Rosalie's here, Deke." I whisper. I grow weak at the thought of her and Ma duking it out over the tofu. And if it's true that the initiates carry daggers, Ma's had better be fake. "I'm going to tell Ma she's here. Or rather, she's sort of here. She's sort of everywhere, really."

Into the inner sanctum I venture on tiptoes, but Ma's not in the heavily-incensed parlor, where several somber-faced gentlemen in black robes are conferring; not in the kitchen, where Pop is scurrying to put the final touches on his ice sculpture, his version of the happy couple in profile (faces only); not in the meeting room where Lady Fortuna is lighting votives and chanting something that sounds like sons of bitches, sons of bitches, while snorting smoke from her nostrils. I thought cigarettes were banned. Well. I guess when you're the head dragon, you can do pretty much as you please. Finally, I knock on the door of the room labelled Womyn. "Ma. You in there? I gotta talk to you. Now!"

The door opens and out she drifts, my mother the Wiccan. "You look lovely," I say, surprised by how much I mean it. The black velvet robe offsets her gray hair and pale skin. She looks regal, like the dark queen in Snow White, only more forgiving. "But listen. I gotta tell you..."

"Rosalie's here. I know," she says, patting my hand reassuringly. "Don't look so worried. What were you expecting, a catfight?"

"Well, uh," I stammer, suddenly embarrassed. "You gotta admit."

She flutters her arms to reveal the dagger entwined in her belt. It looks real enough to me. She removes it, flashes it around.

"Ma. Put that away. You're making me nervous."

"Oh, that. History. You don't have to worry. I'm not out for blood anymore." She cackles, a silly sound that sends chills up my spine. Has she been reincarnated as a goat? Maaa, I plead silently, don't be baaad. "That's all behind me."

"Well, uh, good," I reply. Can I believe her? I see she's wearing the enameled cross I brought her from Montréal. Is this a sign she's veering toward the conventional?

"Deke here?" she asks, shifting focus, eager to move on. "Well, good. Now all we need is the happy couple. Hee hee. And the blessing of the god and goddess."

At least she knows I'm nervous. What's she got up her sleeve? Something.

Irene

Did she really think I'd punch Ro, or worse, slash her? What a grotesque scene that'd be. I mean, the woman is the size of an elephant seal, compared to the sleek little gazelle she used to be. Teddy didn't recognize her at first. He was setting up his vegan hors-d'oeuvres in the dining room when she beached beside him. She reached out to grab two of his tofu finger snacks. The flesh on her upper arms, displayed shamelessly in the sleeveless gown she must have special-ordered from the Big Beautiful Women Catalogue, jiggled with anticipation as she popped tofu chunks into her mouth. "Euw," she exclaimed. "I thought it was cheese. What is it?"

"Oh, madame," Teddy replied, ever the polite party-giver, "the dwellers in this house are vegans, and eat no animal products—including cheese." Obviously, he didn't know who had the pleasure of his company. "Here. Try the tempeh croustades, or the tabouli croquettes with tahini dressing. They won't clog your arteries!"

"I should've guessed," Ro said, mournfully eyeing Teddy's prize spread. "Uh, do you have any potatoes? Baked, with a dollop of real sour cream and just a teeny sprinkling of...oh, never mind." She reached for a croustade, sniffed it, then popped it in her mouth. "Mm. Not bad."

"Rosalie," I said. "It is Rosalie, is it not?" Underneath the layers of fat, I know you're there.

"Is," she said, between mouthfuls of garlicky hummus on toast points, a staple of Teddy's vegetarian cuisine. "Do I know you?"

Have I changed as much as she has? "Only too well," I snapped, then brought myself up short. "I mean, yes, we know each other."

"That voice." Tiny drops of tahini dressing glistened on her chin, then slid down to spot the collar of her dress.

"It hasn't changed."

"Oh, my. Irene. I should have expected you'd be here! After all, you're Junior's grandmother! That'll make you the baby's great-grand-mother! Oh, my!" She giggled, setting rings of flesh in motion, waiting for me to respond. When I didn't, she paused as if wondering what to say next, then she leaned forward and touched my arm. My first instinct was to pull away, but then I saw in her eyes something I'd never seen before—desperation. After all these years, she actually needed my forgiveness. "Antoinette's told me all about you. I used Forever Young for a month before I knew it was your product! What a shame you had to take it off the market. Come now," she fluttered her eyelashes, offering me a glimpse of the younger, svelter Ro, "what was the real reason?"

I tried to imagine Rosalie in her bath, deposited in the tub by a derrick operated by a blindfolded butler, then lifted out, all slimy, pink, and dripping, to be fluffed and buffed in a terry wrap the size of Texas. I decided this woman didn't need to hear my saga. "Where's the father of the bride?" I sidetracked.

"Oh, Maxwell's in Europe on business. He just hated to miss this."

I just bet. I could imagine that stuffed shirt heaving a big sigh, excusing himself from having to consort with witches. As if Wall Street doesn't have hobgoblins of its own. Look what Moldred was able to do! In one day, Forever Young's stock plummeted, and with it my dreams of a carefree future.

"I begged Antoinette to wait for her dad, but she said she couldn't. Of course, I understand. I mean, they're getting on with this not a moment too soon. I can't wait to be a grandmother! Is it as much fun as everybody says? And you!" She pushed her strong forefinger into my now-solid veganized solar plexus, making me wince. "You'll be a great-gran! My, my. Oops. I said that already, didn't I?"

"My, my indeed," I muttered, wanting her to let go of my arm, fearing I'd be left with a bruise if she didn't. This Mama had steel fingers! What happened to those little fluttery digits that used to caress Teddy's prick? Just when I thought I'd forgotten that tape recorded assignation in the Caribbean, those whispered sweet nothings became something again.

Just when I felt myself being overwhelmed by bitter memories, Teddy sashayed in, bearing a tray of hummus this-and-thats. "Madame," he addressed Ro, still clueless. "Try these. Very delicate, yet, ah, somehow altogether satisfying."

Ro reached out to clasp a canape. On the third finger of her right hand glinted an emerald baguette, the ring Teddy brought her from Ukraine when he lectured to doctors about the dangers of diets relying solely on bran flakes. I got a blanket woven by color-blind gypsies.

"Rosalie?" Teddy gasped.

"Teddy?"

I held my breath, half-expecting them to fly into each other's arms, but they just stood there, staring. If there was a flame, after all these years, I didn't detect so much as a spark. I counted to ten, slowly. Not even a smoldering wick. Finally, I said, "Well, I'll leave you two to get reacquainted," and exited grandly (I thought.) The blade of my ceremonial dagger flashed points of reflected candle light across the ceiling as I strode from the room. Wrapped in my mantle of dignity, I'd be the grandest great-grand-anything they'd ever laid eyes on.

Lord Revell sounded the ram's horn and shouted, "Let the Hallowmas handfasting begin!" But long before his voice evoked an excited, anticipatory response, my heart was pounding away and my body was clammy with sweat. Seeing Ro set me back. Could I recoup? I prayed to all powers it might be so.

Shirleen

"Didn't someone yell that the show was about to begin?" Deke asks. I can tell by the way he's pacing that he's anxious for this to be over. Well, so am I. I guess I'm still nervous about Ma and Rosalie. I'd hate to have any stale rivalries spoil Junior's wedding night. "I saw your dad and Irene and Rosalie in the dining room. Whoa."

"Yeah. Wonder how that went."

"What about Junior and Antoinette? They haven't been changed into pumpkins, have they?" he laughs nervously. "Oops, sorry."

"They aren't supposed to be seen until their part of the ceremony. You forget that this isn't just their wedding we're celebrating. It's Ma's party, too. Her coming out as a Wiccan. And it's Hallowmas."

"Oh, yeah. Halloween. Trick or treat." He nuzzles my neck. "Does that mean I get goodies?"

"Come on, Deke. Behave," I scold, flattered nonetheless. We've had some good times lately. Apparently, making up was just the tonic we needed. Just thinking about it makes parts of me tingle. "Hey, big guy. Later."

He smiles.

Irene

There are times I'd like to be from the twelfth century, and invisible. For instance, now. I'd like to be eavesdropping. I'd like to know what the two ex-lovers have to say to each other after all these years. But right now, I wish I could find my notes. I know I won't be able to remember my part of the corn ceremony without notes. I am the seed of the husk that lies dead. Uh huh. What comes after that? In me the circle is ever turning. No, that comes after all living things flourishing. Shit. I'm getting mushbrained. Can't even remember the spells from last Halloween, the chant I used to call up the King of Rock and Roll when the person I really wanted was the Prince of Darkness. What was that phrase? *Denizen, Venizen...*

"Don't even think about it," Moldred says. She's changed her clothes. Now she's wearing her party duds, burgundy brocade with ermine trim. *Très* medieval. Too bad nobody but me can see. "When we're in the circle, I'll be beside you, but only you'll know I'm there," she reminds me.

"I wish you could prompt me. I know I'm going to flub my lines."

"You'll be fine, Irene. Or should I say Cybele? You've matured nicely, come into your own, left all that bibbity-bobbity-boo nonsense well behind you."

But if this is so mature, why am I falling apart here? Gauze binds my tongue. Concepts sift through my brain. I'm visited by ghosts of my past. Would it be so terrible if Ro disappeared for a while? What harm could be done by just one little spell? What am I thinking? She's the mother of the bride, a granny-to-be. She's gotta stick. And I've gotta live with that.

Moldred shoots me a look. I shoot her one back. Satisfied I'll behave, she shows me a crooked-tooth, lopsided, twelfth-century grin. There's my girl.

Fortuna beckons. It's showtime. I've read the script; I know what to expect: In the meeting room, visitors will stand in a big circle holding unlit candles, while an inner circle will be composed of initiates and members. Guinevere taps her bongos, my signal to advance. "Do you come bearing the light, Cybele?" Fortuna intones. What light? Am I supposed to say something? "Ahem!" she says, louder. So?

"Yes, I come bearing the light," someone prompts softly.

"Yes, I come bearing the light," I repeat, then freeze. What light? Nobody said anything about a light. Wait a mo. We made up a rhyme, so I'd remember: she'll flick her Bic and fire my wick. Sure enough, old nicotine breath leans forward and lights my candle. "Cat got your tongue?" she taunts. I hate Fortuna. But I gotta admit, she's right; I can't call up a single word. Seconds pass.

"My candle flickers but does not dim," the prompter whispers. "Get a grip, Cybele."

Thank you, Moldred. "My candle flickers but does not dim," I repeat, my voice stronger. I, who enthralled audiences on Oprah and Sally Jessy, can do this! "I will pass the flame around the circle," I announce. At once a slew of candles are thrust toward me. Hands shaking, I light each one. The ritual unfolds: the passing of the flame, the anointing of our foreheads with fragrant oils, the stirring of herbs and spices into the cauldron of mulled wine.

When I take my place in the inner circle, I leave a small space for Moldred, who squeezes in next to Deke. Were I her, I wouldn't be able to resist pinching, just for fun, but she remains a stalwart, respectful, invisible observer. Hallowmas is, after all, a solemn occasion marking the end of summer and the beginning of winter, and deserves our devout attention. I have studied my lessons well.

Deke, a great big sponge, is sopping it all up. What I love about the guy is that he's always eager, even when skeptical. He and Shirleen are holding hands, scanning the crowd for a glimpse of Junior, but I know my boy is still in the men's dormitory, waiting to be called. Not yet, my little man, my finest treasure. Not yet.

Shirleen

"Here comes Antoinette. Can you see her, Deke? Over there, beside Rosalie. She's coming into the circle, and now Junior's joining her, helping her to kneel."

"I know, Shirleen. I can see. Remember, I'm taller than you. I should be calling the play-by-play."

"Kneeling can't be easy in her condition. Oh, look, Junior's holding her tightly, making sure she doesn't topple forward. There. Deep breath, my girl. That's right."

"Who's gonna do the honors? Perform the ceremony?"

"I don't know. Maybe they have a circuit rider, a wedding-witch."

"Well, somebody has to officiate. They can't just marry themselves."

As Deke is speaking, Pop steps forward, doffs his chef's hat and slips a black robe over his apron. Can anybody be a justice of the peace? I wonder. Yes, I decide. You probably have to have a license, is all. Well. Pop is a free agent. He can be anything he wants. "Dearly beloved, we are gathered here," he begins, reading from a small black book that looks official.

Ma approaches Junior and Antoinette to sprinkle them with cornmeal. Makes sense, I guess, since this is the festival of the harvest we're celebrating. Can't have a harvest without corn. Fertility and all that.

"Will you, Donald Kenneth McClure, Junior, have this woman, Antoinette Sophia Bixby, in marriage?" Pop asks.

A murmur of pleasure ripples around the room as the vows are exchanged. Inner circle participants mouth syllables that make no sense to me. Their faces are glowing, their gazes rapt. "Bless them both," are the words I hear and repeat at the end of a long prayer-like segment. "And the babe, also."

I nudge Deke. "Babe also," he echoes solemnly.

Teddy raises his arms, inviting the couple to rise, but when Junior bends to help his bride she refuses to stand up. "Ow," she says loudly.

"Time for the grand march," Teddy booms. "All around the circle, youngsters, so everyone can share in your joy."

"OW," Antoinette repeats, continuing to kneel.

Rosalie waddles to her daughter's side. "What's wrong, honey?"

"I'm in fucking labor, that's what's wrong, Mummy!"

"We're having a baby here!" Rosalie yells to the crowd, her chins reacting to the force of her voice, wobble wobble. "Somebody do something."

"Hee hee," Ma giggles nervously.

"That's right. Breathe, honey," Junior instructs. "Whoo whoo whoo haah. Stay calm."

"Easy for you to say! Hon, these contractions are getting closer and closer!" Antoinette reaches for his hand. "Don't leave me!"

"Is there a doctor in the house?" someone asks.

"Teddy?" Deke calls. "Teddy? You haven't forgotten how to deliver a baby, have you?"

Teddy stands still for a minute. Then he says, "Why, no. I don't imagine I have," and stoops down on the floor beside Antoinette. "I used to be a doctor," he recalls softly. "I mean, I am a doctor. I just haven't practiced in a while. But," he adds reassuringly, "babies aren't something you forget. So, don't you worry. I'll see you through."

"No doctor. Midwife!" Antoinette insists.

"I already called the midwife. She'll be here in ten minutes," Junior says. "Hang in there, baby. Whoo whoo whoo haah." He's trying to stand up, attempting, valiantly, to disengage his hand, but she won't let go.

"Whoo whoo whoo," Antoinette repeats. "OW fucking OW! I'm dying here. Haah."

"Hee hee," Ma giggles.

"Give us some room," Teddy pleads. "Antoinette, I'm going to do a pelvic."

"NO!" Antoinette bellows. "I want Mary Sue."

"Mary Sue's the midwife," Rosalie explains. "Has anybody called 911?"

"Can't we just take her to the hospital?" Deke asks.

"No hospital. Home." Antoinette pants. "Whoo whoo whoo haah! Baby's being born at home. We planned it that way. Tell them, Junior."

"Let's all do our Soothing Chant," Fortuna interjects nervously "Guinny, you provide accompaniment." Lady Guinevere picks up her bongos, jams them between her knobby knees, and taps lightly. "Ta da, ta da, ta da da da da. Join in, anytime." Gradually the room fills with the timid sounds of celebrants cranking up a chant. They link hands and form a circle around Antoinette, Junior and Teddy. "From the earth, much rebirth, sow the seeds a-plenty," Fortuna trills shrilly.

"Sow the seeds a-plenty," the others chorus.

"That part's been done nine months ago," Deke says. "We're way beyond that."

"Watch them sprout, push them out…"

"Please don't push, hon," says Junior. "At least not until Mary Sue arrives."

Ma, at a loss for something to do, throws another handful of cornmeal on the floor. I half expect Pop to leap up and do a soft shoe routine. Tonight, we're all performers. Somewhere there's an emcee who's in charge. I wish I knew that person's name.

Irene

Where's Moldred? I can't see her anywhere. Wouldn't you know. Just when she could be really helpful—*pouf!* Probably off on another time warp, meddling with somebody else's wedding. "What's keeping the midwife, anyway? I thought she was on her way."

"The agency sent someone else," Shirleen says. "Antoinette doesn't seem worried."

"Brave new world. My great grandchild's being born on the floor."

"Of a covenhouse," says Teddy.

"On Halloween," says Deke.

"Shush!" yell the others. "We want to hear what's going on."

"She's giving Antoinette some herbs for the pain," Rosalie says. "Do you think that's wise? I mean, anything could be in the mix."

"Oh, God. Rosemary's Baby."

"Shut up, Deke. Look, the little lady is rubbing Antoinette's feet." The little lady?

"And singing her a peaceful song," Teddy adds. "I'm very impressed! It seems to be having a calming effect."

"Now she's taking out her beads," Rosalie observes.

I can't believe what I'm thinking. "Wait a minute. This is a midwife? It sounds more like…"

"Mildred," Deke says. I heard her say her name was Mildred."

"Why d'you suppose midwives only use first names?" Rosalie asks.

"I dunno," Teddy replies, "but I'm very impressed."

"Ah. Mildred," I say, thinking this is all adding up. "And what does she look like, this Mildred?"

"She's very short," says Deke, peering over the crowd. He whispers. "Almost too short. And, well, I hate to say it, but she's sorta...bumpy. Eyes bulgy. Arms too short. Stumpy. Very wrinkled." He shrugs his shoulders. "I gotta say, she's ugly."

"What, Ma." Shirleen sidles up, eyeballs me. "You know something we don't?"

I take a deep breath, then let it out slowly. "Here's what I know: I know everything's going to be all right. Let's just try to relax. It takes a while for a baby to be delivered." Yech. How saccharine can I get and still be me? Well, if it helps, I guess it's okay.

"I hope this Mildred knows what she's doing," Rosalie says. "I was hoping Teddy would step in. I'd feel better if a doctor did the actual delivery, wouldn't you, Irene?"

"Oh, I don't know." I trust Moldred. But how can I tell them why?

"You do know something!" Shirleen says. "Come on, Ma. Fess up."

Everything's at a standstill. The music has stopped. People are standing quietly, waiting, watching. Incense and expectation hang in the air, one heavier than the other. Then Rosalie breaks the tension. "What a shame. All those wonderful veggie creations going to waste. How about I bring in a trayful? Eating will be a nice distraction."

"I'll help you," I say, a fish happy to be off my daughter's very sharp hook. Ro and I link arms. "How's Antoinette doing?"

"Resting, for now. Exhausted."

"Mm. It's hard work. Remember?"

"I do. Crêpe?"

"Don't mind if I do." And the two of us sample the goods, then scoop up plates of hors d'oeuvres and make the rounds. Deke and Shirleen follow close behind with pitchers of mulled wine. The room is bathed in the glow of a hundred candles. Fortuna strums her guitar.

Guinevere bongos softly and the male chorus made up of initiates and led by Lord Revell sings a soft lullaby.

Antoinette sleeps.

Everyone waits.

Shirleen

Something—the sweet, spiced wine, the tasty food, the subtle yet unmistakable odor of incense, the soothing music—perhaps all of these elements combined make us drowsy, so we lie ourselves down on the floor of the meeting hall, our heads resting on the bodies of our friends and loved ones.

When I wake it's to the sound of a low-pitched moan. Antoinette is pushing. Junior sits on the floor with his bride's head cradled in his lap. "Deke, honey. Wake up. Look how tenderly he's stroking her face."

"Good girl," Junior coaches. "Now PUSH!"

Antoinette's knees are draped with one of Pop's banquet cloths, but I can see how hard she's straining. Rosalie's lying beside her, holding one hand, her face red with empathic effort. When Antoinette pushes, so does she. The midwife's waving something, a tree branch. Back and forth across her body, waving and muttering. Deke, you watching? You've gotta see this. It's totally weird. Why doesn't Pop do something?"

"Huh?" Deke says, waking. "Wha?"

"The midwife. There's something odd about her. Get Ma."

"Hey, Shirleen. You're missing the best part. Antoinette's pushing hard. Any minute now, we'll be gram and gramps!"

Irene

Teddy and I look on, helpless but lending our strength. I can't help but imagine what my mother would say: That's how it was with the shepherds who watched in the fields. Well, this is no Christ child being born, but this is our special child, and I'm praying with all my might that my faith in Moldred will be...

"Don't push," says the Midwife From Another Time. "Breathe. Now push. That's it. Big push. Don't push." On and on it goes, the pain coming in waves that have us clenching our fists in empathy. Antoinette's knees slump and shiver, slump and shiver.

"Hard work," I say to anybody.

"I know," Teddy says. "Remember? I was there with you."

"I said I hated you."

"I never believed you."

"It was true," I tell him. "And then, there she was, our beautiful girl."

"Yes." He glances tenderly at Shirleen. "She is beautiful. Like her mother."

"GOOD GIRL!" Junior yells.

"Almost there. I can see the head," Teddy says. "Oh, Irene!" He dabs his eyes. Like her mother. Rosalie's face is a glowing red lamp of excitement and delight, but Teddy's attention is elsewhere. Like her mother.

Suddenly the yoke of anger drops from my shoulders.

I can now be me. No more silly spells, no more bogus bubble bath, no more new-age nonsense. They'd never miss me, here. Lady Fortuna's snuck off to sneak a smoke (or take a toke.) Lady G's fallen asleep over her bongos—too much mulled wine, again. And over there in the shadows, Lord Revell's living up to his name, pursuing the younger initiates. The folks in here are no different than the ones out there. Everybody's in a muddle. Cybele, my ass; my name is Irene, for peace.

There's an apartment complex on the west side of town, nice and homey, just the place for a sweet little old couple like us.

I'll keep it in mind for the future.

That old hotel on the mountain. Wonder how much they're asking?

"One more good one," Our Lady of the Herbs instructs. "You can do it, Antoinette. Push!

"Yes, PUSH!" The room vibrates with the force of all our voices. Antoinette pushes and pushes until at last Shyrena Rose slips into our world.

About the Author

Ann Robinson's short fiction has appeared in her collection *Ordinary Perils* (Peter E. Randall Publisher, 2002); *Yankee* magazine; and in many literary and commercial publications, as well as on New Hampshire Public Radio. She is a graduate of Connecticut College. As the owner of Ann Robinson Productions, she wrote and produced award-winning radio commercials for local entrepreneurs and advertising agencies. In her many years as a freelance writer, she also worked as an editorial assistant in the University of Rochester's publications department; a feature writer for the *Keene* (NH) *Sentinel*; a capsule reviewer for *Publishers Weekly*; a proofreader for NK Graphics; an advertising copywriter for WKBK Radio (where she was a CLIO Finalist); and a lecturer on the writer Shirley Jackson, a self-declared witch, whose life and work was the subject of Robinson's focus as a graduate student at Vermont College.

Visit www.annsrobinsonauthor.com to learn more about Ann.

—